A Park Heights Tale

A Park Heights Tale

The Paper Chase

Kevin Miller

a.k.a. Cakes

CHAPTER ONE

"**D**AMN, IT'S HOT as a motherfucker!" Smoove said to himself as he entered the driver's seat of his burgundy Acura TL. Manny had his car shining like new money. He was ready to go.

"Ain't nothing like a fresh car wash on a Friday by the one and only Manny the motherfucking connoisseur." Smoove handed Black Manny fifty one-dollar bills before closing the door of his car.

It was ninety-eight degrees, and the beads of perspiration trickling down his face confirmed it. *Thank god for AC*, he thought as he set the air conditioner on High Cool. He became more relaxed as the cool breeze began to overpower the humidity in the car.

"Got money and didn't know it. Take it out cha pocket," was all Li'l Wayne got to say before he cut the ringtone short by hitting the Chirp button on the side of his Nextel phone. He glanced at the alert Heavy just sent to his phone.

"Yo, Heavy! What's up?" *Chirp, chirp.*

"You already know my nigg!" Chirp, chirp.

"Aight, give me Tracy." That was all Smoove had to say, and automatically, Heavy knew that Smoove would be spinning the bend in about three minutes.

Being in the game for ten years, Smoove learned at an early age that one careless mistake could bring you a lifetime of trouble. So talking in codes over the phone was always a must, never an option.

Getting ready to pull off, he hit the playlist. G-Unit ripped through the speakers. "Every hood we go through, all the gangsters around know my whole crew." Goosebumps exploded all over his body; he cracked the sunroof and adjusted the volume.

The remaining occupants at the car wash began bopping their heads to the music. Some began admiring the tattooed, chiseled chocolate physique seated at the steering wheel. Smoove sat there, mesmerized by the physical attractiveness of a curvaceous petite female decked out in an all-white Bebe shorts set with a pair of white Bebe flip-flops to match. The flip-flops she wore exposed a fresh french pedicure and a tattoo of two butterflies in the center of her right foot. She definitely stood out amongst the rest of the onlookers. She had a look that made you get weak in the knees just by looking at her.

Got damn, this li'l bitch is phat as a motherfucker! He gestured for her to come over. As she got closer, it suddenly hit him. The sexy li'l broad standing before him was no other than Mrs. Jones!

Mrs. Jones was a correctional officer who worked at the Baltimore City jail downtown. He met her two years prior while awaiting trial on a dope case. He vowed that if he ever ran across her on the streets, he would lay his stunt game down on sight. *Now was the time for me to pop my collar on this bitch*, he thought. With another sweeping gesture, he began blowing air kisses in her direction to reassure her that he was talking to her and not one of the tack heads standing in her vicinity.

Mrs. Jones went straight into flirtation mode. She switched her way over to get a closer look at the gentleman who she thought resembled a tattooed street version of Tyrese. With every step, her thighs jiggled uncontrollably, and her shorts rose deeper in her crotch, revealing the plumpness of her pussy.

Smoove couldn't help but get sexually aroused at the sight of her manicured hands tugging at her shorts, trying to prevent them from rising deeper. He had to admit, she was a stallion. She was honey complexioned with hazel eyes. She rocked a wet and wavy hairstyle that went perfect with her seductive look. He began snickering as she approached his vehicle.

Scuuuured! Was the last sound she heard before the remaining water from the wet pavement splashed all over her face and wardrobe. Her hands flew in the air trying to cover her face. Wiping away the wet debris her face contorted in disgust. She let out a deep sigh.

"Ugh!" Instantly, she went into a temper tantrum. She started screaming and sobbing uncontrollably. "You bitch-ass nigga! I can't believe this shit, oh my god!" She looked down, dumbstruck at her ruined outfit. If she had her gun, she would have shot him.

Laughing, Smoove zipped up Reisterstown Road. He headed toward Shirley Avenue to hook up with Heavy. *I told that bitch I would get back at her for spraying me in the face with that mace. Stupid bitch got the nerve to be in my hood getting a car wash*, Smoove thought, beating the red light. *I bet next time that will teach that bitch a lesson how to treat a nigga like a man and not get power-struck 'cause she a CO. Bitch lucky I didn't run her over.*

******

As Smoove approached S h i r l e y   A v e n u e, he couldn't help but notice how alive the block was. Instead of picking Heavy up and conducting business in the car as usual, he decided to park his car and hang around in the hood for a few.

It was mid- June, three thirty on a Friday afternoon. Everybody and their mother were outside. Dudes were zooming up and down the block on dirt bikes and performing tricks on the corner of Shirley and Cottage Avenues. The fire hydrant was open, giving the kids in the neighborhood a chance to cool off and have fun at the same time.

Breezing through the block, he leaned his seat back and turned the radio down in hopes of being unnoticed. He knew from experience that people could identify you by your car. So he switched up whips to stay off the radar. He would rent a different car every two weeks.

His main objective in the game was to stay out of the limelight, get money, and avoid going to prison. So he made moves as if his life was a big game of chess. He was sharp to be twenty-five years old. He was constantly told by the old heads that he was a young dude with an old soul.

"Stupid Motherfucker!" He cursed out loud seeing nobody took the time to look inside his car while driving pass. *These have to be some of the dumbest dudes in the world. They don't even have the sense to pay attention to their surroundings*, thought Smoove. I could have been the narcs or anybody.

He parked and exited his car, leaving his keys and his gun inside. If the narcs ever searched you in the hood and found car keys, they would look relentlessly for the car in hopes of finding drugs stashed inside.

"Smoove! Smoove! Smoove!" yelled a snot-nosed little girl named Poochie. "Gimme a dollar, gimme a dollar", as she stood there with her hands on her hips, pouting in an attempt to look innocent.

"Now if I give you a dollar, what can you do for me?" Smoove said in a joking manner.

"I won't ask you for nothing else for a long, long time. I promise."

"How about I give you ten dollars to clean up Ms. Janice's front yard? And to keep all the kids safe while their playing in the fire hydrant?" Before he could even get his hand inside his pants pocket, Poochie had her hand out, palm facing up, ready to receive her blessing from God. Being a child of a dope fiend mother, she found money was rare. When it was around, it was quickly snorted up.

Smoove took pride in providing for the less fortunate in the neighborhood. It kept the home owners on his side—less haters, the law off his back, and a lot of happy faces.

"Thank you! Thank you! I love you, Smoove!" shouted Poochie as she began dancing around like a break dancer.

Everybody in the neighborhood loved and respected Smoove because he was very genuine. Everything he did, he tried to do it in a respectable way, and he strived to keep the unity within the hood. The slightest sign of taking his kindness for weakness was like wiping a lion's ass with sandpaper. The few that did either squashed their differences or, soon after, bit the dust. Even though Smoove was a good dude, he played by all the rules in the game. If you got out of line, you got your head busted. No one was exempt.

As he proceeded to make his way towards the corner of Shirley and Cottage, all the people he passed by poured out love and paid their respects.

"Hey, Smoove! Mmph, mmph, mmph. That's a sexy-ass nigga," one girl screamed as Smoove walked past a porch full of thirsty bitches.

It was rare that he came through the hood, but when he did, he was given the royal treatment. Even dressed in a pair of black LRG sweatpants, a white tank top, some black-and-silver Nike Foamposites, and a White Sox fitted cap turned backward, he had swagger. Smoove stood at 6'3", 211 pounds, had a chocolate complexion, and was cut up like a bag of dope. He rocked a bald head with a five o'clock shadow. His upper body was covered in tattoos. He worked out five days a week, ate healthy, and took care of himself physically, spiritually, and mentally in hopes of staying on top of his game.

The scenery in the neighborhood rattled his nerves. He realized all the commotion from the dirt bikes, the loud music people had been playing, and the females scattered out in a frenzy had all the drug dealers off their toes. Fiends were all over throughout the block, waiting to get served; none of the lookouts were posted. Smoove instantly got irritated at the sight of this major technicality.

"Everybody, clear this shit up!" he screamed as he wedged his way through the crowd. "What the fuck you niggas think this shit is legal? All this money floating around and you li'l niggas is worrying about these nothing ass bitches and these dirty ass niggas riding fucking dirt bikes? Come on, clear this shit up. Everybody, roll out!" Smoove screamed out in hopes of clearing out the block in a peaceful manner.

Making sure his demand resignated with everybody the open hand slapped a dude in the face who stood in the street dancing so hard the dude hat flew off his head. The four dudes who were zooming up and down the block on their dirt bikes weren't from around the neighborhood. Smoove gave them the benefit of the doubt and motioned them to pull their bikes over. He decided to assassinate them with words, instead of punishing one of the reckless youngsters for being unaware of who they were dealing with. Before he could even offer them an ultimatum, the police swarmed the block and left everybody no choice but to evaporate or spend the night in Central Booking.

The whole block scattered like roaches running from raid. The guys on the dirt bikes sped off in the opposite direction; people could be seen jumping gates, running through alleyways, and throwing blunts and liquor bottles—all because the police in this neighborhood was at zero tolerance. Their main objective was to lock up everything moving, unless you had an unfamiliar face. Even the junkies took off, 'cause they too knew the neighborhood all too well. The police knew what was going on. If they felt that you weren't a part of the solution, then you were definitely a part of the problem. If you looked like you got high, you either hauled ass, or your ass was hauled off.

"Hey, you! Where the fuck you think you're going?" One of the officers said as Smoove was walking into Ms. Janice's front yard.

Even before Smoove could respond, Ms. Janice stormed through the front door, screaming and motioning the officers to leave her property.

"That's all you slime balls know how to do—harass people? My nephew isn't a hoodlum. He's a working-class citizen, just like y'all."

"Ma'am, slow down. We apologize. We're just here to do our job," a redneck doughnut-belly officer replied while squinting his eyes from the cigarette dangling from his mouth.

"Thanks, Officer," Smoove said after the officer motioned him to continue going about his business.

Ms. Janice had the best house on the block. She lived in a two-story red brick row house that had a distinctive look, separating it from all the other houses on the block. She kept her lawn neatly manicured, and at the foot of her porch, she had a beautiful rose garden filled with green and yellow tulips, bearing large cup-shaped flowers. Her porch was freshly painted all white. She had a burgundy carpet to match the red bricks that surrounded her dwelling. She had a cream chair-and-table set that was custom-designed to withstand the four seasons while providing you with the comfort of feeling like you were sitting in a love sofa that was converted into a porch chair. Unfortunately, she still lived in the hood. A chain and two padlocks surrounded her chair-and-table set to avoid being victimized by the neighborhood junkies.

Her doormat read, "Welcome to paradise," and once inside, you would realize her sanctuary paradise seemed more of an understatement.

"You always seem to know all the right words to say at all the right times," Smoove stated as he was led inside by a voluptuous and plump Ms. Janice.

He was instantly ecstatic and no longer irritated by the previous events once he was in the presence of Ms. Janice. She lived alone, so she had no problem walking around in the most seductive, appealing outfits, especially when Smoove came around.

"You know I'm not going to let nothing happen to my baby," Ms. Janice said as she removed her turquoise robe, allowing the floor to catch it, as she proceeded into the kitchen to finish the food she was cooking.

Ms. Janice had Smoove captivated by the sight of her monstrous ass, which was shaking and wiggling like Jell-O with each step she took. She was a stallion that defined the true definition of a dime. She stood six feet two inches tall and had a caramel complexion, with no scars, no stretch marks, and a body that made heads turn. She resembled Clair Huxtable in the face, the mother from *The Cosby Show*.

With the exception that she wore glasses and had an ass like the porn star Cherokee, Ms. Janice was forty-five years old. She knew all the tricks and trades on how to keep a young dude like Smoove open his nose wide and walking around on cloud nine.

Smoove was astonished and amazed by the breathtaking, erotic costume she was wearing. The bulge growing in his pants made it evident. She revealed enough to be enticing but covered enough to let him use his imagination. She was wearing a short see-through satin and lace negligee. It was a crotch less one-piece, which exposed every inch of her flawless feminine physique. She had just got out of the shower, so she had that moist look.

Smoove had to admit she had her house decked out from top to bottom. She had a big screen TV inside her living room, with a black leather La-Z-Boy couch. A love seat and a recliner surrounding a glass table were decorated with various ornaments. Beneath the table was a black persian rug, which covered the whole area where the table and chair were. Throughout the entire downstairs, the floors were made out of black-and-white marble, which shined as if someone had just applied a fresh wax job to it. The living room was immaculate, so exquisite that he could tell it was only used as a showcase and never occupied by anyone. A sparkling chandelier hung from the ceiling, directly over the center of another glass table. In the corner sat a glass china closet filled with crystal-looking figurines. The chairs set up around the table resembled the chairs that judges sat in. Plastered on the wall was a large portrait of the Baltimore Harbor. Underneath it was a cozy-looking bar area.

Smoove knew Ms. Janice for over ten years. Out of all the residents in the neighborhood, she didn't praise him because he was the star of the hood. Because of it, he always had a great deal of respect for her. It wasn't until three weeks ago that she opened up to his advances and allowed him to take her out.

Ever since that day, she couldn't get enough of him, but she refused to give in so soon. This was already his second time inside her palace in a week. He was making a lot of progress, he thought as he continued admiring her home.

"Have a seat, baby, and relax. Don't be acting all shy. Make yourself comfortable," Ms. Janice suggested before she made her way upstairs. Once upstairs, she began applying her Chanel gloss on her lips and transforming her room into a sex haven.

Downstairs, Smoove watched from the window as one by one, his crew was getting put into the back of a patrol wagon. *Damn, I'm about to chill. It's too hot around this motherfucker*, he thought. His crew needed a break. Everyday somebody was getting locked up, their stash was stolen, or the stick-up kids were stinging them. The charges ranged from trespassing and resisting arrest to numerous drug offenses. The good thing about it, though, was, his entire crew was juveniles, with the exception of Heavy. So for the most part, they always came straight home. Smoove hoped that Heavy was only getting arrested for something minor and nothing serious, because after you passed juvenile stages, all that "coming home all the time" was out the door. Once everybody got out, he planned to inform them of a well-needed vacation they would be taking, in hopes of allowing the block to cool down and to give them a break from hanging in the hood all day.

"Got money and didn't know it," came blasting through his phone again, instantly snapping him out of his daydream and sending his attention to his phone. Looking at his phone a smile spread across his face reading a text from Ms. Janice.

> Turn the burners on the stove off. Let's skip dinner and come upstairs for pleasure

Smoove smiled and instantly obliged to her request. Upon entering the room, he was stunned and blown away by the kinky and intimate atmosphere that she had going on in her room. He never thought that after all the years she screamed on drug dealers—she who was portrayed to be a Ms. Goody Two-shoes—he would be in her house getting ready to put his dick all in her. Just last week, he couldn't even help her carry her groceries to her porch, so to be this far was surreal to him. He could smell the victoria's Secret she had on, lingering in the air. Before another thought entered his mind, he started taking his clothes off slowly and teasingly, imitating a male stripper. "Beauty" by Dru Hill kept her from hearing him enter the room.

Ms. Janice was lying on her back with her legs spread wide open, sliding a peeled banana in and out of her pussy. Her inner lips were pink and plump, and the juices flowing from her entrance only made it more appealing. She slid the banana in and out of her pussy with ease, extracting more moisture with each stroke. With the banana saturated with her wetness, she slid it down to her asshole then back to her pussy in an up-and-down motion. She had her eyes closed, so she didn't see Smoove at the foot of her bed stroking his dick and enjoying his trip to paradise, all the while trying not to scare her with the size of his penis.

Smoove was well endowed; he had one of those penises that would scare a female to the point that he would have to literally promise not to put it all in. This wasn't the case tonight, as he would soon find out.

Ms. Janice had so many different kinds of sexual treats scattered throughout the dimly lit room that Smoove didn't even know where to begin. Handcuffs, edible dildos, strawberries, whipped cream, butt plugs, a Silver Bullet, K-Y Jelly, a vibrating penis ring, and an assortment of condoms, which ranged from Magnums to glow-in-the-dark Trojans.

She began biting her bottom lip and rubbing on her clitoris with her vibrator in a circular motion while using her other hand to caress her nipples.

Smoove entered the bed knees first with his tongue leading the way. He lifted and spread her legs and started nibbling and sucking on her clitoris. She was so thick that her thighs wiggled uncontrollably with the slightest touch.

With his tongue, he stayed zoned in on her clitoris and inserted the butt plug to intensify and enhance the sexual stimulation. The juices from her pussy allowed the butt plug to enter with ease. Ms. Janice could no longer hold back the emotions building up inside her. Soon as the butt plug eased its way in, she engaged in pillow talk. She started moaning and jerking her body to the point that he had to literally hold her down to keep her still.

"Ooh, this pussy taste good, don't it?"

"Mmm, hmm," Smoove muttered.

"Yes, right there, keep it right there. Don't stop. I'm about to cum! Ooh yes! That's it, baby! I'm cumming! I'm cumming!" Her body began to shake and quiver as the juices from her orgasm poured out her pussy, leaving Smoove soaked from his nose to his neck.

"Please, daddy, put that dick in me. Momma need to feel that dick," she begged seductively.

Smoove grabbed one of the Magnum condoms from the nightstand, ripped it open, then slowly put it on his throbbing erection while Ms. Janice stared in amazement at the length of his dick.

Good God! she thought as she set her eyes on his family jewels. If dicks could exercise, she sure as hell could see his dick lifting a ten-pound weight. He was huge.

Before she let him penetrate her guts she decided to have fun and get to know her new toy a little better. In one swift motion, she grabbed him by his dick, pushed him on his back, then removed the condom from his dick. She retrieved the broken-up banana, which was lingering inside her pussy then covered his dick in whipped cream, turning his dick into a banana split. Within minutes, she managed to clear his dick completely of the treats she covered it with. She began moaning and making slurping sounds as she slowly sucked his dick.

"Mmm . . . mmm . . . This young dick is so big." She moaned as she began rubbing his dick all over her face and in and out her mouth.

She began encircling the head of his dick with the tip of her tongue teasingly. She applied more than enough spit to allow his dick to glide in and out easily. With each stroke, she took in more of his dick until she couldn't take in another inch. She started gagging as the tip of his dick reached her tonsils. With each gag, she gripped his dick with her hands harder, massaging his scrotum in the process.

With one hand tangled in her hair, Smoove used his other hand to massage her face and ears as he lay back with his eyes closed, enjoying his blow job.

"Ooh yeah, suck that dick, baby." Smoove moaned from the feeling he got when she pulled all the excess skin on his dick down toward his pelvic with both her hands and focused on his head only. "Ah yeah, that shit feel so good. This ya dick, baby. Suck that dick."

Smoove wanted to bust a nut inside her pussy, so as he felt the eruption building up inside him, he called it quits.

"Oh shit, that's enough. I can't take it!" Smoove jerked away from her in an attempt to regain his composure.

Ms. Janice still had on her crotch less negligee, so as Smoove was putting on another condom, she slipped out of her costume then covered her whole body in baby oil. Smoove was baffled by her figure; he couldn't understand how a forty-five-year-old woman could have such a banging body. The only thing on her that was big was her thighs and her ass. She had one of those butts that looked heavy, so even looking at her from the front; he still could see her ass.

Ms. Janice was eager to have her insides filled with his manhood. Wasting no time, she sprawled onto the bed and got on all fours. Smoove's dick reached its fullest potential; he was amped up and ready to go. As soon as she got on all fours, he made his way over to her tunnel of love. He rubbed the tip of his dick along the opening of her pussy, taunting and teasing her before penetrating her womb. With each stroke, her entrance became more slippery than before. She desperately wanted to feel his dick inside her.

"Oooh, daddy, you making mama pussy feel so good." Smoove long-dicked her slow, proclaiming with each thrust that he owned her pussy. She passionately agreed.

"Yes, you can have this pussy. It's yours, daddy. Fuck me like you mean it. Make me bust!"

Within seconds, she collapsed onto her stomach with Smoove right on her heels pounding away. Unsatisfied with her reactions, he closed her legs before thrusting his dick inside her as deep as he could. He gripped her ass cheeks with both hands, spread them apart, then watched his dick slide in and out of her soaked pussy. Her ass shook and wiggled in every direction.

"Whose pussy is this?" he asked mid thrust.

"It's yours, daddy! It's yours!"

Smoove pulled out of her only to find that the condom had popped. So instead of having to pull the condom off to blast all over her, he inserted the head of his dick inside her asshole, splashing his babies all over her small intestines.

"Oh my fucking god, Smoove! I love how you feel in my ass, daddy! Put all that meat inside me, young nigga! I'm a vet at this shit. Every hole I got is yours. I love pain!" Ms. Janice pushed back hard, forcing the rest of him into her ass while she frantically rubbed her clit until another orgasm racked her body.

"You like it rough, huh? You freak bitch, take it all! Take it!" Smoove held her by the waist, fucking her butthole until every drop was gone and he became limp. Pulling out of her, he watched his cum run out of her anus, down the crack of her ass. He fell back in exhaustion.

"Uum, uum," moaned Ms. Janice as she rubbed her hand between her ass cheeks, coating her fingers in Smoove's semen. She moved her hands from between her legs to her mouth. Tasting his cum, she started kissing him up his thighs as he lay still.

Ms. Janice was a pure freak; she was insatiable and nasty as they came. No pun intended. She took Smoove's fresh-out-of-her-asshole penis and put it in her mouth.

"Oh shit, what are you doing to me, Ms. Janice?" Smoove grabbed the back of her head, trying to control the sensations at the head of his dick. Licking his lips, looking down the crown of her head, Smoove enjoyed her over and over and over and over.

CHAPTER TWO

"**A**NTWON JEFFERSON!" A young female correctional officer yelled from outside of a holding cell inside the Central Booking intake facility.

Central Booking was a place where adults were housed at if they got arrested. Either you stayed there for thirty to sixty days then got transferred to the city jail across the street, made bail, or your charge was so minor that you only stayed for twelve to twenty-four hours before being released on your own recognizance.

Heavy jumped off the bench he was sleeping on. "Yeah, that's me."

"What's your ID number?"

"It's 207890."

After confirming he was indeed Antwon Jefferson, she slid his charge papers under the door.

The arresting officers never informed him of what he was being charged with. Butterflies began forming in his stomach as he started reading the first line. He thought that he was only being charged with loitering. When he read his charge papers and found out he had an outstanding warrant for a parole violation, he was enraged. All kinds of thoughts flooded his mind, like spending the next ten years behind the wall. Outside of being dope sick and needing a fix fast, Carlita was weighing heavy on his mind, knowing she was pregnant and had a vicious dope habit, two kids to fend for, and no source of income outside of him. He imagined his situation only getting worse by the minute.

The holding cell was designed to hold only ten inmates at a time, but due to the fact that it was Friday, every holding cell was over crowded. Nineteen people scattered throughout the 10' × 4' tiny cell. Bodies were spread out across the entire floor. It was so crowded some people even slept standing up. No sooner than Heavy got up from his seat, a skinny, toothless-looking pipe head hurried over and took advantage of the open space before it could be claimed.

"I'm sitting there, slim," Heavy told the skinny crackhead before tapping his leg to reassure him that it was him he was talking to.

"On your feet, lose your seat," the crackhead told Heavy before turning back over to finish enjoying the privilege of having a whole bench to himself.

"Take my seat, lose your teeth," Heavy mumbled before unloading a fury of punches on the harmless crackhead in an attempt to live out his threat. One by one each blow landed directly on his mouth.

"CO! CO!" the crackhead cried out. "All right, you can have your seat!"

It was only after seeing him open his mouth and holler that Heavy realized the mission at hand was impossible due to the fact that he was already missing all thirty-two of his teeth. Within seconds, officers came running from all directions, only to find the toothless crackhead trampled in the corner lying in a pool of blood and no one to point the finger at.

CHAPTER THREE

T WO DAYS WENT by, and Smoove hadn't heard from Heavy or Ms. Janice, and it bothered him a lot. It didn't bother him that he was worrying about Heavy. That was normal, if he considered the fact that they did business together. It felt strange to him that Ms. Janice occupied his every thought. Smoove was a big boy, so he was accustomed to the finer things in life, but when it came to Ms. Janice, it was a different story.

She was an active member in her church; no men were ever seen leaving her house. She never did anything to make Smoove think she was nothing more than a loving, down-to-earth church lady. He couldn't believe that just two days ago, he was sexing Ms. Janice throughout the wee hours in the morning.

He started devising a plan as he paced back and forth on his living- room floor. Smoove lived in a two-bedroom apartment in Randallstown, located just on the outskirts of the city. It would only take him twenty minutes to get to Park Heights from where he lived. He knew that he either had to take a trip to the neighborhood in order to find out what was up with Heavy or call the local bail-bond in-charge Sharon Mason to find out about his status. Calling Sharon was the best option he thought before scrolling through the list of numbers stored in his phone.

"Bail Bonds, this is Jessica. How may I help you?"

"Yeah, is Sharon in?"

"Yes, she is. May I ask whose calling?"

"Tell her it's the smoovest nigga in the world."

"Hey, Smoove! How you doing, baby?"

"I'm fine. How about you?"

"I can't complain. I'm living."

"Same here."

"Well, let me get Sharon for you."

Seconds later, a cheerful-sounding Sharon came through the receiver. "Marcus Tillman, what can I do for not only the smoovest nigga in the world but also the sexiest nigga in the world. Well, not the sexiest in the world, 'cause my man is number one, but you right on his ass, baby."

"Sharon, your ass is crazy."

"What's up, Smoove? What can I do for you?"

"Heavy got locked up again, and he hasn't called me in two days, so either he lost his phone, or he's still in there."

"What did he get locked up for?"

"I thought loitering or trespassing 'cause of the way they swept the block and he couldn't have been dirty."

"Well, I'll check the system and call you back in a few minutes."

Minutes later, Sharon called back only to inform him that Heavy was being held without bail for violating the terms of his parole. Finding out that Heavy was being held without bail put a major dent in his street operations. Heavy took care of everything, from making sure the drugs got packaged to making sure the workers were paid for distributing the drugs. Smoove didn't even know the workers. That was what he had Heavy for. It was his job to deal with them on a daily basis. With Heavy gone, he was left with no choice but to hit the streets and put a plan in motion.

His train of thought was abruptly interrupted by the sound of his roommate's keys jingling at the door. Before she could get the door completely opened, Smoove came to her aid, grabbing the shopping bags she was carrying.

"Whew! I gotta pee! Watch out!" Keisha said, brushing past Smoove, dashing toward the bathroom. Smoove was amazed at how bubbly she looked in the Juicy Couture liquid sequined dress with the plunging neckline he picked out for her. It accentuated all the right spots, bringing her hourglass figure to the surface.

"Damn, no hello? Thank you for the shopping spree? Nothing?" Smoove asked before she closed the bathroom door.

Smoove's roommate was a childhood friend of his named Keisha Tillman. He and Keisha had a brother-and-sister relationship due to the fact that Smoove's parents adopted Keisha at the tender age of seven. Keisha was four years his junior so he was more her father than her big brother. She played a very significant role in his life, and every move he made, he informed her on it.

It was Keisha who rented the cars for him, the hotels, and the apartment they lived in, and every bill or piece of mail that came to their home was in her name. With no record, good credit, and a license to carry a weapon, she was more his partner in crime. She would do anything to please Smoove. It was her job to keep the house in order and cater to his every need. In return, she lived rent free, drove different rental cars, and was provided with the finer things in life.

Smoove's parents were deep into the church, so living under their roof was like being in boot camp. Either you lived their way, or you hit the highway. Once Smoove turned eighteen, he moved out and never looked back. When Keisha turned eighteen, she followed in the same footsteps as her big brother. The only advice they got from their parents was that, if you make your bed, then prepare to lie in it. They knew once they left, there was no going back.

Shortly after Keisha's eighteenth birthday, their parents were killed in a botched robbery. They had no choice but to stick together. Smoove vowed to always look after his sister and provide her with the life their parents wanted her to have. Every move he made wasn't just for him; it was for Keisha also. Smoove spent the next couple of minutes informing Keisha on the latest events that transpired before making his way toward Park Heights.

CHAPTER FOUR

PARK HEIGHTS WAS one of the roughest neighborhoods located in the West Baltimore area.

Every corner was occupied by drug dealers, junkies, and liquor stores. Violence plagued the neighborhood. As of June, the murder rate was at 153, and 32 of them came out of Park Heights. Even though Smoove wasn't beefing, he kept a pistol close by. At any given moment, anything was liable to happen. Staying strapped was a way of life for him.

Upon entering Shirley Avenue, Smoove noticed that the block was empty with the exception of a few kids. People were lounging on their porches, and a few junkies walked through, searching for the drug dealers in hopes of getting their fix. Though the block was known to produce thousands a day, nobody moved work through Shirley but him.

The last competition he had was a well-known gunner named Swift. They both occupied the block together at one point, eating off the same plate. Their workers looked after one another, and Smoove and Swift had a mutual respect for each other. That was until all the fiends took their money to one person. Out of nowhere, Smoove came out with some dope that was killing people. Strangely enough, every dope head in the city was trying to get their hands on that killer dope. In one day, it went from them being neck to neck to Swift barely making one hundred dollars a day. Three weeks under those conditions, Swift secretly started eating with Smoove. At the other end of the block, Swift would catch all the customers before they made it to Smoove's crew, selling them garbage dope, convincing them it was the same product. From that point, their rivalry ensued. Eventually, they got into a shoot-out, which left them both wounded and Swift behind bars after being caught with the gun he shot Smoove with on the scene. Since then, Smoove controlled the open market.

Today Smoove's plan was to find the dudes whom Heavy had on the block and see if they had any work before making them aware of the changes that lay ahead.

Cars began slowing down, some even pulling over as Smoove walked through the block. "Where y'all hittin' at?"

"Y'all come out yet?"

"Where Alice in wonderland?"

Fiends began swarming Smoove once they'd seen the head honcho of their favorite dope, Alice in wonderland.

Though he didn't come around often, everybody knew that he was in charge of everything that moved through Shirley Avenue.

"Nothing happening. Shop closed for about a week." Disappointment set in everybody's face as they returned to their cars or walked off without receiving their daily dosage.

"Smoove!" Black Manny yelled out, trying to get his attention across the street.

"Nah, we ain't out, Manny. We chilling for about a week," Smoove said as he tried to brush Manny off and keep it moving.

"Ya li'l crew back there." Manny pointed to the alley behind Shirley Avenue.

Behind the houses on Shirley Avenue was a basketball court and also a spot where hand-to-hand transactions took place. It was more of a secluded area and not in the open. Smoove went over toward him to make sure what he heard was true.

"What chu say, Manny?"

"I was tryna tell you that ya li'l crew is back there on the basketball court serving people right now."

Hearing that, Smoove ran down toward the basketball court in an attempt to stop them before he ended up suffering another casualty. As Smoove reached the foot of the alley, he heard one of them yell to the crowd of junkies waiting to get served, "That was the last one!"

Smoove was happy to hear that they managed to sell their last bag. Even though they didn't have anybody watching the corner, they were able to make it without getting locked up.

"Aye, all you li'l niggas come here," Smoove said while motioning them to come in his direction.

There were four of them, and their age ranged from fifteen to seventeen. Smoove spent three hours getting to know them—from where they lived and what their numbers were—and he schooled them on how to run a dope shop successfully. After talking to them, he realized that it wasn't they who were making careless mistakes on the block. It was Heavy's lack of guidance that led them to believe that the way he was showing them was the right way. He also found out after talking to them that Heavy had a serious dope habit. A lot of thoughts clouded his mind after finding out that Heavy was getting high, especially about money.

On numerous occasions, Heavy told Smoove one of the workers got robbed or their stash was stolen. To make matters worse, some of the customers complained regularly to him about how small the bags were. Everytime he came around, somebody would complain about how small the portion of heroin was inside the bags, but the dope was so good they still bought it.

It all started to hit him as the crew Heavy had out there continued spilling their guts to him. He couldn't believe that Heavy, his childhood friend of over ten years, chose to do him dirty like that after all they been through. Smoove trusted Heavy with everything. Finding out that he crossed him, Smoove had to change up his whole operation.

He also found out that Heavy and his crew managed to get rid of the $20,000 worth of dope with the exception of $2,500 which the li'l runners sold themselves. Knowing that Heavy would have paid them that Friday, Smoove informed them of their new duties before giving each of them $500.

Heavy had $17,500, which belonged to him. When he left the area, he headed straight to Heavy's house in search of his girlfriend, Carlita.

Smoove constantly advised Heavy to always keep money at home so when times like this occurred, Carlita would be able to give it to him. Unlike Smoove, Heavy lived in the city, so he made it to Carlita in less than five minutes.

Their house was located in Walbrook Junction at the intersection of Elgin and Denison Avenues. He noticed that Heavy's car was parked in front of his house. *That's a good sign that she's been in contact with Heavy. How else would she have gotten his car? She had to talk to him. That's the only way she would've been able to get ahold of his keys*, Smoove thought as he put his car in park.

A funny feeling came over him seeing Heavy's kids playing in the front yard, especially that knowing their father made him a distant uncle.

"Uncle Smoove! Uncle Smoove! My daddy got locked up. Him not here," Heavy's six-year-old daughter said in the cutest voice in the world before jumping in his arms and giving him a kiss.

His two-year-old son continued playing with his Legos, laughing while Smoove chased his big sister playfully around the yard.

All the commotion going on outside caused Carlita to burst through the front door only to find that it was Smoove causing her daughter to scream and not a real emergency.

"Girl, what I tell you about making all that noise? You had me scared to death," Carlita sent her and her brother in the house to prepare for lunch.

Carlita was your typical hood chick. You could take her out the hood, but you couldn't take the hood out of her. Everything within her character made it evident. She was five months pregnant, but the outfit she wore exposed more than her swollen belly. She was wearing a white silk see-through nightgown, which revealed her sagging titties and the red panties she wore. She had red-and-yellow tracks piled on top of piles of fake hair.

The bottom of her feet was smoke black from walking around barefoot all day.

He thought about telling her to go inside and cover up, but he knew that would only trigger her to release her innermost ghetto ways.

"Lita, you talk to Heavy?" Smoove asked as he walked onto the porch.

"Yeah, the day he got locked up. He told me you would be stopping by to pick up your money. He also told me to tell you that he needed you to leave me $5,000 so I can get him a lawyer to represent him at his parole hearing. Plus I saw that his window was shattered he told me to get his car for him 'cause there was some money in the glove compartment. When I went up there to get his car, the window was shattered and the glove compartment was hanging open with nothing in it."

Every word she spoke was going through one ear and out the other. Smoove could sense they were both in cahoots once he noticed the track marks on her arms. Everything he heard from the young boys confirmed his intuition. Antwon Jefferson, a.k.a. Heavy, was nothing but a backstabbing junkie. Due to the fact that he always kept a fresh haircut and fresh gear on, Smoove never noticed that Heavy was falling offtrack. But like the old saying goes, what happens in the dark always comes to the light. He hoped Heavy at least had the decency to follow his orders when he told him to never keep over $5,000 outside. If so, at least Carlita would have something to give him.

After asking Lita for the money Heavy had her holding, she came back with a shoebox that looked like it contained nowhere near the $17,500 he owed. Smoove took the money then told her he would be back in two weeks to give her the money for the lawyer. Which was a lie.

"When did you pick the car up?"

"About an hour ago."

"Why you let it sit so long?"

"My first time hearing from him was today, and as soon as he told me, I went straight up there."

This lying bitch just told me she talked to him the first day he got locked up. As he left the porch, Smoove noticed neither one of the car windows were broken. *All I ever did was help that nigga*, Smoove said to himself as he drove up Elgin toward his next destination.

For the remainder of the day, Smoove took care of everything from hiring a new bagger, appointing a new street lieutenant, to thinking up a new name to label his dope. Heavy became a distant memory to him. He had no intentions on getting him a lawyer, nor did he care about helping him or his family while he was in jail. All Smoove cared about at this point was making back the money Heavy just fucked off. Chilling and letting the block cool off wasn't an option anymore. Smoove went home to get some rest. He planned to be on the block by 6:00 a.m. to introduce the world to Crush Groove, the name of his new dope.

CHAPTER FIVE

S MOOVE HAD a peculiar night. He was up and ready to hit the streets at 5:30 a.m. He stayed up until 1:00 a.m. talking to Ms. Janice on the phone. That alone had him in a good mood. Although he was infuriated over the fact that Heavy did the unthinkable, he was blessed to be in the financial position he was in. Refusing to let the minor setback hinder his ability to think straight, he calculated his earnings in his head.

In a bank account he and his sister shared through the will their parents left them was $300,000. From their parents' house in Essex that they rented out, $1,200 a month was automatically deposited into a separate account in Keisha's name. Never touching the money in the bank, they used the money he made in the streets for everything.

Stashed and buried deep in Lincoln Park was $175,000 worth of drug money that only he and Keisha knew about. He had $100,000 tucked away at his Uncle Pete's house and $25,000 inside their apartment. He never brought drugs or large amounts of money to their home by any means. He kept his drugs, along with the weekly profits, at his Cousin Jerry's house.

Jerry was four years older than him, and he lived a total different lifestyle. But due to the struggling economy, he was more than willing to allow him to use his house as a stash house. In return, Smoove gave him $2,500 a month, had a secret compartment built inside the attic, and vowed to always come alone.

Jerry owned a four-bedroom, two-story house located in Owings Mills, Maryland, inside a gated community. Owings Mills was about forty minutes away from the city. Smoove could take numerous back roads to get there. Being followed would be almost impossible. Jerry was a local truck driver who only delivered goods in the surrounding Maryland area. He had a loving wife and two kids.

Growing up, he and Smoove were like peanut butter and jelly, sugar and Kool-Aid. It just wasn't right if the two of them weren't together.

They did everything together growing up—threw rocks at cars, played hooky from school, and played 7-11 and truth or dare with the girls. They participated in all the neighborhood brawls. After losing a close friend to violence in the streets, Jerry quickly turned his life over to God and never looked back. Smoove, on the other hand, was lured in the opposite direction.

Back in the early nineties, Jerry, Smoove, and Kendal were like the Three Amigos. They rolled together every day up until Kendal's untimely death. Back then, their thing was house parties. Every house party they frequented, they were always the life of the party, causing all the girls to gravitate toward them. One particular event at a house party in the projects on the eastside changed their lives forever.

Owning the dance floor, the Three Amigos had the crowd of onlookers chanting as they rocked the latest dance moves. "Hey! Hey! Hey!"

Feeling their movement, two of the cutest girls in the party made their way through the circle formed around them.

"Go, Krissy! Go, Ty-Ty!" They jumped directly in the middle of the circle, stealing the show. The crowd went bananas, seeing the dance-off ensue. Gyrating to the beat, Ty-Ty and Krissy went straight into routine, never once missing a beat. After going back and forth busting impressive moves, they were locked in a tie. Wanting to keep their reputation, Kendal went to the extreme in his attempt to solidify their spot as the reigning champs.

Moving his body with some fancy footwork, he moonwalked in the direction of one of the girls, busting a few moves in the process. "Go! Go! Go!" With the crowd on his side, his mind was dead-set on ending this dance off once and for all. Grabbing her waist, he spun her around, pulled her skirt down, then thrust his pelvic against her backside so hard that it sent her frail body flying into some of the onlookers. All hell broke loose.

Unbeknownst to Kendal, Ty-Ty and Krissy were from Latrobe Projects. So were their boyfriends and majority of the party. At the same time, half the party jumped on Kendal, one guy wielding a pocket knife. Seeing the knife, Smoove rushed in their direction.

"You bitch-ass nigga! That's my girl!" The first swing sent Kendal to the floor. With so many people involved in the melee, Kendal's body disappeared. The majority of the party pulverized him. With all the ruckus going on, the housing authority patrolling the grounds got wind after hearing a window break.

"Oh shit! Housing! Housing!" one kid yelled. On cue, the whole party dispersed. Still zoned in on the guy with the knife, Smoove didn't even see Kendal lying in his own pool of blood.

In a hurry to dispose the knife out the back window, he was caught off guard when Smoove ran behind him. After a brief struggle, Smoove managed to throw him out the window, sending him crashing onto the fire escape below. The impact knocked the screws loose that held the fire escape to the building. Falling down fourteen stories, he screamed at the top of his lungs as his body flip-flopped in the air on its way to the pavement. Seeing his body slam against the concrete sent a rush through Smoove's body.

"Police! Police! " Hearing the police running up the stairs, he climbed out the same window, scaling the building until he reached the nearest fire escape.

"Thank God!" He felt like the luckiest man alive, climbing through the open window on the thirteenth floor.

"Ooh! Please don't kill me!" Paying the frantic woman no mind, Smoove jumped over her bed before bolting out her front door as quickly as he came. In the end, the police had two dead teenagers with no one to point the finger at.

As an adult, Jerry worked, went to church, and lived the life of a family man. Still, for the money involved, he was happy to provide Smoove with a safe haven.

Currently, Smoove had $80,000 stashed there, and once he gained $20,000 more, he planned to bury it with the $175,000 he had in Lincoln Park.

He never kept over a hundred thousand dollars there. Once he reached that mark, he quickly retrieved it and put it in another location. He didn't have any work stashed there at the moment, 'cause he just took his last kilo to his other cousin Tony's house to get bagged up.

Tony would bag up one hundred grams at a time, making $16,000 and some change off each one hundred grams. Tony's job was to bag up one hundred grams at a time, and once he finished, he would separate what he made off the one hundred grams. So during all the transactions that would occur, no one would get confused. When Tony's younger brother A-wax needed more drugs for the block, he would send Tony a text, stating, "You know what it is." Tony would automatically take what he made off the next one hundred grams and drop it off at their neutral stash location in a wooded area not far from the block. After the drop, Tony would send A-wax the same text, letting him know that the drop was made. A-wax would only give the runners $2,500 worth of dope at a time.

A-wax was Smoove's new lieutenant; he was responsible for everything that touched the streets. He had to know where the runners' stash spots were, where the runners lived, and make sure they got paid and keep them on their toes. Blood is thicker than water, so after finding out about Heavy, Smoove put all his trust in his family by cutting off all ties Heavy knew about. In one day, he managed to change up his whole operation with the exception of the li'l runners. He felt comfortable with them due to the fact they were the ones who exposed Heavy. Plus, they earned extra credit for being honest about the amount of drugs they were left with.

Smoove was happy to see his people when he walked onto the basketball court behind Shirley Avenue. A-wax and the four runners were out bright and early, ready to open up shop. Given that he changed the name Alice in wonderland to Crush Groove, it would only be right to give out one hundred testers. Although it was the same dope, it was always a good hustling tactic to get a name established the right way.

Dope sold by how good the heroin was. If you had the best dope in the city, you made the most money. Unlike weed and crack, a dope fiend didn't care about the quantity or the fact that they liked you or wanted to help put money in your pocket. That was never the case. When it came to dope, it was never personal; it was always business. The addicts looked for a strong high, one that would last long. That was it. If you provided them with that quality, you were in good shape. If not, you were stuck holding bad dope.

Smoove planned to give out one hundred bags of dope for free, just to let all the fiends know that Crush Groove was coming out swinging. In return, he knew that they would be back for more and that word would travel throughout the city that Crush Groove was a missile. It was now 6:30 a.m. Smoove wrapped up his speech, gave them their final instructions, then made his way to Essex, Maryland. With Smoove gone, A-wax and his crew spent the next hour and a half going around to different dope shops, letting all the fiends know that Crush

Groove would be giving out testers at 8:00 a.m. Crush Groove raked in $15,220 on its opening day. For the first time in a while, none of the workers were robbed or arrested, nor was their stash hit.

******

Pulling up in front of his old house as always, he instantly thought about some of his childhood memories. He never really liked going inside due to the chilling feeling that accompanied him. His plan was to do his normal routine, mow the lawn, trim the hedges, and get with the tenants about the plumbing issues they were having. Smoove never gave them his cell number, so it was only this morning when he checked his voice mail on his house phone that he found out about the major flood they had.

The two young tenants were good renters, when they called upon him, which was rare; he made it his business to accommodate them at his earliest convenience. He tried calling them back, only reaching their voice recorder each time. *Maybe I'm too damn early*, he thought. With both their cars in the driveway, it was safe to say they were home. His first knock pushed the door open, which, to his surprise, was unlocked. Immediately, he could see that the water problem was something major. In a split second, his eyes popped out of his head. His stomach felt like it just fell onto the floor.

"Oh shit! What the fuck!" he screamed as he backpedaled toward the door. There on the couch, the young married couple sat motionless, holding hands, with their severed heads sitting in their laps.

In an instance a masked gunman appeared from the kitchen. Puzzled by the noise, the gunman emerged with his hands tightly gripping his .40 caliber.

On sight he sent two shots at Smoove's face. Then the gun jammed.

Reaching for his gun, Smoove felt his heart skip a beat as he realized he left it in the car.

With a bullet jammed in the chamber, on instinct, the gunman charged at Smoove in an attempt to pistol-whip him. Smoove blocked the first blow with his forearm. The force the gunman brought by rushing him sent them both crashing through the glass table, sending shards of glass everywhere.

They both rolled over the floor in their effort to gain control of the situation. Using all his strength, Smoove tried to pry the gun away from the intruder while the frantic gunman tried his best to overpower him. Lying on his back, staring down the barrel of a gun only intensified his desire to live.

Mustering all the strength in him, Smoove managed to maneuver his way on top. Using his right hand, Smoove unloaded haymaker after haymaker.

Dazed by the fury of blows crashing into his face, the masked gunman tried his best to get the gun to shoot.

Just as the jammed bullet fell out the chamber, Smoove, using all his might, bashed him in the center of his forehead with the steel table leg that lay beside them, instantly knocking him out cold.

Grabbing the gun, Smoove quickly slid one into the chamber. *Bang!Bang!Bang!* Fourteen shots later, the lone assailant lay motionless with his face mask covered with holes.

Curious to see his face, Smoove snatched the mask off. Not only did the close range shots kill him instantly, it also turned his face into a mush and beyond recognition. As he searched him frantically, an electrical fire broke out from a broken lamp submerged in water. Seeing the curtains engulfed in flames, he went into a frenzy, trying to find some type of identification on him.

Smoove coughed from the smoke. The mere thought of the police catching him like this sent his mind into overdrive. *Who the fuck is this? I gotta hurry up and get the fuck outta here. This smoke is killing me.* He flipped him over, finding nothing in his back pockets. Knowing time was working against him, he hurried toward the back door and left without being noticed. It was only after he got two blocks away that his consciousness reminded him that he left his car parked out front, not to mention his fingerprints on the murder weapon he left behind. Wiping the blood leaking down his face, he came back to his senses before disappearing into a wooded area.

CHAPTER SIX

"**Y**OUR NEXT PAYMENT is due in ninety days, so I'll see you on the thirteenth of September," the manager of Rent-A-Center told Ms. Janice before walking out her front door and heading toward his truck.

"Thank you, sweetie! God bless you for stopping by," Ms. Janice told him while he was leaving. "Hallelujah! One down two to go!" she shouted and raised her hands toward the ceiling.

She had a busy schedule for today. No sooner than she closed the door, she began getting herself together. She had to go to work, pay some bills, and do a little bit of shopping to buy an outfit for her date with Smoove next week. She took a quick shower, got dressed, grabbed her workbag, and headed toward the door.

She was wearing a pink summer dress by DKNY, which stopped just above her calves, and some white DKNY flip-flops, which had glittery rhinestones. Her hair was hanging down to the middle of her back. She was African American mixed with Cherokee. Ms. Janice had a natural beauty.

She entered her black 2013 Honda Accord coupé. She immediately turned on her AC and rolled the windows down to allow the heat lingering inside to evaporate. She threw on her DKNY sunglasses, moisturized her lips with her Chanel Lip Gloss, found her favorite Kirk Franklin CD then proceeded toward her destination.

Her first stop was Mr. Burns' house. Mr. Burns was an elderly Jewish man, an eighty-three-year-old retired lawyer. Ms. Janice was his in-home care provider. It was her job to clean his condo, prepare his meals, and tend to his every need Monday to Friday. In return, he signed her time sheet every two weeks and gave her an extra $1,500 out of his pocket every month due to the extra service she provided him with.

She had a key. She let herself inside and went straight to work. Placing him inside the tub, she turned on the plasma TV he had located on the wall directly across the tub, gave him his medicine, then told him to be a good boy until she came back.

While Mr. Burns waited in the tub, she straightened up his room, packed up his dirty clothes, then put on her work clothes. Mr. Burns wasn't the average eighty-three-year-old. He still walked around on his own, drove his car, and he exercised regularly. To her, it wasn't a bad job. She could take his clothes home to wash them, take out his trash, bathe him, and keep his house neat. She would only work one hour a day with the exception of Monday, the day she cooked.

Mr. Burns would sign her time sheet as if she worked eight hours a day at a rate of eighteen dollars an hour. He didn't mind because his retirement funds paid for her to provide him with in-home care. Plus, she provided him with a trip to paradise once a week. He was more than happy to have her around for an hour.

Ms. Janice reentered the bathroom dressed in a black-and-white maid suit that only covered the front top of her body. Her whole back was open, exposing her entire backside. The only thing showing besides skin on her backside was the straps that held her maid suit together and a tiny piece of her black thong that managed to escape suffocation.

"Hey, daddy! Were you a good boy while I was gone?"

Mr. Burns smiled so hard that his teeth fell out.

"Oops!" Ms. Janice said while shrugging and placing her hands over her mouth.

She dug her hands in the water to retrieve his teeth, but before she could find them, he grabbed ahold of her hand and placed it on his erection.

"Mr. Burns, that viagra isn't suppose to work that fast. I just gave it to you." Ms. Janice laughed teasingly.

"Mmm. Mmm," muttered Mr. Burns.

"I can't understand a word you're saying. Let me find those teeth."

Once she found his teeth, she washed him up then helped him into his bedroom to begin putting him to sleep.

He was wrinkled all over with a hump in his back. As she walked behind him, she realized how sometimes she didn't like the things she did. She just liked the money that came along with it.

"You know you don't have to help me walk. I'm a grown man."
"I know, daddy. I'm just over-protective of you." Knowing everything was a fantasy to him, she instantly went into role-playing.

Mr. Burns flopped down onto the bed, spread his legs, and started rubbing his thumb across the head of his dick.

"Ooh, Mr. Burns, you have a big dick. Don't rub it all. Save some rubbin' for me, daddy."

Mr. Burns's dick was the size of a vienna sausage even when it was hard. His nuts were the size of two plums.

Ms. Janice crawled onto the bed, imitating a cat. "Purr. Purr. Purr." Within seconds of her wrapping her soup coolers around his dick, Mr. Burns started moaning as tiny driblets of semen leaked from his pee hole.

Ms. Janice wiped him down and tucked him in as his limp and frail body lay motionless in bed. She slipped on her gym clothes and grabbed his dirty clothes she had packed by the front door before making her way toward her next destination.

******

Heads turned as she strutted through the front door of the YMCA located on 33rd Street. "Good morning, I'm here to meet Eric. I have a ten thirty appointment."

"And your name is?" asked a short, stocky thirty-ish-looking receptionist seated behind the front desk.

"Janice Walker."

After calling Eric, moments later, he came around the corner and led her around to his office.

Eric was a handsome-looking young massage therapist. Following him back to his office, she couldn't help but admire his sexy physique. He had on a red YMCA muscle shirt that showed off every inch of his muscular frame. He was 5'9", had a mocha complexion, with short curly hair. He was 185 pounds of pure lean muscle. His veins were protruding all over his body from the quick workout he just did before she arrived.

In a skintight emerald-green Apple Bottoms sweat suit, Ms. Janice looked drop-dead gorgeous. After closing the door to his office, he had his hands and tongue wander all over her voluptuous body.

"Mmm . . . Baby, you smell so good," Eric whispered in between kisses.

One thing led to another, and shortly after her arrival, Ms. Janice was getting long-dicked from the back as she stood in an upright position. Both of them were covered in sweat. The steamy atmosphere made every stroke feel like a sensational high.

Everything located inside the steam room was made of wood—the floor, the ceiling, the walls, and even the seating area. He had Ms. Janice standing up with her legs closed while he slid his dick in and out of her asshole. She gave him easier access by spreading her ass cheeks apart and stooping down. She was taller than him, so with each stroke, he ended up on his tippy-toes, trying to fill her insides.

"Oh shit. Mmm. Yes! Yes! Ooh! Ooh! Oooh my god!" she was screaming at the top of her lungs from the pain and pleasure he was providing her with. Each scream made him dig deeper and deeper. Even with her hands full of ass, he was able to find areas to smack and grasp hold of.

Thwack! Thwack! "This how you like it, bitch!"

"Yes! Yes! Punish me, daddy. I been a bad bitch!"

With every smack he applied to her cheeks came louder screams and more shit-talking.

Thwack! "Ooh yes, fuck me!" *Thwack!* "Ooh yes. Mmm. Punish me, pull my hair!"

Before he could grant her last request, all the blood circulating in his body rushed straight to his dick. "Ah shit, I'm, I'm cumming." Swiftly, he pulled out of her asshole and snatched off his condom while Ms. Janice hurried to turn around to finish him off.

She was on her knees with her mouth wide open when he grabbed her by the hair and exploded all over her tonsils. She swallowed every drop and sucked his dick until he begged her to stop.

"Damn girl, my dick numb as a motherfucker." His knees buckled as his dick went limp from the workout session it just endured with Ms. Janice's tonsils.

He no longer could take it, so he pulled away from her death grip and ended his session with Paradise, the sensational specialist. Ms. Janice showered in his private shower then grabbed her $250 before leaving yet another satisfied customer with a limp dick.

CHAPTER SEVEN

T HE FOLLOWING WEEK, Smoove was over the fear of the police getting his prints from the gun. After watching the news that same night, he found out that the house was so badly burned it would take the investigators weeks to salvage through the wreckage. Seeing the condition of the house firsthand was even more convincing. By the time the firefighters reached the scene, the house was already fully engulfed. Due to it being an electrical fire, the water from the fire trucks only made it worse. It was only after the house burnt to the ground that they were able to manage it. With the autopsy still pending, he was curious to know who was behind the invasion. One part of him believed he just so happened to be at the wrong place at the wrong time. Then on the other hand, he somehow thought it was meant for him. Whatever the case, he was lucky to have left the scene with only a few scrapes and bruises.

Tonight he planned to do it big with Ms. Janice. Even though they just recently had sex, he knew her good enough to know that she was wifey material. He was tired of bouncing from broad to broad; he vowed that if he ever found Ms. Right, he would settle down. He wanted Ms. Janice in every way possible, and tonight he would announce his proposal. He was used to having his way with women, but she was more than a challenge. She was a mission. Everything she did was with class.

He wasn't able to pick her up at her house. Because of their age difference and his occupation, she wouldn't even go out in public with him. Tonight they were headed to DC. The only reason he was allowed in her house on those few occasions was because it was normal for him to be in someone's house on Shirley Avenue. Before anyone came under suspicion, she planned to put an end to that. She lived a very secretive life due to the fact that she was a call girl. She took pride in portraying a different image in public. None of her associates outside her clients knew about her scandalous ways except her best friend, Wanda. Her plan was to keep it that way.

It was a little after 7:30 p.m. when Smoove pulled up in front of Wanda's house on Monroe Street to pick her up. Seconds after blowing his horn, a stunning-looking Ms. Janice stepped outside, looking like a bona fide fashionista.

Smoove was once again awed by her ability to look so young. She had on a pink skintight mini dress by Vera Wang, black snakeskin boots, which came to her knees, and a black Gucci handbag. Her hair was braided into one french braid, which hung down to the middle of her back. Wearing a pair of Gucci shades with platinum trimmings on the side, a platinum tennis bracelet, along with her diamond-studded earrings, she illuminated through the night.

She made her way over to the candy apple-red Audi R8 v10. Smoove hopped from behind the wheel and greeted her with a dozen white roses then planted a soft wet kiss on her cheek before helping her into the car. Once inside the car, they started complimenting each other's elegant and classy attire.

Smoove had on a pair of black True Religion dress pants, black Prada shoes, a tight v-neck T-shirt and a black velvet True Religion blazer. His leather Italian black belt had a cross decorated with rhinestones in the middle. The watch he was wearing was a timepiece made by Ten a Key Jewelers. Lighting up his left ear was a three-karat diamond-cut earring. He had a clean bald head along with a neatly trimmed beard.

"Thank you for the flowers. You sure know how to treat a lady." Ms. Janice admired the beautiful roses.

"It's just a small token of my appreciation."

"Appreciation for what?"

"For being able to have you in my life."

"That's so sweet of you." Ms. Janice blushed.

"It's not me you should be thanking. You should be thanking yourself."

"And why is that?"

"Because it's you that got me wanting to do what a man's supposed to do for a queen."

"You're my king now?"

"I'm just trying to be everything I'm sure you want in a man and more."

She looked at Smoove with wise eyes. "What have I always wanted in a man?"

"The same thing every woman wants—stability, a concrete future, and everything that surrounds love."

"Boy, you still got breast milk in your mouth. What does a twenty-five-year-old young man even know about love?"

"Enough to know what it takes to keep a woman in it. You see, Ms. Janice I—"

"Boy, if you don't stop calling me Ms."

"See, that's just the point I'm trying to make, Ms.—I—I mean Janice. Ever since I've known you, I always held you in high regard because of the way you carry yourself as a woman. I never imagined in a million years I would be putting dick all in Ms. Janice. I mean, messing around with you," he stuttered.

"You're a church lady with the best house on the block. You've known me since I was a kid. You've never gave me any sign that you were into street dudes. I never even saw you with a man."

"Well, Marcus, that's the way I choose to live in order to keep my personal life private. I'm human, so I do have vices, and for the most part, I'm not perfect."

"Well, you seem pretty close to it."

Child, if you only knew, she thought to herself as she thought about Paradise the sensation.

It was times like this that made her regret living the life she lived on a daily basis. She wanted to settle down, get married, and live happily ever after. She was so caught up and accustomed to the lifestyle she was living that she never really gave it any real consideration. It felt good to her that she was single, had no kids, and held her own. She still felt empty inside as if her life was missing something. She wanted to settle down and have a normal life, but she feared investing then losing everything in the end. At forty-five years old, she couldn't afford to put herself all into a relationship and then, in the end, have to start all over. Her clock was ticking; she had no time to waste in a relationship.

She was eager to know what Smoove had planned. He never told her anything but what time he would be picking her up and warned her to be prepared to stay out all night. He urged her not to bring any changing clothes, no money, nothing, just herself. She had the slightest idea what he had up his sleeve. From the flowers down to the Audi coupé, it felt like it was going to be an exciting night.

Looking at the navigation system on the dashboard, Ms. Janice could see that they would be reaching their destination in less than three minutes. Throughout the forty-five-minute ride, it took to get from Baltimore to DC, they talked about everything under the sun. This was the first time they got to hear each other's goals, each other's plans, and they were beginning to see eye to eye. Neither one of them had kids, they both were financially stable, and they both had some of the same dreams. Approaching The Sweet Georgia Brown restaurant located on Fifteenth and vermont Streets in Northwest DC, Ms. Janice became silent as she surveyed the elegant restaurant.

The view from the parking lot to the front door was exclusive looking, instantly giving her a rush. On both sides of the street, valets in red tuxedos worked the block at a fast pace in order to clear the block from the cars that were lined up waiting to get parked. All the cars that pulled up were luxury vehicles.

From the uppity scenery, Ms. Janice knew she was attending something very exquisite.

The block was flooded with Bentleys, Ferraris, Range Rovers, limos, and various assortments of showroom-floor cars. Pulling along the sidewalk, they were greeted by two slender-built g u y s who opened the door for both of them at the same time.

"Easy on the gas. She's tender," Smoove told the valet as he handed him a crisp one-hundred-dollar bill he had folded up in his hand.

Together they walked hand in hand headed toward the door keeper to get properly seated.

"Good evening, sir, I have a table reserved for two under Marcus Tillman." The doorman scanned his list then gave Ms. Janice a red rose.

Ms. Janice was speechless by the effort he was putting into his attempt to pamper her.

"Smoove, you are going to make me fall in love with this lavish lifestyle. How can a twenty-five-year-old boy be doing this to me?" she said, sliding her arm under his. "Boy, I got to see some ID. I need to give you a lie-detector test or something. Boy, you too advanced to be twenty-five years old."

"Woman, you've known me for too long. Just think back to ten years ago. I was a young snot-nosed lil kid running around."

"I know, baby. I just never imagined you being so romantic." Before Smoove could respond, she grabbed his face with both hands and kissed him.

They were abruptly interrupted by the hostess, who purposely cleared his throat to announce his presence. They were led to a beautifully decorated table that was located in the corner of the dining area. A waiter stood behind Ms. Janice's chair, and pulled it out for her. The restaurant was very classy, and everybody was dressed to impress. Expensive-looking paintings were hung throughout the building, and on each table sat a bouquet of colorful flowers. A live jazz band was on the stage, which was set directly on the opposite side of the dining room. A few couples danced along the foot of the stage.

Waiters dressed in red attire roamed around, carrying silver trays filled with hors d'oeuvres while at their table stood a waiter holding a pepper mill ready to cater to their every need.

"Ladies first," Smoove told Ms. Janice, giving her the cue to order.

The waiter informed them of tonight's specials. He took their orders and returned minutes later with two bowls of clam chowder, a fresh basket of hot dinner rolls, accompanied with a bottle of white Zinfandel.

Smoove only drank on special occasions; tonight was one of them. After returning with the appetizers and wine, their waiter filled their glasses.

"I would like to propose a toast." Smoove grabbed her by her hand. They were seated directly across each other, so with every word he spoke, he looked her straight in the eyes to reassure her of his sincerity. "Janice, this is a very wonderful and special moment to me. This is the beginning of a life-changing event for the both of us. I would like to toast to a long-lasting, beautiful, and prosperous future together." They both toasted to his proposal then engaged in conversation until the waiter returned to serve them their entrées.

Ms. Janice ordered steamed shrimp, two lobster tails stuffed with crabmeat and a chef's salad, along with ranch dressing. Smoove had crab imperial for his main course and six oysters that were topped with melted shredded cheese, lemon juice, green onions, and bacon bits. He also had a side dish of caviar. After they finished up their meals, Smoove took the bill to the front and paid for their dining, then they left, looking like the perfect couple.

A little behind schedule, he sped off in a rush to make it to H street, located in Northeast DC. All their destinations were programmed inside the navigation system. Zooming up the street, he touched one button on the screen, and the navigation system responded by advising him that he was en route to the Lincoln Theatre. The wine he just consumed had him feeling tipsy. He cracked the sunroof, leaned his seat back, and hit "Watch the Throne" on his playlist.

"Ball so hard make niggas wanna find me," Kanye and Jay-Z blasted through the speakers.

Ms. Janice was turned on by the music and the rough ride mixed with the wine. Being in Smoove's company brought out her inner youth. She no longer felt forty-five; she felt like she was in her twenties. She was beginning to love every minute of being around him.

They reached the Lincoln Theatre in less than the ten minutes predicted by the navigation system. They had ten minutes to park and make it to their seat before the show started.

The Lincoln Theatre was packed with people from all walks of life. They came out to see Mike Epps, a.k.a. Day-Day, from *Friday* perform live. Smoove was glad to see that they had valet parking also, 'cause that would give him just enough time to grab a few things from the concession stands before being seated.

Within minutes of being seated, they saw an energetic Mike Epps emerge from behind the curtains, dancing to Meek Mill's "Ima Boss" anthem that was being played.

"Cut the motherfucking music off! It's time to get this bitch crack a-lacking!" Mike Epps screamed through the crowd. "It is some beautiful woman in this bitch. If you know you looking good and your pussy good than a motherfucker, make some motherfucking noise!" The females broke out in an uproar.

"Now, lady, if you don't sit cho old ass down," he said, pointing to a big-boned sixty-something-year-old-looking lady.

"If my grandmother wouldn't whip my ass for letting you have it, I would kick yo ass. Life is crazy because I think that some people was meant to be creatures, animals, or some shit. It's some ugly motherfuckers out here as well. I seen a nigga so ugly tonight that he need to send a few motherfuckers in front of him to let people know his ugly ass is coming through. That nigga was so ugly he a fuck a nigga whole day up. I can see me now about to get up in some pussy then that ugly motherfucker pop up."

By the end of the show, Mike Epps got a standing ovation from the crowd and gave everybody their money's worth. It was eleven forty-five, and Smoove still had a few tricks up his sleeve. They left the Lincoln Theatre and headed toward New York Avenue to the hottest club in DC—the LOVE Nightclub.

LOVE was an upscale, plush, twenty-one, and over night club that played the latest hip-hop and R & B music. You couldn't even get inside
unless you had on casual attire from head to toe. The atmosphere was for the grown and sexy. After finding a parking spot two blocks away, they walked hand in hand toward the entrance.

The block that the club was located on was flooded with people and cars playing loud music. To make matters worse, the line to get inside the club stretched around the corner, and it would take at least forty-five minutes before they could gain entry.

"What are you doing, baby? We can't just jump in front of all these people," Ms. Janice told Smoove as they walked past everybody in line and headed toward the front entrance.

"Boys do what they can. Men do what they want. I'm joking. Just chill out. I got this," Smoove told her, leading the way.

Smoove approached one of the doormen who was outside the club, giving people pat-downs, and placed three one-hundred-dollar bills in his hand. In return, the doorman patted him down then sent Ms. Janice in the direction of a female security guard to be searched, and into the club they went.

Once inside the club, Smoove paid a cover charge, bought two VIP wristbands, then headed straight toward the VIP section with Ms. Janice. The place was packed to capacity. Not touching somebody going through the crowd was impossible. They wedged their way through constantly excusing themselves. It was so hot that the walls were sweating; nothing seemed to calm the crowd down. The entire club gyrated to Waka Flocka Flame "No Hands" song. Different groups of women could be seen leaving the bar area to join in all the action, so it was only right when Ms. Janice followed suit.
She pushed Smoove against the wall and started grinding and gyrating against him.

It was dark inside the club, so she went unnoticed, sliding two fingers along the entrance of her pussy. With her juices on her fingers, she turned around to give Smoove a taste.

"I think we need to go up to VIP and get us a booth!" Smoove yelled in her ear after sucking her fingers and placing her other hand over the large bulge growing inside his pants.

The mere thought of his long black dick sent tingles straight to her pussy.

"That's the same thing I was thinking!" she yelled while placing his hand between her dripping legs.

The second floor was like a whole different club. It seemed like the second floor was occupied by the stars of the hood, celebrities, and the baddest groupies money could attract. It was an all-you-can-eat buffet, a bar, a DJ, and six different booths. The DJ was playing "Shot Caller" by French Montana, sending the whole room into a frenzy.

"Isn't that that new rapper guy?" Smoove looked in the direction she was pointing at.

"You sure the hell is right." Even though he only could see the back of his head, he was sure it was French Montana, because damn near everybody in that vicinity wore Bad Boy or Cîroc shirts.

There was about twenty dudes and eight girls dancing in the skimpiest outfits. One of the girls was laid back on the table with her legs cracked up high in the air while another broad looked like she was devouring everything between her thighs. Some of the dudes were pouring champagne on the broads. Some were getting lap dances. The rest of the dudes watched two girls grind on each other on one of the sofas inside their booth. The dance floor and every booth were jammed packed with the exception of one booth. Smoove knew that it wouldn't be vacant for long. For that reason, he rushed over with Ms. Janice in hand and claimed their spot.

Each booth had its own color and a security guard on post. He ordered a bottle of Cîroc then lay back on the sofa, tongue-kissing Ms. Janice while she gave him a lap dance. "Smoove, I want to be your girl." She managed to say in between kisses. That was like music to his ears.

"Baby, you make me feel so good. I never want to leave your side."

Normally, if a broad told Smoove that, he would rarely take it into consideration, simply because he knew that money would make a person do anything. That wasn't the case with Ms. Janice. She had her own

40

money, her own home, car, and job, and in his eyes, she was always independent. He felt that any type of love and affection coming from her was genuine. "You know, I been feeling the same way about you for years. Believe me when I tell you the feeling is mutual."

"Smoove, you are still young. Are you sure you're ready to settle down? I mean, I probably can't give you kids. In five years, I'll be fifty. What's going to happen when them young girls come at you?"

"It's different. I've been infatuated with you for years. I been in love with you before we even started dating. To finally have the woman of my dreams, the only thing on my mind is enjoying the rest of my life with you."

A short, slender model-looking young girl rocking a Mohawk and a black skintight cat suit came through the door. "One bottle of Cîroc for the lovely couple." She placed two glasses on the table.

"Thank you," Smoove replied."

"Would you guys like anything else?"

"No, thanks."

"All right, you guys enjoy the rest of your evening."

With that said she switched her way out of the booth then disappeared into the crowd.

Smoove filled two champagne glasses to the rim. "This toast is for a new beginning. Our future together and a lifetime of joy." They clinked glasses.

Ms. Janice downed her glass then poured another glass before Smoove took one sip.

"Damn you, don't be playing."

"But I see you do. You still got a whole glass full." She laughed.

"I told you I don't drink like that, so you lucky I'm even taking a sip." Due to his weak system, he was still feeling the wine from dinner. Having a booth, they were provided with a great deal of privacy. Each booth had slightly tinted windows and a light you had to turn on and off to adjust your own setting. Once Smoove finished his first glass, he turned the light completely off and started looking around to see if they could be seen. He never even got the chance to make sure the coast was clear. Before he could, she was on her knees, tugging away at his belt, begging him to slut her out.

"Please, baby, treat me like a slut." She was moaning even before she managed to pull his dick out. He was rock hard. So as soon as his dick was free, the taunting began.

"You want this dick?"

"Yes, daddy, please give mama that young dick. Please let mama taste it." He grabbed her by her ponytail and started pulling it while smacking her face with his dick.

Ms. Janice had her mouth wide open waiting with her tongue hanging out for Smoove to give her a taste. He entered her mouth head first.

Ms. Janice massaged his balls with one hand, and with the other, she held his dick and focused on his head.

"Hold up, baby, let me sit down." His dick stayed in her mouth while he walked backward toward the sofa.

Ms. Janice crawled as he was backing up, managing to keep his dick inside her mouth. On the sofa, he stripped completely naked, and cocked his legs wide open. She slipped out of her mini dress, squeezed his dick between her perfectly round titties, and bounced them along the shaft on his dick. She placed a tittie on each side of his dick, only allowing the head to stick out. Once she positioned her titties properly, she began spitting directly onto his tip and in the crevices of her breast. Knowing from experience the wetter the better, she covered the entire area with her fluids. She slid her titties up and down Smoove's dick while deep-throating him at the same time.

"All right, baby, that's enough. You 'bout to make me bust." As usual, he was ready to get up in that pussy before she sucked him into submission.

Her head was a beast, but the thought of bouncing behind her big ass overpowered him.

"Bend that big ass over and keep your legs closed." Before following instructions, she grabbed the bottle of Cîroc, took a gulp, then pulled her one-piece mini dress over her head.

"Keep those on." Smoove told her, referring to her knee-high boots. Even with the lights off, they still could see a little from the light glaring from the dance floor. She still could not believe how big his dick was. It seemed unreal.

"If I didn't know you for all these years, there's no way I would believe that you are twenty-five years old."

His dick was the size of a miniature bat. Never once did it stop her from taking every inch like a pro. She walked over toward him, turned around, and assumed the position on all fours. Smoove smacked her on her ass hard. Each time she screamed for more.

"Punish me. Ooh . . . Treat me like a slut." He spanked her again. "Yes, daddy." It was like smacking an ass full of Jell-O the way her ass shook.

The sensation she felt once he rubbed the head of his dick along the entrance of her pussy caused her pussy to become warm and slippery.

"Ooh yes. Give me that dick."

"Beg for it." It was like somebody turned a faucet on inside her pussy. Juices just started flowing rapidly.

"I'm cumming! Oooh. Oh, daddy, I'm cumming!" To enhance her orgasm, Smoove slow-stroked her and massaged her clit with two fingers while sucking on her neck. With his other hand, he played with her ear and rubbed her face, all the while loving how easy it was to make her cum.

"Daddy, just like that! Don't stop! Keep it right there! I'm cumming again! Oh my god, I!" Before she could say another word, her entire body started to tremble. "Stop! Stop! Take it out! I can't take it anymore!" In mid stroke and approaching an orgasm, Smoove body flew backward onto the floor.

"What the fuck?" His heart fell at the sight of her having a seizure.

"Stop, don't touch me!" she yelled, smacking his hand away.

"Are you having a seizure?"

"No, boy. Just give me a second."

It was like a chill was running through her body. She was gritting her teeth and squirming around like she had a charley horse all over her body.

Little did Smoove know she was having multiple orgasms, which were causing her entire body to quiver. Regaining her composure after the numb feeling subsided, they both laughed together after she explained to him what was happening to her. This was the first time for Smoove, so he really felt like he laid it down. They fucked in every position possible until they both couldn't take anymore. By the time they left the club, they both were physically exhausted. The only thing on their mind was sleep.

All the sexing and the drinks they consumed took a toll on them both. Smoove had to almost carry Ms. Janice back to the car. She was so impaired she barely could walk straight. Once inside the car, she went straight to sleep. Though Smoove was drunk, he didn't drink the amount she did, so he still maintained his composure. They had one more stop to make. The Hilton Plaza Hotel. His mission was now complete. After tonight, he knew she was hooked. Tomorrow would be the nail in the coffin.

CHAPTER EIGHT

THE NEXT MORNING, Ms. Janice was awakened by a loud knock at the door.

"Room service!"

"All right! Gimme a second!" She woke up with a banging migraine, instantly irritated by the loud knocking at the door.

"Who ordered room service, and where the hell is Smoove at?" she said to herself, trying to regain her consciousness.

She couldn't recall any of the events that transpired once they left the club. Waking up inside a plush five-star continental suite, she was now anxious to see what room service wanted. She climbed out the bed then covered her naked body with a blanket. Opening the door, she found a short-looking Mexican lady with a cartful of accessories.

"Ms. Wallcah?" the Mexican lady said with a Spanish accent. "This is for you, complimentary of Mr. Tinmen."

Peeping out the door, Ms. Janice grabbed the cart, thanked the housekeeper, and then closed the door.

Excitement filled her body as she pulled the little silver cart inside. She was speechless. On top of the cart was a complete entrée. Her meal was separated between three trays, which consisted of eggs, turkey bacon, raisin bread, a fruit salad, and a bowl of Honey Bunches with oats cereal. She also had a pitcher of hot coffee, a glass of cold milk and orange juice, along with a pack of aspirin and two packs of Alka-Seltzer tablets. At the bottom of the cart was a white robe, a pair of white house slippers, and a pink and white Juicy Couture sweat suit folded neatly on top of each other.

She was really beginning to take Smoove seriously. As of this day forward, she promised herself that she would let all her guards down and allow him to have her in any way he wanted. In the beginning, she never looked at him as more than a sponsor. Her plan was to add him to the list of bill payers. She never imagined that a twenty-five-year-old street hustler would be the one to make her settle down. Happy tears streamed down her face. He was everything she always wanted in a man—in fact, more. She was starting to realize how grateful she was to have a young man of his caliber.

"Thank you, Jesus!" she shouted out loud. Kneeling down at the foot of the bed, she began praying. "Dear Lord, I do believe that you sent your Son Jesus Christ down on the cross to sacrifice his life so that I could live. I do believe you did all that because of the sin being committed on earth. I do believe that he died on the cross and that he rose from the dead on the third day. I do accept you in my life as my Lord and personal savior. I believe in you. I do believe that you are the ruler of the world, the Almighty God, the Most High, and I will worship you and you only. I'm not perfect, I have sinned, and I pray that you forgive me and help me to rid my life of sin. Thank you, Lord, for blessing me with such a wonderful man as Marcus. I pray that you give us strength and wisdom to maintain a loving and bonding relationship. In Jesus's name. Amen."

The only thing on her mind after answering the door was Smoove. After praying, she rushed over to the nightstand in search of her phone. Before she could even dial his number, she noticed a text message from him. "You have a 10:00 a.m. beauty appointment. Don't be late. I'll be picking you up at 1:00 p.m. for lunch. Follow the rose petals."

Instead of following her gut feeling to call him, she dismissed the notion and went searching for the rose petals.

The suite they were staying in was the size of a two-bedroom apartment. She followed the rose petals, which led to the rear of the suit. Stopping in front of a closed door her heart raced wondering what was inside. Smiling she opened it slow. She was once again full of joy setting her eyes on the numerous gift bags, flowers, and women's accessories that were before her. For the remainder of the weekend, all they did was shop, party, and make love nonstop. Indeed, that was the nail in the coffin. She was hooked.

CHAPTER NINE

H EAVY FELT LIKE a brand-new man walking out of Baltimore City jail. His parole was reinstated by the courts after serving a sixty-day sanction for violating. If it wasn't for his probation officer vouching for him, he would have been back in prison serving the remainder of his sentence, which was ten years. He felt like he just dodged a bullet. To come back to the streets and bullshit around was something he couldn't afford to do. He realized that he needed that time to sort out a lot of things in his head and make a lot of changes in his life.

Seeing Carlita when she pulled up made him realize how much his life was really on the edge. He never realized how drugs could bring a person down so low. Due to him living the fast life, he never took the time out to pay attention to his family. While incarcerated, everything surrounding his family problems hit him dead in the face. He neglected his family for the streets; inside he got a taste of his own medicine. Carlita never wrote him, didn't bring the kids to see him, and stopped accepting his calls. He couldn't blame anybody but himself. It was he who introduced her to heroin. To see her in this state brought tears to his eyes.

Even though he had a vicious dope habit, he was a fly-dressing dude. When he first met Carlita, so was she. She once kept her hair and nails done, drove a brand-new Mercedes ML 430 SUV, and wore all the high-end fashion clothing. To see her pulling up in her old beat-up, white two-door 1989 Ford Escort with a scarf on her head made it clear to him that he had a lot of work ahead of him.

The sight of her made him sick to his stomach. She had a cigarette dangling from her mouth and a white robe that had all kinds of stains on it. The inside of the car was a complete mess. Trash, empty bottles, cigarette butts, and spoiled food was everywhere. Her car appeared as though a homeless person who collected cans for a living lived in it. Sadly, it was close to one hundred degrees outside, and she didn't even have the decency to drive his car. Instead, she drove her hoopty with a broken AC.

At that moment, it hit him. *Where the fuck is my car?* Not clear on why she chose to driver her bucket when she had the keys to his 2010 champagne-colored special edition DTS Cadillac, he felt his stomach fall straight to his feet. It felt as if he was riding a roller coaster downhill. He was furious. All he could think of was how fucked up she carried him while he was in jail. Now to possibly find out some bad news about his car, his pressure started to boil.

He didn't even acknowledge his kids jumping around, screaming his name, when he got inside the car. All his attention was on Carlita.

"Hey, ba—" Before she could even mutter another word, his face transformed into a demon. He grabbed her by her jaw, digging his fingers in so deeply it felt like her teeth were about to crumble. His temple veins were pulsating

"Bitch, where the fuck is my motherfucking car at?"

"Mmm. Mmm." Having a cigarette and a death grip around her mouth hindered her from speaking. He released her with a spiteful shove, causing the back of her head to crash against the window. She instantly shrieked in pain. "You stupid motherfucker! I'm pregnant with your child!" Carlita wasn't no slouch, nor was she a stranger to danger.

No sooner than he released his death grip, she started acting a fool. She threw her cigarette in his face, causing him to duck, giving her just the time she needed to reach on the side of her chair to grab her nigga knocker.

Her nigga knocker was nothing but a broken wooden chair leg that had Nigga Knocker written on it in big black letters. "Bitch, don't chu ever put cho motherfucking hands on me!" Carlita screamed as the first blow landed on his forearm then the side of his head.

The impact from the first blow caused Heavy's natural reflexes to kick in. Instead of trying to block the next blow, he went for the stick. A brief struggle over the stick ensued. Before he could retrieve the stick, Carlita looked in shock as two correctional officers across the street began walking in their direction.

"Police! Police!" Carlita yelled out the window.

He was scared shitless seeing the look on her face and hearing her scream "Police." *This shit ain't supposed to be happening,* he thought, letting go of the stick. He had no intentions of going back to jail. He turned around to see how close they were. She smacked him again with the stick.

The second blow crashed dead in the back of his head, stopping him from getting a good look at what he thought was the police. Refusing to be caught fighting with her, he covered up in the corner, hoping that if, indeed, the police was close by; they would see him being assaulted and not the other way around.

She never gave him a chance to see that it was just two female COs getting off work. Before he noticed, she pulled off, making him believe the two cops were running toward their cars to give pursuit. "Go! Go! Go! Shit, I cannot go back to jail!" he exclaimed.

"Then next time, you should think before you put cho hands on a bitch like me."

"Just pay attention to the road. Are they still behind us?" Heavy asked, trying to get a good look through the rearview mirror.

"Boy, their cars were parked a half block away!" she lied. "We good. For your information, your car is parked in front of the house."

"Why you ain't say that in the first place?"

"'Cause, nigga, I don't know sign language, and for damn sure, I don't have muscles in my mouth to pry your stinkin' ass hands up off me."

Heavy felt bad. She was right. He never even gave her a chance to tell him that the car was safely parked in front of the house.

He began rubbing her face where he left scratches, asking her with intense sincerity if was she all right. "Baby, I'm sorry. It's just these last two months been very hectic for me, and I guess I just snapped and took it out on you. I mean, baby, I love you. You're the mother of my children, and we been through so much that I hate to see you letting yourself go like this."

"Well, guess what, Antwon? This is what you created. You introduced me to this shit in the first place. What you see is what you made."

"You right, so if it's anybody I should be mad at, it should be me."

"Exactly."

"I love you, baby, and I promise that we're going to get our shit together as of this day forth. After today, ain't no looking back."

"Antwon, you say that all the time. Baby, we going to do this, baby, we going to do that, and what do you end up doing?"

"I know, I know, baby. But this time I'm serious we goin' to make it." Heavy reassured her while rubbing her stomach. "Momma, your tummy getting bigger. How many months are you now?"

"Seven." For the remainder of the ride home, Heavy enjoyed playing with the kids while listening to Carlita as she replayed all the events that occurred while he was away.

She told him that she checked herself into a rehab facility two weeks after he got arrested. Although she quickly relapsed, going on a get-high frenzy with the money she took out of his glove compartment, he was happy she tried. She also informed him that she talked to his parole officer in person, finding out early on that he would be reinstated when he appeared in court. He also found out why she didn't write him, accept his calls, or bring the kids to see him. It hurt him to hear the truth.

Her theory was when he was on the streets, he didn't come home every night. He didn't spend time with the kids, and they didn't talk on the phone at all. She needed him to feel what she was so accustomed to: neglect. She told him how she hadn't heard from Smoove since he came by to pick up his money and how strange it seemed that he never came back with the money for his lawyer—or to check on her and the kids.

Just hearing Smoove's name rattled Heavy's nerves. He knew that one day he would have to face the music. He wasn't prepared for that day to come any time soon. There was no such thing as an easy way to tell your best friend that you were nothing but a dope fiend. He never planned to tell him that he stole from him, but he did plan to tell him that he was getting high. Telling a nigga in the game you stole from him was like telling him you wore a wire. Some things just weren't tolerated, and he knew that stealing was one of them. He figured that Smoove must have found out something while he was locked up, 'cause it was unlike him to leave anybody hanging—unless you put the rope around your own neck, and in his case, he did. He just hoped that Smoove didn't know everything.

Two weeks went by, and Heavy lived out every plan he had for his family. For two weeks straight, he stayed in the house, spending an enormous amount of time with his family. He was even able to get Carlita to start taking pride in how she looked again. With two months clean under his belt, he admired himself in the mirror, liking what he saw. Heavy was 6'1" and 286 pounds, and he was always one of those slick fat dudes. He could dress, always smelled good, and had a mouthpiece that was out of this world. He knew that being aggressive wasn't always a strategy to get out of a situation. Using his mouthpiece was something he was accustomed to at a young age.

Like the average dude growing up in the hood, his parents were strung out on drugs. He was left with two choices: either allow social services to find him a suitable family setting or hit the streets, like the rest of his peers. Unfortunately, he couldn't make his mind up fast enough before social service placed him in foster care. His social worker, Ms. Nolan, thought that placing him in the Tillman residence was the best thing to do for his situation. At the time he was fourteen years old, with a fifth-grade education, one would have thought he possessed a bachelor's degree in ignorance. Due to him never having to listen to his parents, he felt the same applied for everyone else. His first day at the Tillman residence was better than he had expected. He had his own room and a whole new wardrobe from Sears, which his social worker, Ms. Nolan, purchased for him through a welfare voucher, and he also had a new brother and sister, named Marcus and Keisha. It was the summer of '99 when he and Smoove first met. Smoove was one year older than he was. They shared the same interest in everything, from girls to video games to clothes and sneakers. They instantly bonded and became inseparable. The summertime came and left too quickly. Before they knew it, it was time for school.

Being that it was summertime w h e n he arrived at their home, he was used to hanging out with Smoove all day. When they were home, they were e i t h e r playing video games, talking to girls on the phone, or sleeping. Other than that, they were beating the streets all day. Mr. and Mrs. Tillman thought that it would be best if they allowed the two boys to enjoy the summer. They were given a weekly allowance and only had to attend church once a month. The week before school, Mrs. Tillman entered Heavy's room with all his school supplies and school clothes in hand.

"Hey, baby, how's my youngest boy?"

"I'm okay, ma. Just tryna make it to the playoffs," he responded, referring to the Madden NFL video game he was playing.

"Well, baby, I came here to talk to you about a few things, so can you please pause that for a minute."

"Sure, Mom. What's up?"

"Well, you know school starts next week. I just wanted to make sure that you're prepared."

For the first time in his life, he was really looking forward to going to school, especially knowing that he and Smoove would be attending the same school.

Seeing the shopping bag she was carrying only made him more anxious. Heavy never liked school, church, or following orders, but as long as his road dog Smoove was involved, so was he.

"Here's all your school supplies, your uniforms, and shoes. School starts at seven thirty, and you'll be getting out at three fifteen. Every morning, I'll be waking you up at six thirty, and breakfast will be ready at seven. Your bus gets here at seven fifteen, so you have to be ready every morning at seven fifteen. I'll pack your lunch and keep your clothes ironed and cleaned. All you gotta do is be ready. Is there anything you wanna know about your new school?"

"You know, Marcus done told me everything about that school I need to know. I feel like I already been there."

"Well, that's good, baby. Are you excited?"

"Yeah, why wouldn't I? Me and my nizzle goin' be up in there mackin'."

"You know someone at this school?"

"My bad, Ma, you ain't up on our slang. I'm talking about Marcus. We goin' be up in there doin' our thang. We goin' do our schoolwork and stay outta trouble and all that, but all the girls g—"

"Baby, baby, hold up. You guys aren't enrolled at the same school. You're in the fifth grade, Antwon, and Marcus is in the eleventh. You didn't know that?" Heavy hadn't been to school in so long that he sure as hell forgot that he was still indeed in elementary school.

Every word she spoke after that never made it to his ears. His whole body went numb. There was no way in hell he was going to elementary school at fourteen years old. So he thought. Eventually, he decided to go after being convinced by Smoove.

"Listen, man! All you gotta do is do your work and stay outta trouble for a month, and I'm telling you they goin' put you in middle school. Once you're in middle school, do the same things. Before you know it, they're gonna put you in your right grade."

Upon his arrival at school, Heavy was teased and taunted by the whole school. He was the size of some of the teachers. On several occasions, he was even harassed by a few of them.

After lunch was over, he decided to leave school early; he could no longer take it. It was bad enough he couldn't go to school with Smoove, then to make matters worse, he had to get teased by some nerds. Before making it to his locker to grab his belongings, the school bell rang, alerting everybody that lunch was over. Moments later, the hallway became flooded with kids trying to make their last runs before they were ushered off back to class. Three fifth graders had another agenda before returning to class.

"Blubber Butt so dumb that I told him it was chilly outside, he went and grabbed a bowl," a kid named Tony said, and everyone laughed. A crowd began forming; laughter could be heard throughout the hallway.

"Nah, hah, I got one, I got one. He so old that every time he farts, dust comes out his butt!" another kid added. The entire hallway erupted into laughter.

"Enough is enough. It's time for me to lie my lick down. That way the whole school know not to fuck with me," Heavy mumbled as he walked in the direction of the kids who was teasing him. Mrs. Tillman had him enrolled into Catholic school, so the kids there were used to fighting with words. If you got into one fight, you got put out. That wasn't the deal with Heavy; he was from the streets. If you talked shit, you better know how to back it up. He outweighed the tiny fifth graders by more than fifty pounds; surprisingly, it didn't matter to them. They kept teasing him.

"Everybody, back to class at this very moment," demanded the school principal, Ms. Burton, who came outside her office.

They all obliged and quickly headed toward their next class—with the exception of Heavy and the three agitators. Before they could make it back to their class, Heavy came from behind and unloaded on all three of them at the same time.

From a distance, it looked like a gorilla in a uniform was pulverizing the three kids. He had all three of them balled up by the lockers, screaming and pleading for mercy. He continued his onslaught with no intentions of letting up. Finally, Ms. Burton was able to break him out of his rage when she grabbed him by his arm, only to receive a vicious upper cut to the chin, which knocked her wig off before sending her flying back against the lockers on the other side of the hallway. By then the hallway was flooded with teachers and staff members, who properly restrained him.

After that stunt he pulled on his first day of school, he was sent to juvenile hall for six months. After serving his short-term sentence, Heavy came home and went full-fledged into the streets. His social worker, Mrs. Nolan, placed him in another foster home his first day home. That same night, he ran away and never looked back ever since. He started selling drugs, committing robberies, and doing whatever it took for him to survive through the epidemic he was living in. In the hood, money could buy you anything—guns, p u s s y , drugs, food stamps, and a place to stay. You name it, if you had money, you had everything you needed. As quickly as he hustled up money, he quickly spent it on prostitutes, w e e d , cigarettes, alcohol, and clothes—anything that fueled his hustle. He never wanted to be rich; he just hustled to make it through the day. All he needed was a place to lay his head, food to eat, a good high, and an orgasm, and he was straight.

During his stay at the Tillman residence, that summer he and Smoove made several trips up to Heavy's neighborhood, Park Heights. Even though Smoove had a good upbringing and didn't have to be always gravitated toward the street life, he fell in love with the fast life and everything that came with it. Shortly after being released from juvenile hall, Heavy was surprised to see that Smoove was still able to hold the block down without him.

Smoove rolled up in his '96 Cadillac Eldorado, which was equipped with chrome-dipped rims and vogue tires. He spotted Heavy hanging on the corner of Shirley and Cottage engaged in a game of cee-low.

"Yo! Heav, there go Smoove right there in that white Caddy!" the cornerman shouted.

A cornerman's job was to post on the corner of the block as a lookout for the dealers, in hopes of spotting the law, the stick-up kids, or potential drug sales, giving the dealers enough time to be prepared for the inevitable. Spotting the Caddy from a half block away, Heavy could tell right away that was his man.

"Smoove! Oh shit, it's on now. My motherfucking n i g g a is pushing now!" Heavy shouted while jumping up and down in the middle of the street in an attempt to catch Smoove's attention.

While away, Heavy had no idea that Smoove stepped his game up the way he did. It was only after he arrived on the block and got word from everybody in the hood that he found out Smoove had the block bubbling. Before he went to juvenile hall, Smoove was just learning the ins and outs of the dope game. Amazingly, in his short time away, Smoove managed to go from buying less than fifty grams to moving keys. Heavy was baffled. They'd been hustling together ever since.

In the beginning, Smoove had no intentions of being a small fry in the game. When it came to the streets, all he knew was what Heavy taught him. When it came to the game, he was green. He just had the money and the hunger for more.

Heavy knew the game like the back of his hand. Being a pawn was his biggest downfall. He hustled for all the wrong reasons—clothes, weed, to trick off, and dumb stuff like that. He had all the connections, so it was his job to take care of everything pertaining to the streets. Smoove, on the other hand, oversaw all the earnings. Smoove never smoked, drank, or tricked off with females. Nor was he able to splurge with his money, being that he had to hide his new hustle from his parents. Because of it, he was holding.

Heavy had every vice imaginable. With his outrageous spending habits, he was always broke. His way of seeing things was simple and plain: "You can't take anything with you when you die. I'm having fun while I'm here."

When they first started out, Smoove gave Heavy $2,500 so he could purchase thirty-five grams of raw heroin. In exchange, he promised Smoove he could turn it into $4,000 in one day. Easily he did. Smoove couldn't believe it. He couldn't comprehend why and how Heavy wasn't rich. Seeing how he treated money, he quickly remembered why. Early on, he realized it would be best if he kept control of all the money. Instead of splitting everything fifty-fifty, he controlled all the profits and just paid Heavy on a daily basis. There was no way that he could count on him to have anything toward the reup if he didn't. Heavy's lack of responsibility only pushed Smoove deeper into the game. Fortunately for him, he made his own connections, learned how to bag up, and without looking back, kept learning from there.

******

Heavy felt out of his comfort zone, making his way onto Shirley Avenue. This was his first time coming through the hood since being released. In no way was he comfortable with having to tell his right-hand man that he was sniffing. Since his release, he was unsuccessful at trying to reach Smoove. He decided it would be best to hit the streets. From Park Heights, it was like the block was under new management. Every corner was occupied by one lookout, who seemed to be good at his job. The streets weren't crowded or in disarray. For the first time in a long time, it looked like a totally different block. Even though there were people roaming around, everything looked discreet.

By the time he parked and got out his car, one of his old workers, by the name of D-Low, rolled up on him on his bike to holler at his used-to-be boss.

"What's up, Heavy? You looking good, man. When you come home?"

"Two weeks ago."

"This the Heavy I know," D-Low said, referring to a rejuvenated and well-put-together-looking Heavy.

He was fresh from head to toe in a pair of blue Indigo Red boot-cut jeans. He also had on a baby-blue Indigo Red hipster nylon jacket with yellow trimmings along the waist and collar. Directly in the center of his back was a yellow dragon with Indigo Red written in fancy lettering beneath it. His crispy-fresh-butter Timberland boots went perfect with his outfit, giving him that got-money look he was so accustomed to.

"Get used to it 'cause the old Heavy is back. I shook that monkey off my back, and I refuse to let that motherfucker jump on me again. You smell me, li'l nigg?" Heavy said while placing his hand on D-Low's shoulder.

"Yeah, I feel you."

"You got a number on Smoove? Since I been home, I haven't been able to reach him."

"Once I seen you parking, I hit his li'l cousin on the phone and told him to call Smoove to let him know that you were around here. He told all of us that if we were to see you, make sure we call him and let him know. His li'l cousin is the only one with his number. I'm waiting for him to call me back. This must be him right here. Hold up," D-Low told him before answering his phone. "Aight, yeah, we standing on Shirley right now." D-Low quickly hung up his phone. He told Heavy that Smoove would be around in about twenty minutes before telling him he was needed on the basketball court.

Damn, Heavy thought after seeing how disappointment set inside D-Low's eyes before he left. Heavy knew that D-Low looked at him differently. Maybe it was because of all the stupid things he witnessed Heavy do. Or maybe he just felt down for some reason. Whatever the reason was, Heavy wasn't too concerned about it; all he worried about was meeting up with Smoove and reclaiming his spot.

Nothing else really mattered to him. In the middle of September, it was chilly outside, and daylight was rapidly descending, allowing darkness to escape from its threshold.

After making small talk with some of the residents and the customers coming through, thirty minutes went by, and there still was no sign of Smoove. Heavy decided to walk to the bar on the corner and snatch up a drink. At least he could be getting tipsy while he waited. After purchasing a pack of Newport shorts, a bottle of water, and a half pint of Rémy Martin VSOP, he thought that it would be best if he just chilled on the basketball court and caught up on things with his old crew.

He was so busy rushing to free one of his cancer sticks that he walked out the bar with his head down, failing to see the lady headed in his direction, pushing a stroller. It was too late. Before he lifted his head, he tripped over the stroller, taking the baby inside with him to the pavement.

"Oh shit, miss, I'm so sorry. I can't believe how stupid I am for not paying attention." In a panic, he went to grab the crying baby lying inches away from him.

Once he reached what he thought was the baby, he no longer was petrified after realizing that it was nothing more than a fake doll baby. "Miss, you had me scared to—"

Toof. Toof. Toof. Toof. She managed to squeeze off four shots from her Taurus 9mm, equipped with a silencer, before her gun jammed. *That wasn't enough damage,* she thought. She instantly bashed his face with the butt of the gun, crushing his facial bones with each landing. The last thing Heavy saw before slipping into unconsciousness was the blow that landed in the middle of his forehead. After knocking Heavy's facial features around, she placed her gun in her coat pocket then walked slowly but cautiously toward an awaiting getaway car.

CHAPTER TEN

"**G**IRL, THIS NEIGHBORHOOD is getting worse by the day." Sitting in her doctor's office, Ms. Janice began explaining to her homegirl Wanda over the phone. "The guy that was killed down the street from my house yesterday was one of Smoove's people. I'm worried like shit that something might happen to him next." "You can't think like that. Maybe he did something to deserve that shit. You just never know these days."

"Wanda, yo ass is pure ghetto. Nobody deserves to be gunned down in cold blood like that."

"I'm just saying people just don't go around killing people for nothing. You know what I'm saying."

"God says that thou shall not kill, so no, I don't understand."

"Girl, if you don't go ahead with that God shit."

"You need to come to church with me one day 'cause you're going down the wrong path."

"Oh, so selling your ass is the right path, huh?" They collapsed into giggles.

"Girl, stop, you got these people up in here looking at me like I'm crazy." Ms. Janice glanced at an elderly couple, who were looking at her.

She was there waiting to see her gynecologist to get her annual checkup, so talking to Wanda was always a tactic she used whenever she needed to kill time.

"Listen, I need your advice, girl. Me and Smoove been seeing each other for a little over three months, and I think he's the one."

"The one what?"

"That special someone. I was thinking about settling down and, you know, being faithful and all that good stuff. Smoove is young, but he's truly everything I've always wanted in a man and more."

"You're right. He is a good man. Maybe it's time for you to settle down, girl."

"I feel the same way, but it's more to the story. I'm forty-five years old. I can't give him any kids. All these young bitches running around. What if he decides to up and leave, then what?"

"Well, you do have a point there. So stop beating around the bush. What are you insinuating, Janice?"

"I was just thinking that it would be a good idea if I did my thing a little longer just to save up some money. At least I would have something to fall back on. If I cut out all the spending I do on shoes, purses, clothes, trips, and everything else I do to splurge, then I know I can easily save up $100,000 in six months."

"Damn, bitch, you make that much fucking money?"

"Oh Lord, why in the hell did I tell you that."

"All this time you been selling ass, you should be rich by now, if you can make $100,000 in six months."

"Yeah, you right. I should have more than that, but trying to keep up with the Joneses comes with a hefty price."

"Before you come up with the money, what do you plan to do about Smoove?"

"He's part of my plan. I figure I can move in with him and live rent free. Cut out all the unnecessary spending I do, plus when he gives me money, I can save that also."

"Sounds like a plan to me."

"Yes, girl, let me finish. I also plan to sell all of my furniture. Once we move together, he's buying everything for the house. It's no need to have my stuff sitting up in storage."

"What about your house?"

"I figure instead of selling it, I could rent it out. That way I always have a house to fall back on."

"Damn, girl, you got this shit mapped out, don't chu?"

"I'm trying, I'm trying. I just feel kinda bad though."

"For what? Shit, you gotta have a security blanket these days. Motherfuckers are crazy out here."

"You're right, but I just hope he never finds out. I can't afford to lose this nigga. Does my plan sound good to you, or should I just step out on fate and not risk the chance of getting caught?"

"What is this, a rhetorical question? Girl, you better stick to your guns. These days you never can be to certain about anything, so I say, stick to your plan."

"That's why I love you, 'cause you see things like I see them."

"Sometimes, not all the time, so don't flatter yourself."

"Hold on one minute, Wanda. The receptionist is calling me. Don't hang up. I'll be right back." Janice put her on hold.

Wanda was her confidante. Even though they were different in some aspects, they loved each other like sisters. The main thing they had in common was beauty. Wanda was drop-dead gorgeous. She was 5'2" and 155 pounds and had light skin with short hair. At thirty-five, she had the aura of a twenty-one-year-old. She rocked Mohawks, feather tucks, and all the Fantasia hairstyles in order to stay in tune with the younger crowd. With her vanilla complexion, she had pretty facial features. Along with dimples, she had a set of beautiful pink full lips, with a lip ring attached to her bottom lip and a Marilyn Monroe piercing above her top lip. She didn't have any bumps, blotches, scars, or blemishes on her face. With a set of pearly white teeth and green eyes, she kept a fresh pedicure and manicure as she made weekly visits to the nail salon. Overall, she was a fashionista diva also.

They shared the same interest in the fashion world, from the shoes, handbags, and clothing to other accessories that were in, such as name-brand eyewear like Louis Vuitton shades, Gucci, Marc Jacobs, Chanel, and of course, jewelry, specifically diamonds. They both had a fair share of jewelry—earrings, bracelets, rings, and necklaces. They stayed draped up. Ms. Janice made six times the amount of money Wanda made. She made sure she kept her road dog fly and up to par just to keep her in the same lane. Every time they went shopping, hit the club, or were on vacation, she would foot the bill.

Wanda was a single mother raising three kids—a seventeen-year-old son, a fourteen-year-old daughter, and a baby girl, who was nine. They all had the same father, who was currently incarcerated. She was ghetto down to the bone gristle. No matter how much Ms. Janice tried to change her ghetto mentality, she never budged or attempted to compromise. She wasn't a hood-rat type of broad by far. She just had ghetto ways that Ms. Janice couldn't understand to save her life. She was the type who would cut a person up, argue in public, and fight. She didn't believe in going to church or praying. One would have thought that she was an atheist if one considered some of the comments she made to Ms. Janice about God. The one thing she wasn't was a whore. She had kids and a baby father, whom she respected. Doing some of the things Ms. Janice did was outta the question. She was a one-man woman; tricking off was something she vowed to never do.

"I'm sorry, Wanda, I had to fill out some insurance papers," Janice said, clicking Wanda back on the phone.

"Well, girl, my lunch break is over, so I guess I'll talk to you a little later."

"Aiight, girl, just call me on your next break."

After hanging up, Ms. Janice began indulging in the latest *Jet* magazine, which was on display on the table inside the waiting room. A few minutes later, her name was called out by her doctor, letting her know that she was ready to be seen.

Due to her active and outrageous sex life, she had a monthly annual checkup, which consisted of a thorough search for any sign of an STD. She practiced safe sex, washed thoroughly before and after sex. She always inspected every sex organ she encountered.

On several occasions, she canceled dates, leaving a few dudes with stiff dicks after seeing a bump, rash, or because of poor hygiene. For the most part, she always played it safe. Condoms weren't 100%safe, so she took every precaution available to prevent contracting any disease. "Here you go, Ms. Walker," Doctor Sanders told her while giving her a hospital gown and bootees to put on. "I'll be back momentarily. Just make yourself comfortable."

"Thanks, Doc," Ms. Janice said in return while looking him straight in the eyes without blinking.

She began admiring herself in the mirror once she put on the robe. "Good God Almighty. Look at all this ass," she said to herself, seeing her ass shake in the mirror. The back of the hospital gown was open. Only the front part of her body was covered, allowing her whole ass to hang free. Goofing off she started twerking, making her ass cheeks clap, they made tidal waves wiggling in every direction. Startled by the knock at the door, she hurried over to the examining table before giving Dr. Sanders the okay to step in.

"Come on in, I'm good."

Dr. Sanders entered the room, carrying her medical chart, smiling ear to ear, puttin' the Kool-Aid man to shame. "How's my favorite patient doing today?"

"I'm fine, I guess. And yourself?'

"I had better days, but who am I to complain?"

Dr. Sanders has been her doctor for the last five years. Her insurance only provided her with a visit to his office every six months; any visit outside of that was on her. To her, it was worth it 'cause it gave her the privilege to stay on top of her health while staying health conscious at the same time. Not only did he check her for STDs, he also was her orthodontist, her hygienist, and her nutrition specialist. He had his own private practice located in Lansdowne, Maryland, which sat on the outskirts of the city.

He specialized and was certified to deal with any and everything pertaining to the human body. Each visit he gave her a Pap smear, a physical, and a pregnancy test and examined every inch of her body, looking for anything that was abnormal. Every six months, she was given an HIV test, was thoroughly screened for cancer, and got her teeth cleaned. It cost her $2,800 every six months for the services he provided her with. Her insurance only covered two visits a year.

Dr. Sanders grabbed his stethoscope and went to work. After listening to her heartbeats and her breathing, he motioned her over to the scale located along the wall near the front door. She was optimistic and confident that her plan would work. On the other hand, she was nervous because of his ethnicity and his demeanor.

He was a fifty-eight-year-old Peruvian man who came to the United States forty years ago from Peru, a country of western South America. Dr. Sanders was a married man with four kids. So with all that combined, his family, race, ethnic background, and the simple fact that he always kept his composure while she was nude left a little doubt in her mind. Plus the fact that she never dated a man of his descent made it even harder.

What the hell, she thought. *Scared money don't make no money.* With each step she took toward the scale, her big, voluptuous ass shook as if an earthquake was erupting underneath her feet.

"It looks like you gained three pounds since your last visit. What's that all about?"

"I knew my ass felt heavier. It's like every time I gain weight, I gain it in my ass. Look at it, Doc. Doesn't it seems like it's getting bigger?" she asked, spreading her ass cheeks apart.

"Well, I-I mean, it always seemed fairly large to me."

"I know you get to see a lot of ass due to your profession."

"I just do my job. Seeing body parts is part of it."

"I know it must be tempting at times. Lord knows if I came in contact with as many dicks as you do pussy, I would lose it."

Seeing him losing his composure when he tugged at his tie and slightly blushed gave her the confidence she needed to turn it up a notch. "Well, time for the fun part, Doc. You get to stick your finger into the cookie jar again," she told him while sashaying over to the examining table.

"Are you okay, Ms. Walker? You seem to be kinda extra jittery today. Is there something you wanna talk about?"

"I just been going through a lot sexually lately, and at times, I just can't control myself."

Not able to take his eyes off her fingering her pussy, he asked. "Sexually? I'm your doctor. There's nothing wrong with your organs or your reproductive system. You seem to be ovulating pretty fine for a woman your age. Is there something you haven't been telling me, Ms. Walker?"

"It's kinda complicated."

"I don't quite understand, so maybe if you elaborate on it, I'll have a better understanding. That way I can provide you with the proper treatment."

"Will it be off the record?"

"Ms. Walker, I'm your doctor. Everything we do is off the record."

"Call me Paradise."

"Like I was saying, Paradise, I'm your doctor. Everything we discuss is off the record. Your medical history is confidential information shared only with me by law."

"Well, in that case I guess I can confide in you."

"Sure, it's my job as your doctor, so feel free to enlighten me on your situation."

"I haven't had an orgasm in the last six months. Then to top it off, I just got laid off from work, so this may be my last visit outside of my scheduled six-month checkup. I'm under a lot of stress, Doc. What do you suggest I do?"

"For beginners, I think it would be appropriate if you took a trip to the local x-rated store to purchase a few accessories that would help you relieve some of that tension you got building up inside you. Secondly, you've been a patient of mine for years. I just couldn't see myself neglecting you. For the next six months, don't worry about making any payments. And lastly, make sure you get plenty of rest. Recent studies showed that lack of sleep can increase weight loss, keep you irritated, slow down your libido, and the list goes on and on about how lack of sleep can be very detrimental to your health. Now with that said, do you feel better, Ms. Walker? I-I mean, Paradise."

"A little bit."

"You just have to take it one day at a time." After reassuring her that she would be okay, Dr. Sanders retrieved a pair of latex gloves from a nearby cabinet and was preparing to move forward with his examination.

Before turning around to face her, he had to say a silent prayer, thanking God for this moment. For years, he masturbated after every visit. There was no way that he would allow her to miss any appointment, money or not. It was patients like her who made him love his occupation. Being in a dead-end relationship with his wife, fondling other women was a bit of an excitement to him. The only time he stepped outside his marriage was once a year during his weekend vacation. Other than that, this was his passion. At home, he got sex once or twice a month. When working, pussy was in his face several times a day.

Seeing Ms. Janice completely naked, sitting up on the examination table with her legs wide open, sent shock waves throughout his body. Her still fingering herself and being disrobed only excited him more. His mind was sent into overdrive.

Maybe this is my lucky day, I wish I could taste, he thought.

"Mr. Sanders." Hearing her voice broke his train of thought. "I think those latex gloves will get in our way. Just wash your hands and use your fingers." Without saying a word, he quickly obliged.

Washing his hands, he felt his heart begin to beat a thousand miles an hour.

He barely could walk straight making his way back over to her. He entered her pussy with his index finger leading the way.

"Ooh, that feels so good!"

"Everything feels fine down here."

"Yes, it does. Thanks to you, Doc. It feels good!"

Dr. Sanders was baffled but decided to just follow her lead.

"Is that right?"

"Yes, this is exactly what I been needing, Doc. Please take all the pain away down there." She moaned in a sexy voice.

By that time, he realized that finally his dream came true. Without second thought, he fell to his knees and began devouring her pussy. "Ooh, Doc, thank you. Mmm. Mmm. This feels so good to me. Don't stop. It's on its way." She knew that if she only allowed him the privilege of eating her out, he would do anything to fuck her. She thought it would be best that after she came in his mouth, she would roll out, leaving him thirsty and willing to do whatever for more.

To her surprise, Dr. Sanders must've been a certified head doctor also. He was hitting nerves she never even knew existed. She came long and hard.

"Ooh yes, you want this pussy, don't you?" she cried out.

He didn't respond verbally; he allowed his work to speak for itself. She came back to back. It got to the point that her pussy was beginning to get numb. After she busted four nuts, she ended her session with Dr. Feel Good. He never even got the chance to pull his dick out.

After giving her a normal checkup, he left the room. Smiling, he came back moments later to give her the best news ever. "Looks like you're pregnant!"

CHAPTER ELEVEN

THE BLOCK WAS flooded with people paying their respects to the fallen soldier. From the turnout of his candlelit visual, it seemed as if Heavy was the star of the hood. It was scheduled to be held at eight, the night after his murder. Barely 7:00 p.m. and the streets were filled to capacity. There were so many people there the Northern District police chief sent several cars to the scene just to make sure things didn't get out of hand.

Officer Frank Batts and Ira Carmicheal were the first to arrive on the scene. They were the most respected officers in the district, so they were more than willing to act as guardians over some of the people they grew up with. They both grew up in the neighborhood, so they had several personal relationships with numerous people in the area. One in particular was Heavy. Even though they were officers of the law, they never changed or turned their backs on the community. In return, they were given a great deal of respect for it.

"Damn. Look at this shit. Another prominent black man's life is taken by the streets he grew to love," Officer Batts stated as the two officers exited their vehicle.

There were well over two hundred people waving candles in the air. The two officers walked through the crowd, greeting everybody, paying their respects by giving out their condolences. Even they were given candles to lift in the air. They had seen a few people try to hide blunts and liquor bottles as they made their way through the crowd, not knowing that the officers were more on their side than anything. Every officer on the scene knew what time it was, so this was a day they allowed the neighborhood to go into a frenzy. All they came to do was keep the peace. It was more of a block party slash candlelit vigil. It was more like they were celebrating his life than mourning his death.

"We'll Always Love Big Poppa" by Faith Evans, Puff Daddy, and the Lox pumped out of a speaker sitting on one of the porches. The whole crowd began chanting Heavy's name in unison.

"Heavy, Heavy, Heavy, Heavy." People could be seen dancing, some crying, and drinks was everywhere. Weed smoke was circulating in the air. The majority of the crowd had on R IP, Heavy shirts.

Smoove sat and watched the entire scenery from Ms. Janice's porch. "Baby, you cannot keep blaming yourself for what happened. When God calls you home, nothing or no one can stop you from going."

"I know, but I just feel bad that I had him waiting on me and I was late, that's all. It's only a matter of time before I find out who did it."

"Then what, Marcus? Are you going to gun down the person or persons responsible?"

Smoove put his head down and had a dull look on his face. "If you think that taking another person's life is going to bring him back, then you have another thing coming. All that is going to do is leave another mother mourning over the loss of her child, plus create problems for you. I know you from the streets, and it's part of the street life that you ride for your homie, or so-called keep it G. Before you do something you'll regret, think about your unborn child."

Smoove looked at her with confusion all over his face. "You're pregnant?"

"Yes, Marcus, I'm going to have your baby." Smoove was caught off guard by her last statement.

"Oh shit, I'm about to be a father!" He ran over into her direction and swept her off her feet before spinning her around in the air.

"Baby, baby, okay, I know you're happy and all that, but don't forget we got people in our business as is."

"Baby, I don't even care 'cause in a few, you're not even going to be living around here. The hell with these nosy motherfuckers."

"Have a baby by me, baby. Be a millionaire. Have a baby by me, baby. Be a millionaire," Smoove sang the lyrics to 50 Cent's "Baby by Me."

Ms. Janice was laughing to death watching her man celebrate the good news he just heard. He was jumping around and dancing, all the while chanting, "Have a baby by me, baby. Be a millionaire." Once he settled down, he sat back down to allow it all to sink in. Not only was he infatuated with her, he was addicted to her. To have her as a girlfriend was something he never thought could happen.

"My baby's mother. I never would've thought in a million years that the infamous Ms. Janice would be my baby mother."

"Well, believe it, 'cause I went to the doctor's, and we don't need Maury, 'cause you are the father. I was shocked as hell when he told me I was pregnant."

"I'm kinda shocked my damn self 'cause it's rare for a woman your age to be having a baby, isn't it?"

"Yeah, that's why I'm shocked too. I mean, I heard about and seen women on TV older than me having babies. I just never thought at forty-five, I would be considering having one."

"Well, it looks like you don't have a choice now, huh?"

"I guess."

"What's wrong, baby? You don't seem too enthusiastic about the situation."

"I am. It's just, what if I lose it?"

"Don't think like that. Think positive. Look, if it'll make you feel better, quit your job and move in with me. I'll foot all the bills, and you can open up a business or something."

"I don't know nothing about running no business, boy."

"Well, you better learn, 'cause I don't want my baby mother out here working for nobody. Fuck that! If anything, you goin' to have people working for you."

"Boy, you need to stop cursing so much. Lord knows you got a filthy mouth."

"Girl, shut up. I'm your baby daddy now. You better get used to it."

"Whatever, boy. Come here. I need to show you something," Ms. Janice said as she led him inside her house.

Once inside, they sat on the sofa. She pulled out a photo album from underneath the couch. She began showing him different pictures. Each page she turned was a picture of a young-looking guy who seemed to be some type of a major figure to Smoove. They were pictures of him standing in front of Lambos, Ferraris, yachts, helicopters, and beach resorts. He was in various photos with different exotic women. He had on big jewelry, and in a few pictures, he was dressed like a pimp from the suit to the cane. Smoove felt a stirring of emotions seeing a younger picture of Ms. Janice wearing a two-piece bathing suit and hugging him on a beach.

"Who's the fake pimp dude?"

She didn't even respond. She kept turning the pages. Tears began to well up in her eyes, and before she could stop them from falling, she broke down. She was crying and sobbing so heavily that snot was oozing outta her nose and her breathing was labored. Handing her a Kleenex, Smoove started rubbing her back in a circular motion.

"I'm all right, baby. I just get a little emotional when I look at these pictures."

"Who is this guy?'

"My baby brother."

She remained silent and allowed the pictures to talk. After flipping through a few more pages, she came across what she was looking for then placed the book in Smoove's lap. There it was, a picture of her brother lying inside a casket, dead.

It all started to make sense to him—the tears, the pictures, and all the times she preached to him about selling drugs. "So your brother was in the game too, huh?"

"Yeah, and this was his retiring plan. Death. So tell me, how do you plan to retire? By going to prison or by dying in these same streets your best friend just died in?"

He knew at that very moment that this was the time he was waiting for. *Fuck reaching a million,* he thought. "You know what, Janice, for a while, I told myself that once I reached a million dollars, I would quit 'cause I thought that would make me happy. Honestly, being with you is the best feeling in the world. Money could never add up to the love I have for you. Before I continue taking chances in the streets, I rather take a chance with my lady and my unborn child."

Every word he spoke he said it with sincerity in his voice and looked her dead in the eyes.

"So what are you insinuating, Marcus?"

"I'm done. This is it."

"Are you serious?"

This time it was her jumping around in excitement. "I can't believe this. Mmm." She placed a sloppy wet kiss on his lips and cupped his face before pleading with him to be serious.

"Marcus, baby, please be serious with me. Tomorrow isn't promised to anyone. We can open up a store together. Just give that street life up."

"It's nothing more to say. I'm done. I don't know how many times I have to reiterate it for it to resonate with you, but real talk I'm done."

"All right, I'm convinced. Now give mama some sugar," she told him, jumping in his lap and planting small kisses on his face.

For over an hour, they sat there, going over different suggestions and ideas in their attempt to solidify a more concrete future. Before coming up with the right idea, Smoove decided to head back outside to finish paying his respects.

"Baby, we got more than enough time to come up with something. Let me get back outside, 'cause you know it wouldn't look right if I wasn't out there."

"I know, baby. Go ahead and handle your business. Oh, one more thing, Marcus. All that you staying at your place, me staying at mine is over. I don't care where you lay your head at as long as you wake up next to this ass," she advised him, grabbing a handful of her ass, stuffed in her black spandex. "As of this day forth, no more of that sleeping alone stuff."

"Woman, yo ass is crazy!"

"I'm not playing with you, chile." She playfully marched toward his direction, tightly gripping one of her slippers in her hand. Smoove stuck his tongue out his mouth then playfully ran out the door, closing it just in time for it to hit the door.

******

"Girl, you will not believe this!" Ms. Janice told Wanda over the phone.

"What?"

"I'm pregnant!"

"What? Bitch, you are lying."

"Nope, I found out at the doctor's office."

"Why you ain't call me back to tell me?"

"I did. You didn't answer your phone."

"After forty-five years of living, you finally got knocked up!"

"I can't even believe it."

"Me either."

"So what are you going to do about the baby, your plan, and how does Smoove feel?"

"Well, for starters, he's happy about the baby, and he's planning on giving me a few hundred thousand dollars to start a business."

"Get out of here."

"Yes, girl, then in less than a week, he's going to be out of the game for good."

"Mmmph, mmmph, mm. You gotta be kidding me. What the hell did you do to him? Shit, I need some of them lessons so I can put it on Chris's ass when he comes home." They both busted out laughing.

"Girl, yo tail is crazy."

"I'm serious, girl. That nigga all up in there talking about he a Muslim now. I told that nigga he might not eat pork but he, for damn sure, goin' to eat this pussy when he gets out. That's for sure." Ms. Janice was cracking up.

"Girl, stop it before you make me pee on myself. Now listen, let me finish telling you the rest. Then in a few weeks, we going to buy a house, and he's putting my name on the deed. Ain't that something?"

"Who you telling? So do you think the baby is his?"

"I hope so. Nah, I'm just joking. Yeah, it's his. He's the only person I let cum inside me."

"How far along are you?"

"Eight and a half weeks."

"Bitch, I'm jealous. You got it going on."

"Yeah, so far so good, I guess."

"Well, it appears that things are going good for you I wish I could say the same for me."

"What do you mean? What's not going good for you?"

"Hold on, girl. Li'l Chris, you better sit cho five-dollar ass down before I make change outta yo ass up in here! I'm back, girl."

"Li'l Chris is still running ya li'l tail crazy, huh?"

"Yeah, he wanna be hogging the computer, eating up all the leftovers, drinking up all the Kool-Aid. Shit, I eat pig feet too." They both burst into laughter as Wanda imitated Pops from the movie *Friday*.

"Like I was saying, things not going too good for me sexually or financially, so a bitch want in." Ms. Janice knew what she was talking about, but at the same time, she couldn't believe it.

"Not the ghetto, stuck-up, stingy pussy prissy Wanda."

"Call me what chu want. I just can't take it anymore."

"Shit, what's the use of letting this pussy marinate and stay in hibernation and be broke? It's like I work just to pay bills and to provide for my kids. Then on top of that, I'm taking care of Chris's ass while he's in jail."

"So now after all this time, you been struggling finally, you see the picture I used to try to paint for you?"

"It wasn't until you told me how much you can make that I got interested. A hundred thousand in six months. Bitch, I would suck a golf ball through a straw."

"So what about Chris?"

"Shit, what about him? The same thing you doing with Smoove. What he doesn't know can't hurt him."

"You been hanging around me too much."

"I figure since most of the clientele would be married businessmen, politicians, doctors, and people like that, it would be easy for me to keep it under the rug and from Chris. Plus I can get some dick in the process of getting paid."

"You damn right, but please answer this one question for me: what the hell took you so long to come to this conclusion? I mean, for the longest time, I couldn't understand how you could give your all to a nigga in jail that treated you like shit when he was home."

"He ain't just any nigga. He's my children's father."

"Yeah, the same nigga that cheated on you, neglected you numerous times."

"Aight, girl, you ain't gotta throw the shit up in a bitch face like that. I know what he did." Ms. Janice couldn't stand him, so every chance she got, she aired him out. She dreaded not telling Wanda about the few times he tried to make a move on her, but she knew if she did, Wanda would only end up taking his side in the end anyway.

"I'm just telling you, you can do better, chile."

"Yeah, I know. So what do I have to do to get set up with some dates? Get on the Internet or something?"

"Nah, I'll just hook you up with my old agent, and he will work you in."

"Why your old agent? What's wrong with the one you got now?"

"I'm out the game. I no longer have an agent. Nor am I a whore anymore."

"What about the plan you just devised?"

"The hell with that plan. My man came up with a better one. I can't afford to blow this one."

"It's like that, huh?"

"You damn right. This is what I been wanting all my life. A good man with money, great sex, a baby, and to be secure. Being that he's going to put my name on the deed, buy an establishment for me, and father my child, I know he'll eventually marry me. I'm really in love with that boy. I feel that it's only right if he's making me financially straight that I be faithful to him and just give us a try. You know what I mean?"

"Yeah, you got a good man, so it ain't no need in jeopardizing that shit. Just hook me up with some of your connections so I can get me some dick."

"What about getting you some money."

"Don't get it twisted. I'm in it for the dick and the money."

"I feel you. Chris been gone, what, three years now?"

"No, it's been three years, two months, and eleven days since I had some dick, and my bullet and dildo just ain't like the real thing." For the remainder of their conversation, Ms. Janice taught her the ins and outs of the game, leaving out none of the details.

******

It was now 12:15 a.m. The streets were empty with the exception of a few stragglers. The police shut the party down at midnight, but before it ended, the whole neighborhood had a ball lighting fireworks, drinking, smoking, and eating all at the expense of Smoove. Smoove noticed that none of Heavy's family attended the visual, not even Carlita. He decided to stop by her house to give his condolences. It was late, but he knew Carlita would be up. Upon pulling up in front of her house, he immediately noticed how deserted their home looked. The swing set that usually was out front was gone, none of their cars were there, and all the porch chairs were gone—nothing seemed to be in place. Once he reached the porch, his suspicions were confirmed. Carlita had indeed moved out. All the curtains were gone, giving him a view of the empty downstairs. He wasn't sure if they moved before or after the murder of Heavy; it just seemed strange to him. This was his first time over there since his last visit when Heavy first got locked up. *Maybe they had moved*, he thought, leaving the porch. Minutes later, he was pulling back up in front of Ms. Janice's house. It was now twelve forty-five; before one, he managed to bust a nut and was sound asleep.

CHAPTER TWELVE

T HE NEXT DAY Wanda was at home, getting ready for her job interview with Charles, the agent Ms. Janice hooked her up with. She was anxious; not only was she going on an interview, Charles also was sending a chauffeur to her house and forewarned her to bring her A game with her. He also told her about the $1,000 incentive she would receive if she was hired. She was eager to get her day moving forward. She dropped her kids off at her mother-in-law's house earlier in the day and was enjoying being at home alone. She stepped out the shower then instantly went to work on her beauty.

Applying an apple scented Bath and Body works moisturizer all over her body; she spent extra time massaging the lotion on her breasts. She applied a dab of Ambi Skincare to her face, giving her a little glow to add to her natural beauty. Next, she gently applied eye shadow to her eyelids to enhance her eyes. After that, she swiped both of her armpits twice with her secret deodorant, brushed her teeth, then made her way over to her wardrobe.

Her walk-in closet was filled to capacity with brand names, from designer clothing to shoes. She even had a section where she stored her purses and handbags that were exclusive. If it was top-notch, she had it—Prada, Christian Dior, Gucci, Dolce & Gabbana, Coach, Fendi, Chanel, Burberry, Apple Bottoms, Coogi, vera Wang, True Religion, and Juicy Couture, just to name a few. Trying to keep up with Ms. Janice kept her broke. *Fortunately, all that would change,* she thought as she began ransacking her closet in search of the perfect outfit.

Her first pick was a pair of black Casadei pumps. Next, she grabbed her cleavage-cut black-and-white m i n i dress by Dior, with the shades and handbag to match. To top it off, she rocked it with a black garter belt by H&M. She went to her jewelry chest and picked out a heart-shaped diamond-encrusted Cartier watch and placed two crater-size diamonds on her ears.

It was so quiet in her house that she was startled when her phone rang. She answered it by the second ring only to hang up on the operator who was advising her that Chris was calling collect. Seconds later, he was calling her again. Instead of hanging up on him again, she just unplugged the phone. Her mind was made up, so there was no way she could allow him to spoil her moment. She felt bad about the whole situation, as it was, and hearing his voice would only intensify the guilt she felt inside. Her ride would be picking her up in any minute now, and she was not about to let him slow her down any longer. She already was on lock for three lonely years; another day was unimaginable.

While at the mirror applying some finishing touches, she heard her cell phone vibrating on her nightstand. Before she even reached it, she became nervous.

"Hello?"

"Yes, is this the lovely Ms. Wanda Jenkins?"

"Yes, this is she."

"I'm calling to let you know that I've safely arrived, ma'am. I'll be out front waiting on your departure."

"Great, I'll be out shortly."

She couldn't believe the moment was here. She was both nervous and excited at the same time. She was nervous over the fact this was her very first day. She didn't know what to expect. Then on the other hand, she was eager to see what it was like. To make matters worse, Ms. Janice only told her the ins and outs of the game. She never told her about the interviewing process at all.

She smoothed on a layer of Mac Lip Gloss and sprayed her Victoria Secret perfume between her legs and along her neck. Before leaving, she stuffed a few toiletries in her handbag and was on her way. Upon stepping outside her house, she was stunned to see her chauffeur leaning against the side of a platinum Maybach. She lived in the hood, so she wasn't the only one mesmerized by the rare beauty.

It was a gorgeous day outside. The sun was beaming, the sky was clear, and the people in the neighborhood were out in great number *I can get used to this*, she thought to herself as she hurried over and climbed in the backseat.

All eyes were on her. The hustlers standing on the corner were catcalling and giving her compliments. People were hanging out their house windows trying to get a good look. The younger kids were jumping around like Santa Claus himself was in their presence over the exotic car. That was a true reminder to her that she needed to get out the hood, and fast. Nothing could be done under the radar in the hood. It was like no matter what time of day it was, somebody was always outside or at their window to hear or see something. There was no such thing as a secret in the hood. What one person knew, everybody and their momma would end up knowing before the day was out. She could hear her baby father now. "Who was that nigga I heard picked you up? What you doing staying out all night?" Like he owned some damn body. In her mind, this would be her first and last time giving her neighbors something to talk about.

To her amazement, her chauffeur was a very handsome-looking man. He was wearing a black tailor-made tuxedo, which gave him a model type of look. Deep jet-black waves sat atop his head. He was dark chocolate with a muscular face. He was clean shaven.

"Greetings, ma'am. How are you today?"

"I'm good, but can we pull off please?"

"Oh, excuse me, ma'am. Anything for the lovely lady."

"No need to excuse yourself. I just hate seeing all these nosy ghetto people all up in my business."

"Oh, I see." He looked at the crowds forming on both sides of the street.

"What type of music do you have up in here?"

"All genres. What type of music do you like?"

"You got R & B and hip-hop?"

"R & B and hip-hop it is."

She was in love with the customized interior, from the seats to the velvet carpet on the floor.

"What is this?" she asked, referring to the curtains on the windows.

"They're curtains for the windows." He pressed a button, and automatically, the curtain covered her window. "Instead of having tinted windows, a Maybach got curtains."

"Well, you can pull them curtains back now. A bitch needs to be seen up in this joint. You feel me?" she playfully told him, all the while looking cute, patting her Mohawk.

They both started laughing. "Motivation" by Li'l Wayne and Kelly Rowland came blasting from the system.

"That's my shit. Turn that up." Every block they rode through before they hit the highway, she felt like a superstar.

People were waving at her from passing cars. When they stopped at red lights, people ran up to the car to get a closer look. This was a feeling she could get used to. The ride was short; they reached their location in little over an hour. They parked in front of a high-rise building on Broad Street, located in Downtown New Jersey. Wanda felt good all over. In her mind, she managed to convince herself that there was no need to panic. With every step, she walked with confidence. Being out of town and going to be meeting with complete strangers, she felt more relaxed and at ease. Upon entering the establishment, s h e walked toward the receptionist's desk to announce her presence.

"Good afternoon, sir. I have a 2:00 pm appointment with Charles."

"It's good to see you made it here on time, Ms. Jenkins. You've passed the first stage of the interviewing process with flying colors," said the receptionist.

She was puzzled. "How do you know my name?"

"I'm Charles. It's my job to know everything that goes on in this building, especially since I'm the head honcho!"

He told her while standing up, extending his hand to greet her. He placed two soft kisses on the top of her hand, which sent chills through her body.

She couldn't believe that this young-looking dude was Charles. *How in the world could a nigga this young run a business like this? And be that damn fine?* she thought as she looked into his hazel-brown eyes. He had a mixture of "I'm a street dude slash intellectual gentleman" style to him that made Wanda feel right at home.

Charles was one of them light-skin brothers who didn't quite fit in the played-out light-skin category of most guys his complexion. He had four freshly braided french braids, which reached the center of his back, along with a crispy, neat shape-up. He rocked a baby-blue V-neck vest with a light-pink button-up shirt, which was open at the collar. His left sleeve was rolled up, revealing a few tattoos and an iced-out Movado watch. The light-blue jeans he rocked with it went perfect with his pink-and-white Pumas.

"You look more beautiful in person than on a picture." Her puzzled look made it evident to him that she wasn't knowledgeable about the picture Ms. Janice emailed him late last night.

"What picture?"

"Janice never told you she sent me a few pictures of you, huh?"

"Nope, she never mentioned a thing to me about no picture." *That heffah*, she thought.

"Here at Divas Inc., it's procedure that we do a little background check on anybody we hire. Each and every individual is different. Take you, for instance. Janice hooked you up with me, so I know you're not an undercover cop or informant. Now if a beautiful woman walked through the front door right now and wanted to work under my agency, the only thing that I would know about her is that she's beautiful, that's it. I wouldn't know how old she is, where she's from, or nothing. She would go through more of a hassle than you would.

"You, on the other hand, you get a head start being that you have such a great reference like Janice. Now about the picture. Being that I didn't get to see what you looked like, I had to think and look at the bigger picture. Time is money, and I make sure I waste none of them. There's no way that I would've been willing to send my chauffeur to pick you up plus have my team of stylists prepare for your photo shoot. Not to mention waste my time interviewing someone I have no intentions on hiring."

"So, in other words, if I was ugly, or should I say not so attractive, then what?" she asked sarcastically with her hands on her hips.

"That's a no-brainer." They both blushed.

"Okay, now that we got a few things out the way, let's get the interviewing process rolling. Why don't you have a seat, and one of my assistants will be out shortly to take you through the next phase. I look forward to seeing you momentarily."

She watched as he went through the door behind his chair. Within seconds, an attractive-looking female of Indian descent emerged from behind the same door Charles exited.

"Welcome to Diva's. I'm Tu-Tu. I'll be your host for the moment. Follow me as I take you on a tour. Don't look at this as an interview. Instead, look at it as an opportunity of a lifetime."

Tu-Tu's appearance didn't quite fit her occupation, Wanda thought. She reminded Wanda of one of those Indians you saw behind the cash register at 7-Eleven. She even had a red dot on her forehead. She was wearing a sari, one of those outer garments worn chiefly by women of India and Pakistan. It consisted of a length of cloth with one end wrapped about her waist, forming a long skirt, and the other end draped over her shoulder. She was very young looking also.

"Charles assigned me the duty of giving you a tour of the building. Relax and make yourself at home."

"Thank you for making me feel comfortable."

"It's my pleasure. First things first. A quick rundown on all the services we here at Diva's provide and what we have going on inside our establishment. The first two floors are occupied by our employees and staff members only. The remaining floors belong to various agencies. A massage parlor, doctor's office, and a swinger's house." The first floor consisted of a fitness center, barbershop, day-care center, hair-and-nail salon, and a classy-looking cafeteria. To her amazement, everything was open twenty-four hours, seven days a week.

"You mean to tell me that as long as I'm an employee, I have access to all of this for free?"

"That's right."

"So let me get this straight, I could bring my daughter with me to work, get my exercise on, then go and get my nails done for free?"

"You said it right."

Wanda was shocked at what she was hearing.

"That's decent. I'm feeling that. So what's next?"

"You see that elevator at the end of the hall?"

"Yeah," Wanda answered nonchalantly.

"It only goes to the second floor. Once you reach the second floor, Charles will be waiting to take you through the next stage." After the elevator doors closed and she was alone, she let her excitement run wild.

"Oh yeah, it's on now. A bitch is about to get paid." She started dancing and bragging to herself out loud. She quickly regained her composure after she realized she reached the second floor. To her surprise, Charles greeted her on the other side with a rose and a glass of champagne.

"This is nice."

"You are a Diva. Every time I see you, I'll treat you like one."

"I need it. Lord knows I do," she said as she lifted her glass in the air.

He led her over to a bar area where there were a few other people sipping on drinks. The atmosphere on the second floor was more to her liking.

Making her way over to the bar area, she was really beginning to feel right at home. "The Motto Remix" by Drake, Li'l Wayne, and Tyga was pumping at a high volume through a jukebox located on the other side of the room. "Tell Uncle Luke I'm out in Miami too, clubbing, hard-fucking women. Ain't much to do," Drake rapped.

To the naked eye, one would have thought a party was going on. This was the normal atmosphere at Diva's. There weren't a lot of people there, but the few who were there seemed to be having a good time.

"So what do you think so far, Ms. Jenkins?"

"When do I start? A sista is feeling everything you got going on up in here. You haven't even finished showing me around, and already I'm hooked."

"Well, that's good, 'cause I look forward to working with you. I must admit, you have something special that a lot of women don't possess. I find you to be very alluring. You have a distinctive character, your swag is on one billion, and you have an aura to you that allows you to fit in wherever you go in life. That I like. But let me warn you, only the strong survive in this game. You gotta be thorough. You know what I mean?" With each word he spoke, he looked her dead in the eyes, not blinking once. "You have to be a thinker and know how to use your brain, 'cause just having good looks won't get you ahead in this game. It's millions of beautiful women in this world, but all don't have what you have."

For the first time during her interview, this was the first time she felt discouraged. "Are you okay? 'Cause if you're having second thoughts about anything, maybe it's a good idea if you gave it a little more thought then came back," Charles asked, seeing her demeanor change.

She downed her glass in one gulp then thought about the well-needed benefits and decided to go forward. "It's no need to think about it, 'cause I know what I'm here for. It's just I'm a little nervous."

"Don't worry about it, baby. You'll do just fine. I'm sure of it. Listen, before we move along, I need to go over a few things with you.

"How far are you willing to go in this game?"

"What do you mean by that?"

"Are you willing to do what it takes to get the job done? Or do you plan on being a small fish in the sea? Here at Diva's, we have two lanes. Either you're moving in the fast lane, or you're just on the highway. It's like this; your position here at Diva's would consist of one or two things. The choice is yours. The first option, which I like to call the premium package, or shall I say the welfare package, is where you make the least amount of money. In return, you work less, and you offer no sexual favors. There's no contract or agreement involved, and there's no $1,000 incentive upon being hired. You would only be required to accompany some of our clients during their travels to and from various events. The furthest you would have to go is giving a massage. That's it. For the services you provide under the welfare package, you will be compensated only after the date is over. The pay varies depending on the time frame. I'll give you an example. Let's say a guy wants some company on a date and afterward wants a massage in his room. You end up being in his presence for six hours—no kiss, no sex, nothing. In return, he would pay the company in advance in order for us to provide him with the services he's requesting. In return, you'll be paid $250 for those six hours. Any hour past six hours, you'll receive one hundred dollars an hour.

"What if I'm only with a client for two hours, then what?"

"You get $250 if you're only with a client one minute. Once a client books you, there's a nonnegotiable refund policy they agree to."

"Now for the platinum package, and what I like to call the VIP package, to start making the big bucks, you gotta be prepared to get your hands dirty. Just like the welfare package, the VIP package varies also. If a guy wants to book you under the VIP section, trust and believe me, he wants some pussy at the end of the night.

"If you get booked under the VIP section and he wants you to accompany him on a date, the price is now $500 just to go on a date."

"When you say date, what type of date would a guy want to take me on for $500?" Wanda asked out of curiosity.

"We're talking about some wealthy individuals. You'll be dealing with politicians, judges, lawyers, the city's councilmen, and even athletes. Some of our regular clients play for the New Jersey Nets. You should have seen Kris Humphries in here after he and Kim Kardashian split. You see that guy over there?" He pointed to a Middle Eastern-looking guy shooting pool.

"Yeah, who's he?"

"He's a multimillion-dollar oil investor from Palestine. He's in town on business. Those two lovely ladies with him are his for the entire week. You do the math."

Wanda couldn't begin calculating the numbers; she just figured it would be a great down payment on her Lexus.

"Aiight, now back to business. Like I was saying, after the date, it's $250 an hour in your pocket for each hour you're alone with him. If he decides to go over the six-hour limit, then it's up to you to negotiate a price. I've seen guys book a date for one day and enjoy themselves so much that they ended up keeping the girl for the entire week. Again you do the math. On the flip side of things, some of the things you're gonna see are going to make you sick to your stomach, like guys with uncircumcised dicks, cigarette-smelling fat slobs. You might be introduced to a threesome and all kinds of shit. The most important thing of them all is always protect yourself. I don't care if you're giving a guy some oral pleasure. Make him wear a condom. He may not like the idea of getting sucked off through plastic, but I guarantee you he'll respect you for it. Now the choice is yours."

Without hesitation, she made her decision. Her mind was made up before he even finished talking. "Give me the platinum to go."

They celebrated by toasting to two shots of Patron before he proceeded to walk her through the next stage of the interview.

"You're doing good, baby. Just one more stop, then you're on your way to making platinum status."

By then Wanda was already envisioning her new lifestyle and what it would feel like moving out of the hood and purchasing that new Lexus she desired. She didn't even care what she had to do to make that kind of money. There was no looking back now. All she could think about was the lifestyle that lay ahead of her. From the messed-up economy to the little hours she received at work and being the sole provider for her three children, plus taking care of the incarcerated father of her baby, she was ready to get started today. They sat at the bar area, going over every detail pertaining to her new soon-to-be duties while downing shot after shot of Patron.

"Now that we got everything clear, are you ready for the last part of your interview? Or did you chicken out?" Charles asked jokingly.

"Chicken out! Boy, pleeease." She was beginning to feel buzzed, so she was feeling boisterous. "This my shit," she said, referring to the Young Jeezy song "I Do," which was being played.

"Good, 'cause this is the part of the interview that counts the most. Do well, 'cause your future depends on it. Follow me." Charles led her to a long hallway that had doors on each side. This section was called Fantasy Lane. At $1,000 an hour, one could come to Fantasy Lane and live out any fantasy they desired. Gently placing a key with 69 engraved on it, he advised her that her first client was waiting on her. "As of this day forth, you're my bitch. When I say jump, you jump, then ask, was that high enough? You follow my drift?"

"Mmm hmm," Wanda answered, nodding.

"Handle your business," he told her, smacking her on the ass. With that said, Wanda knew what time it was.

She entered the room nervously, only to find a familiar face lying on his back, butt naked, stroking his dick.

"Aren't you the guy that picked me up?" she asked, full of surprise.

"Yeah, but enough of the small talk. You got a job to do, don't you?"

Without responding, she started getting undressed. Wearing no panties or bra to begin with, she had nothing but her black garter belt on once she slipped out of her mini dress.

"Got damn you ah sexy li'l bitch."

Wanda's body was banging. Her measurements were thirty-six, twenty-four, forty, and for her to have three kids, one would've never known due to her flat waistline. She had a butterfly belly ring, pretty small feet, a clean-shaven pussy, and a curvaceous figure. Her pussy was throbbing and screaming to be filled. The last time she was face-to-face with a dick was three years ago. She was pleased to see that her first client was cute, but strangely, she didn't even know his name. From his demeanor, she thought it would be best if she didn't bother asking and just went straight to business. Her pussy was soaked just knowing that pleasure was on its way. She was feeling the few shots she consumed. The remaining inches of fear left her body once she crawled onto the bed, knees first.

Her first client was gorgeous from head to toe. He was tall and slender and had a six-pack that complimented his brazilian body wax. His skin looked like caramel. To top it off, he looked like someone who just stepped out of a *GQ* magazine.

Once within his reach, he grabbed her by the hair and started taunting her with his dick. His dick was the size of an Eckrich sausage. Each time he smacked it against her face, she was turned on more. In her mind, this was no longer an interview; it was time to get some dick. Grabbing the shaft of his dick, she arched her back then deep-throated him. She took in every inch of his dick, allowing the head of his dick to reach her tonsils. Her mouth was watering as if she were sucking a T-bone steak, giving Jordan the chauffer a sensational feeling.

Suddenly Charles walked into the room wearing a black robe, black house slippers, and some black shades. The ecstasy pills Charles allowed to dissolve in Wanda's drink was beginning to take its toll. She didn't pay him any mind as she felt him enter her from behind. Charles was amazed at how small her entrance was. Her pussy was so tight it felt like he was trying to stick his dick inside a virgin. When his dick pierced her insides, Wanda shrieked out in pain. Her pussy was so wet that once his head found its way inside, his dick slid in and out with ease. She felt pain and pleasure at the same time but enjoyed every moment of it. Charles had one foot on the bed while his other foot stayed on the floor, giving him the opportunity to watch every inch of his dick glide in and out of her pussy. To Wanda, Charles had an average-size dick. It was the dick she had in her mouth she feared.

Jordan had a dick that was so big she knew it would rip her insides. Before he got the chance to do just that, she decided to try sucking him into submission. Little did she know Jordan was high off ecstasy also. This, indeed, would be a long day.

Wanda was performing like a porn star. All the years she missed without sex she was making up for it. With one hand, she tightly gripped Jordan's dick while tongue-kissing his head. With her other hand, she had it pressed against his six-pack, giving her the leverage she needed in keeping her balance. Charles was behind her, laying it down. He was no longer long-dicking her slow; he was pounding away. He went unobserved, slipping an ecstasy pill inside her asshole.

From their previous discussion, she warned him about the time frame it had been since the last time she had sex. Being the hustler that Charles was, he had a backup plan for any and all his investments. He slipped her the ecstasy pill in hopes of giving her the ability to loosen up. He also knew that from the torture she was about to endure, she would need more than a drink and $1,000 to keep her coming back. He wanted her to reach heights of passion she never reached before.

He also knew that he wasn't well endowed. That was how Jordan came into the picture.

Jordan was frequently talked about among the women who worked at Diva's over the size of his dick. He was introduced to the threesome just to do exactly what she thought: rip her insides. In Charles's mind, she needed to be turned out in order to make it at Diva's. Working in this industry could easily make or break a person.

Wanda was experiencing orgasm after orgasm. With the ending of each one, her body screamed for more. Each time she came, she took Jordan's dick outta her mouth and screamed out in pleasure at the top of her lungs.

"Ahhh! Ooh yes! Oh my god, this shit feels so good!" Charles dick was feeling so good that she ventured off into a whole different world. She no longer could focus on sucking Jordan's dick. Instead, she turned around to look Charles in the eyes as he drilled her.

She had her mouth wide open, screaming at the top of her lungs as she watched Charles pump harder and harder behind her. Her pussy was so wet it sounded like juices were spitting out her pussy. Both of his thighs and balls were covered in her wetness. Each time she came, juices rapidly emerged from her pussy, leaving the sheets beneath her soaked.

"I'm coming again! Ahhh! Ahhh! Smack my ass!"

Not able to handle it, Charles pulled out, pulled his condom off, and shoved his dick deep inside Wanda's throat. She never even swallowed the cum of her babies' father. The taste was unfamiliar to her taste buds. Like a pro, she swallowed every drop.

Charles got up, slipped on his robe, then left, leaving Wanda alone with Jordan. By that time, the triple-stack naked lady E pill reached its highest peak in both their systems, fueling their sexual appetites. "Stand up, bitch!" Once Charles was gone, Jordan transformed instantly.

As weird as it seemed to her, she was turned on by it. Wanda quickly hopped off the bed and rose to her feet.

"Yes, daddy."

He placed an unwrapped condom in her hand. "Use your mouth and not your hands."

With no problem, she was able to roll the condom down his entire dick without gagging. The sensation he felt from having his dick deep inside Wanda's throat brought his erection to its fullest potential. Forcing her on her knees, Jordan looked in admiration as every inch of his dick found its way deep inside her neck. Unable to manage the eruption building inside, Jordan pulled away in a hurry before an orgasm worked its way through his body.

"Got damn!" Wiping sweat from his forehead, he frantically backed away. Sensing it, Wanda gripped his butt cheeks and forced his entire dick past her tonsils. Finally escaping her hold, Jordan aggressively snatched her up on her feet by her hair, only to push her down on the bed. To his surprise, Wanda loved every minute of the ordeal. Not once in her life did she feel this drunk or as horny as she was now. She didn't give a fuck what he did because each time he touched her, she felt as if she was about to melt. The ecstasy heightened all her senses, making the smallest touch feel like the best touch she ever received in the world.

Jordan placed two pillows under her stomach, placed a blindfold over her eyes, then handcuffed her hands to the bedpost. After properly positioning her, Jordan rammed his dick inside her, only to reach her walls before even half of his dick was in. It was time to go in for the kill. Spreading her ass cheeks apart, he pushed his dick in as far and as fast as he could.

"Ooh yes, daddy! Ungh! This dick is so big!" As her screams became louder, the pounding became harder. It was no longer a feeling of passion; pain overtook her body as Jordan manhandled her backside.

Twenty minutes went by, and finally, it was over. For the entire twenty minutes, she screamed at the top of her lungs. Never in her life did she ever encounter a dick that was as big as Jordan's. He was more than packing; he was working with a monster. Jordan freed her hands then slid the blindfold from her face.

He slipped on his robe then left Wanda in the fetal position, clutching her stomach on the bed. No sooner than he left the room, Charles was coming back in for seconds.

Damn, when is this shit over! she thought. *Maybe he's just here to talk.* Her pussy was on fire.

"Come on, let's get you cleaned up," Charles told her before helping her to her feet.

She was still clutching her stomach. Each step she took was painful and slow. To make her feel even worse, her pussy was bleeding.

"Damn, you niggas done brought my period down."

"You look like shit compared to how you looked when you first came through the door."

"I feel like it, but I don't need you throwing it all up in a bitch face like that." Charles burst out laughing.

A PARK HEIGHTS TALE

"See what I mean? Even in the darkest moments, you still shine. Here it is. You just got the dog shit-fucked outta you, but you still got the nerve to talk shit."

"You damn right. Now hurry up and get me to the bathroom." She was surprised to see a hot tub filled with bubbles, two bottles of champagne on ice, a stand-up shower, plus a fifty-two-inch plasma Tv, along with a toilet and sink. As she slowly sat inside the hot tub, a tingling and burning sensation rushed to her womb.

"This feels so good," she said, referring to the massage she was receiving from the various holes that shot out the water. "I feel dehydrated. Can you get me some water please? Not only am I thirsty, I'm horny than a motherfucker."

"I guess missing out on some dick for all that time took its toll on you, huh?"

"I guess."

"Here's your water, baby."

"Thanks. You're such a good host."

"I try to be."

Wanda was so thirsty she gulped down three bottles of spring water back to back. After taking turns washing each other's bodies, Charles popped one of the bottles of Rozay. Wanda was squirming around and touching all over herself while Charles sucked along the nape of her neck. She sat on his lap and began tongue-kissing him. She was in a zone; nothing but his touch mattered at the moment. She wanted to tell him that she loved him due to the unfamiliar heights of passion she was experiencing. She wanted to suck his dick, to be fucked for hours, and go at it nonstop.

He pulled her away from his mouth to put the bottle of champagne to her lips. After finishing the bottle of champagne together, they were at it again—kissing, pulling each other's hair, moaning, and touching. They were both ready for penetration. Wanda grabbed his dick and was guiding it toward her entrance when Charles stopped her.

"Always remember rule number 1, protect yourself. Always." He then reached on the outside of the hot tub to retrieve a condom and a bag of E pills.

"What's that?" Wanda asked as Charles put two pills in his mouth.

"That feeling running through your body. Open up. These are for you." Dropping two pills in her mouth, Charles slid a condom on and enjoyed the ride of his life.

"Ecstasy?" she asked.

"Yeah, ecstasy."

CHAPTER THIRTEEN

MS. JANICE WAS lying in bed, cracking up on the phone as Wanda gave her the scoop on her rendezvous at Diva's.

"Bitch, you did not tell me that I would be getting my insides ripped the fuck open by some linky dick, big-foot lurch-ass nigga name. Damn, what is his name?" They both burst out laughing.

"Wanda, your tail is crazy. How in the hell don't you know his name? It's Jordan."

"Shit, all I remember calling him was daddy, baby, and something big dick."

"Girl, you silly."

"All right, be quiet, let me finish."

Wanda gave her the rundown on all the events that transpired from the previous day.

"Then to top it off, after all the sucking and fucking, my motherfucking period came down."

"You lying."

"I shit chu not."

"How did they react?"

"It didn't stop Charles from running up in me in the hot tub. Besides, I wouldn't give a fuck how they felt. It was their fault my shit came down in the first place."

"Did you take your head and full body shots yet?"

"Yes, girl, that was so fun. Let me tell you. I was hooked up with the works. I got a full-body massage by two sexy-ass niggas while I was naked for starters. Next I got my nails, hair, and makeup done. Girl, they had this li'l tank that had a bunch of baby fish in it. Soon as you put your feet in the tank, the fish eat all the dead skin on your feet."

"Damn, I never even had that treatment before. I need to call Charles up. So what happened next?"

"Before the photo shoot, the stylist took all of my measurements then hooked a bitch up with all kinds of clothes. I took a few shots in some lingerie first then some casual shots in business suits and, of course, some hoochie outfits."

The sound of Smoove entering the house gave Ms. Janice the chills. Just his mere presence was enough to give him her undivided attention.

"My baby just came in. I'll hit you up a little later." Before Wanda could even protest, she hung up the phone then made her way downstairs.

"That girl is crazy," she said to herself. Today was a good day for Ms. Janice. It was the beginning of her and Smoove's new life and the ending of their past. Being with Smoove brought out a special feeling. No sooner than he entered the door, she felt like a big kid again. With the front door still open, she jumped in his arms, wrapped her legs around his waist, then planted big, soft, wet kisses along his face and neck.

Within seconds, her future flashed right before her eyes. Dion the manager at Rent-A-Center was walking up the steps that led to the porch. The ending of Paradise meant the ending of all her clients. Dion just didn't get the picture. She thought she was able to shake him when she told him she had a boyfriend and changed her number.

"Save that for one minute, baby. I gotta piss like a racehorse," Smoove said, motioning for her to release her grip. With Smoove rushing up the steps toward the bathroom, she hurried to the front porch.

"Dion! What did I tell you? I have a man now. That life is over."

"We still can be friends. He don't have to know about us," he protested, reaching to wrap his hands around her waist.

"Please, Dion, just leave me alone. You're starting to scare me," she whispered, smacking his hands away.

"Are you serious?"

"Yes, I told you I cannot see you like that anymore."

"Oh, so all the money and free furniture I gave you didn't mean shit?"

With her neighbors looking in their direction and the possibility of Smoove coming back, she decided to give in.

"All right, fine, Dion, you win. I'll call you later and set up a date, I promise. Can you just leave before my boyfriend comes back?"

"Bitch, don't play with me. This shit will be all over YouTube," he told her, showing her a scene on his phone from the sex tape they made.

Oh shit, she thought. This nigga is crazy. Knowing that he had her on camera participating in a threesome, sexing another woman, she was

A PARK HEIGHTS TALE

in a no-win situation. Hearing Smoove walking behind her only made things worse.

"I'm going to call you. Just let me get rid of him."

"So I will be seeing you today, right?"

"Yes! I promise. Now I have to go. I'll see you later."

"Whew!" Gasping in shock, she was startled to bump into Smoove soon as she turned around.

"Who was that?" Smoove asked, seeing Dion leave the front porch.

"Oh, that's just, um, the, ah, manager from Rent-A-Center."

"You wasting money on renting furniture from that place?"

"I sure do. Everybody doesn't have money to just go around buying stuff at will," she lied.

"How much you owe?" Smoove asked, pulling out a wad of money. "We can pay him in full right now."

"No, baby, I can't let you do that. I got myself in this situation. I'll get myself out of it."

"I respect that and all, but as a man, I don't see it appropriate that a bill collector has my woman promising him anything. Let alone asking you like he's demanding to see you today. So how much do you owe on it?"

"One hundred fifty dollars."

"That's it. Hey, hold up!" Smoove called out, trying to get Dion's attention as he was pulling off.

"Relax, baby. Let's go inside. I'm all out here half dressed."

"Well, here's $150 right here. Make sure you pay it today, 'cause I don't like his demeanor."

"You know how those bill collectors can be, baby, but if it makes you feel better, I'll take this money this time. Don't think that you have to do everything for me. I can hold my own, you know."

Once inside, she felt as if the weight of the world was just taken off her shoulder. She wasn't sure of everything he heard, but from his response, she was almost certain that he bought into her story.

"I love you, baby," Smoove told her as he looked her deeply in her eyes.

"I love you more, baby. How was your day?" she asked, rubbing on his face.

"Besides saying good-bye to the hood, I'm feeling all right."

"I know it must be hard on you to just up and leave so suddenly, but, baby, this is the best choice you could've ever made."

"I know. It's just not as easy as it may seem."

"Let's sit down, baby. I'm here to talk and listen to you. Regardless of whatever, we're in this together," Ms. Janice told him, leading the way to the sofa. Seated, she stood behind him, massaging his neck and shoulders, listening to him.

"Do you know what effect I will have on other people's lives once I step away? By me leaving the game, it's no telling what will happen to this neighborhood. For years, it's been me that stopped certain things from going down. It's me that made sure all the elderly people get treated with respect around here.

"I'm responsible for a lot of people eating. For instance, I been paying my cousin mortgage for years. If I was to stop today, it's no telling what would happen to him financially in this fucked-up economy. It's bigger than just me. Then today when I told all of my workers that this was it, they acted as if I just told them the world was coming to an end, like, these dudes don't know how to make it on their own out here. All they know how to do is get a package in their hand and sell it. They don't know how to buy and measure weight, package it, not to mention they don't even have a connect. I'm literally the only connect that they have right now, so to just up and leave them without putting them in position to make it out here is something I can't do."

"But, Smoove," Ms. Janice protested, "what about us? Our baby? Our store?"

"Chill, baby, you got it all wrong. Let me explain."

Smoove got up and grabbed hold of her hand and led the way toward her bedroom. Once they were seated on the bed, Smoove proceeded to give her his spiel.

"Baby, listen. I'm not saying that I'm getting back in the game. All I'm saying is that I gotta find a way for the people I was in the game with to eat. Not to mention I still got work that I gotta get rid of. Don't get me wrong. I'm done. It's just a transition that I have to go through before I officially can call it quits." He could tell by her reaction that she wasn't quite feeling his decision.

She sat beside him with her arms crossed over her chest, pouting her lips. "I mean, Marcus, break it down to me better than that, 'cause I'm not understanding the point you're trying to make. Either you going to continue selling drugs or not. Which one is it?"

He wasn't ready to give her a straight answer. That wasn't a part of his plan.

"I knew it, I knew it. All that shit you talked was a lie, Marcus."

This was the first time in their relationship that they hit a bump in the road, and Smoove was on the verge of seeing a side of Ms. Janice he never knew existed. She fell to the floor and began crying, causing Smoove to not only rush to her side but to also feel bad, knowing he was the cause of the pain she was feeling.

"I'm done with you, Smoove. Just leave. I don't want nothing to do with you! I'm not having this baby. I don't wanna be with you anymore. It's over. Just leave. I'm done."

"Baby, baby."

"Baby my ass. Just leave me alone, liar." She rose to her feet to begin showing him that she was serious. "Get out of my house now!" she screamed, throwing some of his belongings at him.

"Listen! Listen! Listen!" Smoove grabbed her by her shoulders. "You got it all twisted."

"No, you got me twisted. What do you think, I'm some type of pushover?"

Sensing things spiraling out of control, he realized he had to act, and act fast. He pushed her on the bed, sat on her chest, then pinned her hands down.

"What the fuck is going on with you? Since when did you start assuming things without hearing what I got to say? Is this how it's gonna be when I need to talk to my baby mother? I love you, woman, and I would never do anything to hurt you."

"So why are you, Marcus?"

"Please tell me how could I possibly be hurting you when all I did was tell you how my day went? I never told you that I was getting back in the game or nothing. You just started flipping on me for nothing."

"Baby, I'm sorry. You're right. It's just that these past couple of months have been pure bliss for me. The thought of losing you or just knowing what these streets can do to you caused me to lose it. I love you, Marcus."

"I know, baby, and I love you too." In unison, their lips met, and they engaged in a passionate kiss.

Smoove took advantage of the situation and turned a bad situation into a passion-filled, heated debate. Ms. Janice was only wearing a nightgown. Smoove took advantage of her weakness before she could protest by burying his face deep between her thighs. "Marcus, I love you so much."

While his face was buried deep inside her pussy, he was working adamantly to free himself. Every thought of the previous events managed to escape her mind once he applied his simple touch. At first, he really did have plans to call it quits, but after realizing the toll it would have on other people's lives, he thought against it. The one and only obstacle in his way that seemed capable of hindering his plans was lying on her back with two fingers and a tongue inside her pussy.

"Marcus, this feels so good, baby! Whatever you do, don't stop."

Smoove moved away from her and took off his clothes only to talk and tease her at the same time. "Baby, I love you. I don't wanna argue. All I want is for us to be happy and stay on the same page," Smoove told her, stroking the length of his dick at the foot of the bed.

"Baby, I'm sorry. You right. I never did give you the opportunity to even finish your story. I was wrong, and I promise, baby, that that's something I'll work on."

Smoove pulled her by her ankle and brought her pelvic area closer to the edge of the bed.

"In order for any relationship to work, it takes understanding, patience, compromising, togetherness, loyalty, love, and seeing things from your partner's perspective," he told her while rubbing the head of his dick up and down the lips of her pussy. Every word he spoke was like music to her ears.

"I know, baby." She moaned. She began rubbing and touching all over her body as the head of Smoove's dick teased and taunted her entrance. "Stick it in, baby! Smoove! Baby, why are you doing this to me? I need to feel you inside of me." Smoove backed away as she was starting to inch closer in her attempt to allow his dick to penetrate her insides. Smoove slid in and out of her insides slow, going deep as he could. She was loving every inch of his long, passion-filled strokes.

"Baby, I need you to understand that I'm a good dude, and I would never leave a person hanging when they need me."

"I-I know that, baby, and I-I-I wouldn't want you to."

"Do you love me, Janice?"

"Ye-ss I do, I-lo-ve you a lot, Marcus."

With each question he asked, he made sure to dig as deep as he could, causing her to moan as she talked.

"How much?"

"Ah, I-I love you so much, baby. I swear I do."

"How come you just spazzed on me like that?"

"Oh my god, this dick is so big."

He put his back into it more and dug deeper before giving her the chance to answer his question.

"I don't know. I was stupid," she whined.

"Bend over so I can punish you for being mean."

"Yes, daddy! Punish me, I been a very bad girl." She was loving the emotional role-playing she was engaging in.

It had been years since she had been in love; it was getting to the point that she was becoming submissive for this feeling. It felt good to have someone claim her and really mean it. She was so used to just being fucked. She no longer wanted to feel unloved or be a whore. Her main focus was to have her baby and spend the rest of her life with the man she loved.

"Whose pussy is this?"

"It's yours, daddy! It's yours!" she cried out.

"Then why you tell me it was over a few minutes ago?"

"I-I." *Thwack!* "Oh, Smoove, punish me. Baby, I'm sorry. I won't do it again."

That was his cue to turn it up a notch. He pushed her head into the mattress to muffle her screams before letting loose a fury of long, fast strokes.

"Whose pussy is this?"

"It's you-r pu-ssy. It's Smoove's pussy!"

"Who will this pussy always belong to?"

"Daddy! You, daddy!"

"Who?"

"Smoove, I—it's a-lways g-oin' b-e Smoove's pussy." *Thwack!* "Ooh, harder!" *Thwack!* "Smack my as harder!" *Thwack!* "Ah, ah, I-I-I'm cumming, I'm cumming!" *Thwack!* "Yes, daddy, this dick is so good. Don't chu ever leave me." She collapsed onto her stomach with Smoove trailing right behind her. Only this time he wanted to make love.

He fell flat on her back once she fell and gripped the sheets for leverage to pull forward in his attempt to push his dick as far as he could inside her.

"Baby," he whispered in her ears, "do you trust me?"

"Yes, baby, I trust you."

He slowed down the pace of their intercourse and continued to slowly but cautiously pick at her brain. "So how come you don't trust that I'll make the right decision for us and the people surrounding me?" he asked her in his sexiest voice. He still managed to suck on her neck, face, and ears while he continued to get her to see things his way.

"I do, baby. I told you I do!"

"It's not like I'm going to not open up the store, and it's not like I'm going to be in the streets all day. All I'm saying is, its people in the streets that need my guidance and assistance right now, 'cause the streets is all they know."

He flipped her over onto her back so not only could he put his dick in her as he gave her his spiel, he also had full access to her titties, her lips, and the advantage of looking her in the eyes as he spoke. Before questioning her again, he tightly gripped her hair and started tongue-kissing her. His hands and lips traveled her entire upper body, hitting all her hot spots.

Having sex with a man she loved was different from having sex for money. It possessed more passion, more energy, and more electrifying, intense moments during intercourse.

"Baby, I trust that you will make the right choices, and as of this day forth, I won't ever doubt you again." Each time she spoke, she spoke with lust and pure passion in her voice.

To Smoove it was evident in her speech that she was becoming vulnerable. He was loving it. In less than thirty minutes, he managed to take their relationship to another level, one that he controlled.

Pillow talk was a motherfucker, he thought as he put on his clothes and watched Ms. Janice purr and roll around in the bed. Seeing the effect his sex had on her stroked his ego.

"Where are you going, baby?"

"To handle some business. Why?"

"I'm just asking, baby, that's all. What, I can't check on my baby daddy?"

"Yeah, you can check on your baby daddy."

"Gimme a kiss before you leave."

Smoove planted a soft kiss on her lips, kissed her stomach, and promised he would return shortly before leaving her lying in bed. After he left, she grabbed her cell phone.

"Hello."

"Dion! Boy, you got some nerve pulling that type of stunt on me. When and where can we meet?"

******

Leaving Janice's porch he wondered if killing Heavy was the right decision. On the corner where the murder took place, a display of stuffed animals and balloons could be seen as far as a block away.

It still seemed odd to him that days after the murder, there was still no sign of Carlita, and nobody knew the whereabouts of the funeral. All eyes were on him as he walked to his car parked directly in front of her house.

"We love you, Smoove! Keep your head up, my nigg!" The whole neighborhood knew how close he and Heavy were. As he made his way to his car, people on the porch next door, the sidewalk, and across the street paid homage to the prince of the hood. He acknowledged them with a phony head nod and a weak fist held in the air. He had too much on his mind and on his agenda to entertain any condolences. Adding to the fact he was strapped, he was more than in a hurry to peel off.

CHAPTER FOURTEEN

MEANWHILE, WHILE EVERYBODY picked their brain over the whereabouts of Heavy's funeral, Carlita was at his bedside rubbing his hand tentatively, reassuring him that everything would be all right. Heavy was in Sinai Hospital with tubes and IVs attached to his motionless body. Gauze covered 98 percent of his face, concealing the reconstructive surgery he just underwent. Not only did the lone assassin managed to break half of Heavy's facial bones, she also managed to lodge one bullet two centimeters away from his heart. The rest of the bullets luckily entered and exited without causing any internal damage. Miraculously he would survive.

Carlita, on the other hand, was an emotional wreck. Not only was her children's father fighting for his life, she also was scared shitless after finding out through many detectives that came in and out of the hospital room that Heavy was a federal informant. They also warned her of the dangers it posed on her and their children. For the time being, their new home was on the fifth floor in a secluded area at Sinai Hospital. After being neglected by Smoove when he got locked up, helping the feds build a case against him was Heavy's way of getting revenge.

Two nurses and one detective stayed on their floor ready to tend to their every need. Leaving wasn't an option. At least that was the way Carlita felt. There was no way she dared walk the streets of Baltimore knowing the persons responsible still lurked the streets. For all she knew, they could be trying to get her too. She knew if the feds were involved, this was something big.

"Hey, how many times do I have to tell you! No smoking in here, ma'am," the detective on guard stated upon entering the room. Heavy coughed. Suddenly for the first time in days, Heavy regained consciousness. Carlita stomped her cigarette out on the floor while the detective ran to get the nurse. Seconds later the two nurses rushed through the door, shooting Carlita a scolding look before going to

Heavy's aid.

"Thank God I was smoking, 'cause it caused him to cough and wake up," Carlita said with attitude before wobbling out into the hallway.

Once inside the hallway, she reached in her pocket and retrieved a card then dialed the number that was on it. The phone rang twice before the person on the other end answered.

"Hello, Agent Randolph speaking." "It's me, Carlita. He's woke."

******

Special Agent Renee Randolph had been a member of the Drug Enforcement Administration since August 2005. In addition, she had completed sixteen weeks of specialized training at the DEA academy located in Quantico, Virginia. She also completed training on telecommunication exploitationn, given by the DEA's special operations division. Due to the aforementioned training and experience, Agent Randolph is familiar with various types of controlled substances, such as heroin, cocaine, marijuana, and other related paraphernalia commonly associated with manufacturing and distributing.

Agent Randolph was currently assigned to the DEA's heroin task force. She focused on investigating drug-trafficking organizations in the Baltimore metropolitan area. Since her arrival, she had participated in numerous arrests and search-and-seizure warrants where narcotics had been seized. This was her biggest case to date.

Upon receiving a call from her number 1 informant's girlfriend, Agent Randolph was conducting a briefing with several law enforcement agencies. In attendance were the FBI, the Organized Crime Division, the Task Force, and a few local undercover detectives who were assigned to the case. Due to her expertise and qualifications, she was appointed the person in charge.

"All right, ladies and gentlemen!" she screamed while holding her hands high in the air. "I just received word that my number 1 man is awake and alert. Let's just hope to God he can give us something to go on."

"What if he can't remember nothing from the accident?" one of the rookie cops asked.

"You got a lot to learn, boy. You got a lot to learn. Come with me. The rest of you guys, get back to work. Follow up on any and every lead.

Marallis, Burress, you two get a team and beat the streets hard. I need undercover purchases. I need any and all informants to be squeezed. I need results fast."

******

She arrived at the hospital in less than ten minutes and was eager to reach the fifth floor. Exiting the elevator, she moved at a fast pace toward room 501, with the rookie cop right on her heels.

"Listen, Ryan, I need you to take notes. I'll do the talking, got it?"

"Gotcha," responded the rookie cop.

She knew from previous experience that timing was crucial in cases like this. The informant could easily slip into a coma, suffer from amnesia, or even worse, succumb to their injuries. Agent Randolph identified herself, greeted the nurses, and sent them on their way.

"I'm Agent Randolph," she said, showing her badge. "Greetings, ladies. I need to have a word with Mr. Jefferson. I'll need for you two to step out of the room."

"Ma'am, Mr. Jefferson is in no shape to—"

She interrupted her in mid-sentence. "Ma'am, I'm a federal agent. I call the shots in here. Unless you want to get arrested and charged with hindering a federal investigation, I suggest that the two of you make like an egg and beat it."

Sucking their teeth, the two nurses quickly followed her direct orders and left the room, feeling defeated.

Carlita sat alongside the bed, smirking at what had just transpired.

"Hey, how you doing, Carlita?"

"I'm—just still tryna take all of this in."

"So what's going on with Antwon?" Agent Randolph asked a fragile-looking Heavy once she made it next to his bedside.

"Mmm. Mmm. Mmm," was all he was able to mutter through the wires that kept his mouth shut.

"Squeeze my hand once if you know who shot you. If you don't know, do it twice."

Heavy managed to squeeze her hand twice, letting her know he didn't know who had shot him. He couldn't believe it; this bitch wasn't even in his presence for two minutes, and now she was drilling him with questions. *Damn, do you even care about a nigga's well-being?* he thought.

Here he was, lying in a hospital bed with tubes running every which way, clinging onto his life, and all she cared about was solving a case.

"If you got a good look at the shooter, squeeze once."

He squeezed twice.

"Do you think Smoove ordered the hit? If so, squeeze once." Seeing his response startled Carlita. She couldn't believe it.

******

After being humiliated at their workplace by Agent Randolph, the two nurses called the local news station in hopes of throwing a fork into her investigation. They were told from day 1 that Heavy was a federal informant. They were advised early on not to alert the media about his condition. Unbeknownst to Agent Randolph, she was messing with the wrong bitches at the wrong time. They were seeking retribution.

******

"Thanks for tuning in to *Fox 45 News at Ten*. I'm Karen Parks standing in for Kevin Glasscho, who has the night off. Here's some of the top stories people are talking about tonight. On Friday we brought you the story first on Antwon Jefferson, the individual that was shot and killed on the corner of Park Heights and Shirley Avenue. Sources close to the victim have given us some breaking news on the case. There live on the scene at Sinai Hospital is *Fox 45* newscaster Shaneria Hill."

"I'm Shaneria Hill, here live on the scene at Sinai Hospital, following the Antwon Jefferson case. Here standing with me are two nurses on duty ready to shed some light on the case. What's your name and affiliation to the case, ma'am?"

"Latoya Tossie. I'm his nurse."

"What can you tell us about the case?"

"Antwon Jefferson isn't dead. He's alive and recovering from multiple gunshot wounds, a broken jaw, and his face has been reconstructed. He's in stable condition, and he has a great chance at fully recovering."

Agent Randolph walked up to the nurse, slapped a pair of cuffs on her, and read her her rights. "Ma'am, you are being charged with hindering a federal investigation."

"Bitch, if you don't get cho motherfucking hands off me!" Latoya shouted, throwing a fit. "You don't know who you fucking with. Bitch, I'm motherfucking Toy-Toy from Douglas Projects! You got me fucked up!"

The second nurse managed to easily slide off unseen. So she thought.

"Hey, rookie!" Agent Randolph hollered. "Grab her." Realizing her liberty was at stake, the second nurse took off, leaving the poor rookie in her dust.

CHAPTER FIFTEEN

SMOOVE SAT MOTIONLESS and perplexed after hearing the news about Heavy. Not only was it a shocker to him, it was also a problem he knew he had to take care of.

"Are you sure you heard right?"

"Yeah, it just came on the news," Keisha told him.

"I cannot believe this shit!" he screamed, banging his hands on the table. "Damn it, Keish, you should've hit that nigga in the head like I told you to. You slippin'. I taught you better than that."

"Well, it's over and done with, Smoove. We can't bring the past back to the present"

"Yeah, but we damn sure can make better choices in the future. The next time, I'll just do the shit myself."

"Fuck you, Smoove!" Keisha yelled, strutting outta the bedroom, slamming the door behind her.

Smoove was right on her heels. "Keish, Keish, come here." Keisha was in her room with her face stuffed inside her pillows, crying, when he entered the room.

She prided herself on being able to please Smoove in every way possible. Whenever she fell short, which was rare, this was the outcome. Since they were kids, Smoove was the only boyfriend she ever had. In spite of being diagnosed with attention deficit disorder she had no problem thinking clearly when it came to Smoove. She never met her biological family, never worked, and due to her illness, all her classes in school were in DEC.

They started out when she was the tender and vulnerable age of twelve. They were engaged in a game of hide-and-seek. Smoove, a few years older than her at the time, gave her more than what she sought upon finding him. On several occasions, they rubbed and kissed but never took it to the next level. At the time Smoove was going through puberty, his manhood was screaming for attention.

"I know you're in there," Keisha said before searching under his bed.

After searching his entire room and coming up empty-handed, her expectations in finding him was beginning to run high, especially after realizing the basement was the only place she hadn't searched yet. She rushed towards the basement.

"You can run, but you can't hide. Come out, come out wherever you are." She could tell by how the pillows were stacked on the bed that he was hiding under them.

Happy and eager to find him, she jumped in the bed and started tickling him to death.

"You got me, all right, you got me!"

"I told you I would find you. Now it's your turn to find me."

"Let's play mother and father," Smoove challenged.

"All right," Keisha answered, knowing all too well what he meant.

"Now get in bed and give your husband a kiss." They both got underneath the covers and allowed their hands and lips to explore areas never explored before.

Though they both were virgins, Smoove was a little more experienced than Keisha. His older cousin showed him porn movies when he went to visit him.

"Listen, Keisha. This is how you kiss." Smoove taught her how to kiss only using her tongue and lips. "You're not supposed to use your teeth when you kiss, Keisha. This is how you do it. Open your legs. Not like that, like this." He told her while pulling her panties down.

"Do you know what you're doing?"

"Yes, I did this before," he lied. "Now lie back and let me put this cock in you," he told her, reciting one of the lines he heard in a nasty movie.

From that point on, they were like Bonnie and Clyde. Growing up, Smoove taught her everything he learned—how to bag up and weigh drugs and their prices and the ins and outs of the game. He also felt the need to train her into a cold-blooded assassin. Keisha had a clean record and held gun permits in a few states.

She frequently visited the shooting range, quickly advancing to marksman status in months. She was more advanced with poppin' her pistol than Smoove. She even went as far as studying the human body to find out what and where the vital spots were. It was like a sport to her. On one occasion, she shot a dude in the wrist and hit a main artery. He bled to death before he made it to the hospital. She had four bodies

under her belt to date, and Heavy surviving forced her to step her game up. Not only was she feeling bad that she let Smoove down, she also was disgusted with herself over the fact she fucked up her perfect record. Hearing Smoove speak on it only added fuel to the fire. Though she was a killer, she still was a woman with feelings, and right now, they were hurt. Smoove loved her like a sister, but when it was time to handle his business, he put love to the side.

"Keish," he whispered to her while climbing on top of her from the back. "Listen, I know you mad about what happened, but you a big girl. You gotta take that shit on the chin and keep it moving. Here, take your medicine and relax. I got a plan. You listening?"

CHAPTER SIXTEEN

" GOOD MORNING, MA'AM, I'm Cathleen James from *Fox45 News*. Is a Ms. Latoya Tossie available?"

"Oh hell no! A bitch is not fucking with you news people again. My ass got booked messing around with y'all the last time. Please leave me alone!" she screamed before slamming the door in the news lady's face.

"Ma'am, there's money involved. No cameras. I promise it'll be strictly confidential, just you and me."

Hearing that money was involved, Toya cracked the door all smiles. "What did you just say?"

"That this interview will be strictly confidential, and you will be paid for your time."

"No camera?"

"Yes, no cameras, just me and you. I have a contract with me binding us to that."

Without even thinking twice, Toya unlatched the chain off the door and allowed the news lady to come in her roach-infested apartment. Entering her apartment was like walking inside a roach nest. Roaches were everywhere. The news lady's skin was crawling at the sight of hundreds of roaches visibly crawling all over. Even in their presence, the roaches didn't scatter. The news lady hated to see the effect that the projects had on some women. Here was Toya, who had on a Louis Vuitton outfit, her hair and nails were done, and her jewelry y was authentic. The inside of her apartment told a different story. She had the nerve to have a puppy pitbull inside a cage filled with feces. The news lady was ready to get this interview over and done after seeing over a hundred roaches attacking a dried-up chicken bone on a Styrofoam plate sitting on the table in front of them. Smacking the plate to the floor, Toya killed the remaining roaches with her hand before clearing the table of everything by knocking it all to the floor.

"You can have a seat while I fix you something to drink."

"I'll pass. I'm just here on business, then I have to cover a story a few blocks away." Without taking Toya up on her offer to sit down or a drink, she got straight down to business. "I'll get straight to the point, Ms. Tossie. I need you to tell me everything that you know about Antwon Jefferson. Leave out none of the details. Here's $500 up front and our confidential contract. Depending on how much you tell me, you might get a $500 bonus." Without bothering to read it, Toya signed the contract, stuffed the $500 into her bra, then instantly started spilling her guts.

"Antwon Jefferson is a black male, heavy set, dark—"

"No, no, Ms. Tossie, I'm talking about his status. What's his room number, and what's the situation surrounding him being a federal informant? You know things that will make a big story on the news."

"Oh, my bad. He was shot four times, once in the chest, shoulder, stomach, and the neck. His face was shattered. The person who shot him struck him with some type of hard object. Maybe the gun that was used in the shooting."

"What does he have to say about the whole ordeal?"

"He can't talk. His jaw is broke. Plus he was so heavily sedated he was out of it until yesterday."

"What happened when he woke up?"

"As soon as he woke up, I paged his doctor. Then me and Ms. Hamilton, the other nurse that was on shift with me, stayed by his bedside, monitoring his vitals. Before his doctor came, we were ushered outta the room by the same stankin' ass bitch that locked my ass up."

"She put you out of his room? Why?"

"She wanted to ask him some questions."

"About what?"

"I'm guessing about what happened to him. She put us out the room before she questioned him."

"What's his room number?"

It's 501, but the chance's of any news reporters making it to see him is outta the question. For one, he has twenty-four-hour protection. Plus he's not under Antwon Jefferson. He's under an alias."

"What's his alias?"

Before answering her question, Toya held her hand out, palm facing up, motioning her four fingers at the news reporter, letting her know that it was that time. Knowing that the alias was important and vital to her, the news reporter quickly granted her request.

"It's Henry Eubanks," she told her after receiving her $500 bonus. Relieved and feeling she had enough; she rushed outside to her van and headed toward Sinai Hospital.

******

After reaching the fifth floor, she stepped off the elevator then went straight for the nurses' station. "Did anybody ever tell you that you look exactly like Meagan Good?" Heavy's doctor asked her once she reached the nurses' station.

"Well, being that I am, yes, I hear that all the time."

"Oh my god, you are Meagan Good! I love all your movies. By the way, you did your thing in *Think Like a Man*."

"Thank you."

"You are more beautiful in person than I would've ever imagined."

"Aw, you are too kind."

"What brings you here? Is this some type of reality show on VH1 or BET?"

"I came here today to put some smiles on a few faces. It's something I try to do in every city that I arrive in. It's like a ritual. I believe that if I can randomly pick a hospital to stop in and show some love to someone in need, then I helped to make the world a better place."

"Well, as you can see, nobody's here to keep happy but me on this floor, but feel free to keep me smiling."

Keisha was confused. "So there are no patients here that I can take pictures and sign my autograph for?" she asked, pulling her camera out her purse.

"Not on this floor. This section of the hospital is only occupied by patients in the Federal Witness Protection Program."

"The Witness Protection Program? What's that?"

"Snitches, rats, or people the feds hide because their lives are in danger."

"Oh, I get it."

"I can imagine you hardly ever having to work around here."

"I wish. I just got rid of a patient yesterday. The only reason he was moved between me and you was because two nurses called themselves,

getting back at this detective by calling the news station and giving up tips about his status and his whereabouts. Here in the program, the media is prohibited from knowing anything about a patient, so just like that, he was gone."

"What do you mean 'just like that, he was gone'? What, the news people came and got him?" she asked.

"No, not the news people, the feds came and moved him to another undisclosed location."

"Damn, they took him to another floor?"

"No, sweetie, the feds don't play. When they hide a person, they're liable to be on the moon."

Convinced that he wouldn't be of any assistance, Keisha aborted her mission for now. After leaving the hospital empty-handed, she drove home.

"You did good, Keisha," Smoove told her after hearing all the work she put in trying to find Heavy.

"Yeah, but if I had killed his ass in the first place, I wouldn't even be looking for him right now."

"That's neither here nor there. What's good is that you actually found the girl that was on the news, posed as a newscaster, and found out a lot of valuable information. Shit, if it wasn't for you, I wouldn't even have known that the feds were on me." Every time he heard or mentioned the name *feds*, he felt uneasy.

Smoove's reason for attempting to have him killed was for the fact that he was stealing from him. In his mind, if Heavy stole from him, then he would do anything. Though enraged to find out that the feds were on his heels, hearing how Keisha put in work made him feel good. She went as far as remembering t h e girl's name from the projects she saw on the news to calling downtown to Central Booking posing as a bail bondsman to get her address. *Now that was some gangsta shit*, he thought. Good thing she wore a good disguise when she attempted to kill him, 'cause the last thing they needed was the feds looking for her also.

CHAPTER SEVENTEEN

WITH THE FEDS and the unidentified murder on his mind, Smoove planned to change things surrounding his life.

"Hey! Don't be dropping none of them boxes like that!" Ms. Janice screamed, referring to the box of dishes one of the movers just dropped inside the U-Haul truck.

"I apologize, ma'am," the youngest of the four movers told her.

It was 3:00 a.m., and they were doing a good job maneuvering in the dark, she thought. She didn't know what had motivated Smoove, but for some odd reason, a day after stating he needed more time in the streets, he came over and told her to pack all her things then place them into storage. She didn't understand why he wanted her to move everything at night, but happy to move forward with their plan, she refused to protest.

"Wanda, girl, watch him. I don't trust these people with my stuff, and make sure that li'l Chris stay with that guy on the back of the truck."

Being that it was such a short notice, she called Wanda and her oldest son over to help keep an eye on the movers Smoove hired. So far they were doing a good job at packaging and moving things around. At the rate they were going, they would be done before the sun came up.

Seeing Smoove walk through the door made her get emotional. "What's wrong, baby?" he asked, rushing to put his arms around her. "I thought you would be happy to move out of here and live the life I told you we would live."

"I am, baby. Don't mind me. I'm crying tears of joy."

"Well, get ready to cry a river, 'cause this is just the beginning."

"Smoove, stop doing this to me. Tell me what you got up your sleeve?" she asked, panting. "Do you know how I feel right now? I mean just put yourself in my shoes. All you did was tell me to put my stuff into storage, 'cause we're moving in a house. You never told me where we were moving or nothing. Then you walk up in here all nonchalantly, telling me that you got something else up your sleeve."

"It wouldn't be a surprise if I told you anything, now would it?"

"I know but—"

"There's no buts. You said you would trust that your baby daddy would make the right choices for his family, right? Or did you forget? I mean, if you did, I'm sure I can make you remember," Smoove teased while grinding his dick in a circular motion against her butt.

"You are so nasty. Do you ever get enough?"

"I don't mean to break y'all li'l party up, but it's still a little work to be done around here. That's why you all knocked up now," Wanda stated, interrupting their little charade.

"You must be Wanda?" Smoove stated, extending his hand.

"And I can see why they call you Smoove. Damn!" Ms. Janice shot her a cold look after her statement.

"Yeah, Smoove is what they call me. I heard a lot about you, and it feels like I know you already. Janice is always speaking very highly of you, so it's my pleasure to finally meet you."

"I feel the same way," Wanda told Smoove as she looked him up and down.

"So do you plan to take my best friend away from me or something?"

"Nah, what makes you say that?"

"I'm just asking. Shit, you moving a bitch up out the hood and all. I don't know you might make her change on me for all I know." Ms. Janice shot her a scolding look, causing the both of them to laugh.

"What did I miss?" Smoove asked, confused.

"Nothing, baby, it's a woman's thing. Let's get the rest of this stuff outta here," Ms. Janice replied.

"Yeah, that sounds like a good idea, 'cause a bitch is tired as a whore," Wanda said while yawning and stretching her arms to the ceiling, exposing her belly ring and a few of her pubic hairs.

The pink spandex she wore hugged every inch of her curves to perfection, leaving Smoove's eyes glued to the knot sitting between her legs. Quickly before turning a simple stare into lust, he turned to Ms. Janice.

"Yeah, you right, baby, let's hurry up so we can get outta here. I'm kinda tired myself."

An hour and fifteen minutes went by, and the house was completely empty.

CHAPTER EIGHTEEN

Two Months Later

"THINGS ARE GOING good," Ms. Janice told her mother and father over the phone.

Her parents were on the speakerphone, listening to their only daughter as she brought them up to date on the new happenings in her life.

"Yes, Mother, he will be in church today. Yes, you will finally get to meet him."

"How long have you known this guy?" her father asked.

"For over ten years."

"You been dating this guy for over ten years, and we're just meeting him? We raised you better than that."

"Daddy, I never said I was dating him for ten years. I said I've known him for over ten years."

"So how long have you been dating him?"

"For a little over a year," she lied.

Without leaving room to be further interrogated, Ms. Janice told her parents she would be picking them up in an hour to take them to church and, afterward, over to her house for dinner.

"All right, you just make sure you're on time. I am not trying to be late," her mother warned.

"Anything for you, Ma. Love y'all. See y'all soon."

"All right, love you too. Bye."

After ending her conversation with her parents, she was all smiles, looking at Smoove holding their new poodle puppy, Precious.

"You are so nosy."

"What did they say?"

"Oh, so Mr. I'm Not Scared to Meet Your Parents is getting butterflies? Let me find out."

"It's not that I'm nervous. I just wanna know what I'm up against. That's all."

"You don't trust that your baby mother will make the right choices for her family? I trusted you," she teased.

"Hell no, not against her parents, I don't. What did they say when you told them I would be coming to church?"

The same thing you told me when you bought me to this house." Nothing. Oh, I almost forgot a new truck and a beauty salon. Can a sister surprise you sometimes?" she asked, adding a little emphasis.

"Aight now, don't start nothing you can't handle. I will act a fool up in church today if I have to. Hallelujah! Thank you, Jesus! I feel the Holy Ghost coming!"

Seeing Smoove jumping around like the Holy Ghost was inside him had Ms. Janice laughing so hard her stomach started hurting.

Witnessing her clutching her stomach, Smoove dropped Precious on the floor and bolted to her aid.

"You all right?" he asked, placing his hand on her stomach.

"It feels like the baby is kicking me, Marcus. Put your hand right here."

He placed his hand on the spot, and seconds later, he too felt the first sign that his baby was moving.

Smoove got on his knees and put his ear to her stomach. Moments later, he felt a kick.

"Oh my god, did you just feel that? He kicked me again."

"You mean she."

"Think what you want to think, woman, but my son is up in there kicking up dust already."

"Boy, you are silly."

After kissing her stomach numerous times, Smoove stood up and planted a sloppy wet kiss on her lips. "I love you, baby."

"I love you back. That's enough, baby. Keep your hands to yourself. You are going to make us late," Ms. Janice pleaded.

"We got time for a quickie." Her body felt so good wrapped inside his arms.

"Now, honey, you know if we're late, that good impression you're trying to make is going to fly right out the window."

Jumping back to reality, Smoove let her off the hook, and they both rushed to get dressed.

A half hour later, they were on their way out the door, holding hands, looking like the perfect couple. *This is the good life*, Smoove thought as they waved to their Jewish neighbors. *This is what it feels like to leave the hood*, he thought, climbing inside her truck.

******

Pulling up in front of her parents' house reminded Ms. Janice just how fortunate she was growing up. The swing set she and her brother used to play in still sat in the front yard, along with the birdhouse and the waterfall. She was brought up in an all-girls school from kindergarten all the way until she graduated high school. Her parents were together all her life, so there was never a time when she was abandoned. Growing up, she was so smothered and under so much strict supervision that once she did get a taste of the real world, she was turned out. Even to this day, her parents were overprotective of her.

After beeping the horn a few times, Ms. Janice watched her parents joyfully exit their front door, looking like the happiest couple in the world.

"Here we go," Smoove said, hopping out the passenger seat to hold the door open.

Like Ms. Janice, her mother had natural beauty and a face that shed twenty years off her age. Her father was more of the pretty-boy type—had thick finger waves, was a smooth dresser, and walked with confidence. Everything about his style of clothes led Smoove to believe that all would go well as long as he was around. Mr. Walker had an "I'm cool" type of vibe with him, one that made people want to be in his presence.

"Pleased to meet you, Mrs. Georgia. I'm Marcus." After handing her a yellow rose and kissing her on the hand, Smoove helped her into the front seat of the truck.

"Aye, watch out now. You already got my daughter. You want my wife too?" Mr. Walker joked.

"It ain't even like that, Mr. Walker."

They both embraced each other before engaging in small talk on the sidewalk while Ms. Janice and her mother had a brief one on one.

"Marcus, you must be a very special man. Buying my daughter a house, new truck, and helping her to get her salon off the ground. I thank you for taking care of my baby."

"It's an honor, sir. As long as I'm alive, I'll see to it that she's well taken care of. And that I promise."

"My kind of guy."

"Theodore, if you don't get cho hind parts inside this truck and stop harassing that young man!" Mrs. Georgia barked.

"It's okay, Mrs. Georgia. He's only doing what's expected of a father."

"Yeah, but at the same time, he's making me late for church."

Without hesitation, her request was granted, and off they were.

******

During the short ride to church, they talked about everything pertaining to their love affair. Though most of his earnings came from the drug trade, they agreed early on to use the fortune his parents left behind upon their death as his resource to money, not to mention the insurance company handling the house fire was nearing a settlement.

He scored mad brownie points on the way to church.

The church was packed to capacity and looked more like a fashion show than anything else, to Smoove's surprise. Everybody was dressed to impress, even the kids were suited up. Service wasn't intended to start for another ten minutes. The Walker family took that time to introduce Smoove to the few family members and close friends. Janice was all smiles introducing her child's father.

"Hey, Janice," said the deacon's wife, sister Clarice, while giving Ms. Janice a hug. "Girl, are you pregnant?"

"I would hope so, big as my stomach is. Now that we're on the subject, I would like you to meet my child's father. Marcus, this is Clarice. Clarice, this is Marcus."

Clarice was one of the few people at church whom Ms. Janice dealt with on a personal level. As youngsters, they came up in church together, lived in the same neighborhood for years, and attended the same schools. It wasn't until adulthood that they went their separate ways. Even still, they kept a close connection.

"Nice to meet you, Mr. Marcus. I pray that you continue to come to service."

"Oh, he will be," Janice said, squeezing his hand.

"Yeah, I'm sure you'll be seeing more of me."

"Praise the Lord. Amen. We always need strong black brothers around here, so it's a pleasure to have you with us today."

"Thank you, ma'am. It's my pleasure."

After introducing Smoove to Clarice, Ms. Janice spent the remaining minutes before service introducing him to a few of her aunts, uncles, cousins, and close friends before heading to the ladies' room. Happy things were going well, Ms. Janice didn't even consider running into whom she just bumped into.

"Well, well, well. Look here. After all this time, I been looking for you. Finally, you decide to come to church."

"What are you doing here, Dion?"

"Waiting on you! Hump, since you just up and moved on me, I knew eventually I could find you here. You can change what gym you go to, your phone number, and even move, but how hard would it be to change churches? What would poor old Mrs. Georgia think of her baby girl abandoning her church?"

"Dion!"

"Dion my ass," he whispered through clenched teeth, snatching her arm, pulling her off to the side. Not wanting to make a scene, she led him into a utility closet out of view.

"Why are you stalking me? "Visibly shaking Ms. Janice started to cry. Tears ran down her face.

"To re-claim what the fuck is mines. I've been watching you prancing around with that young boy. What you think you're Stella when she got her groove back bitch? You're a whore, my whore!" Dion hawk spit directly into her face. Gaining the upper hand before she got too loud and brought attention onto them he pulled his phone out and she quickly calmed down. "Facebook, Instagram, the church website." "The next fucking time I have to hunt cho ass down I'm taking this shit viral!" Trying to wipe a gooey blob of spit from the crevices of her eyelids Ms. Janice watched the video on his phone, in horror thinking about the devastation having those images all over the net would have on her life. When his hands reached up inside her summer dress she frantically tried to squirm from his grip he had around her neck.

"Move again bitch and I'll cut cho ass up in this bitch."

Producing a knife Dion held the sharp blade inches away from her throat. Dropping his pants he then shoved her against the concrete wall. He aggressively tugged at her underwear until they were down then spit in his hand before coating his penis in saliva.

I can't believe this shit, thought Ms. Janice, Giving up her fight she just gave in and cried as Dion savagely pushed his erection inch by inch into her anal cavity.

******

Embarrassed and feeling violated, Ms. Janice staggered out the dark utility closet and headed straight for the ladies' room. Locking the door behind her, she was glad that church was in session, leaving the lobby area empty. She couldn't believe it. She trusted Dion so much that he knew where she worked, went to church, and even what stores she shopped at.

"Hello."

"Yeah, Charles, it's me, Janice," she whispered with panic in her voice.

"Hey! I thought you retired."

"I am, but one of your clients keeps stalking me."

"Who is it?"

"Dion, the guy from Rent-A-Center."

"What do you mean he's stalking you?"

"He just raped me."

"What?"

******

"Sorry, y'all," Ms. Janice said after being reunited with her family. "I got so caught up talking then had to use the restroom. What did I miss?" she asked, squeezing Smoove's hand.

"Not much," Smoove said.

"Even when you're on time, you're late," her mother teased.

"All right now," Mr. Walker chimed in, smiling at them.

"God is good!"

"All the time!"

"God is good!"

"All the time!"

Each time the preacher proclaimed that God was good, the sanctuary became louder and louder as they screamed all the time.

"It seems like some of y'all folk still asleep up in here, or maybe some of y'all devoted all y'all energy to the club last night."

"Hump, preach, Reverend!" Gladice yelled from the second pew.

"The way some of y'all dressed up in here today, I think a few of y'all still think y'all at the club."

"Mmm hmm. Preach, brother. Amen!" The elders of the church gave the preacher the fuel he needed to keep coming strong. With every statement he made came a gesture.

"The Lord said, come as you are! This is God's house! Whose house?"

A few people yelled.

"I don't think that everybody clearly understood what I said. This is *w-h-oo-s-e* house!"

"God's house!"

"Who-se house?"

"God's house! Hallelujah! Talk to us, Reverend!"

"For those of you who may have a misinterpretation of the definition of God's house, you are in deep trouble. I get the feeling that some folk up in here today truly don't know the significance of the matter at hand. You see, the Bible says that this church is his house, not the reverend's house, not your house, but God's house. Now does anybody not believe that this is God's house?'

The whole sanctuary became quiet after that statement.

"That's good. Amen."

"Hallelujah! Thank ya, Jesus!"

"But not for everybody. You see some folk up in here faking today, and they were faking last Sunday and the Sunday before that and so on. Showing up in church is in no way a free ticket into heaven, so I have to save some of you today. Today it's time to jump down one's throat and identify the fakers. Can I get an amen?"

"Amen!" People could be seen throughout the pew whispering among each other as the reverend dabbed the perspiration trickling down his face with a handkerchief before making his next statement.

"You see, if everybody here tonight truly believed that this was God's house, then brother Rodney wouldn't be pulling up in his Mustang convertible blasting Soldier Boy, Chris Brown, and all that other gangster rap stuff. What about sister Charlene? Stand up for me for one moment, sister."

Sister Charlene looked stone-faced as she slowly rose to her feet.

"Now, sister, with all due respect, do you believe that this is God's house?"

Sister Charlene, with a dumbfounded look on her face, answered, "Yes."

"Do you believe in the saying 'Come as you are'?"

"Yes." With each question, a puzzled expression that appeared on her face seemed to deepen.

"Would you please make us aware of your occupation and what you stand for as a woman?"

Clearing her throat, Charlene started speaking in a sophisticated manner. "For the last ten years, I worked as an event planner for a marketing and promting corporation based out of Washington, DC. Over a ten-year time frame, our establishment has been able to successfully obtain over 2.8 billion in sales and revenue. As the chief executive in the firm, I'm in control of 90 percent of the enterprise's yearly revenue and sales. In the company's first fiscal year, we started a nonprofit organization catered toward the development and growth of young African American girls in our country. Initially, our goal was to prevent, protect, and prepare—Triple P—which was our logo.

Due to the massive amount of poverty plaguing our community, we quickly evaluated our goals and formulated a more concrete, stabilized improvisation. We quickly became aware through town-hall meetings, public lectures, and through PTA meetings in our school systems that not only did we, as a people, need to support our young black sisters, we also needed to find more ways to facilitate our brothers as well. Gradually we adopted a more feasible solution toward inspiring young adolescents, in hopes of contributing to the success rates in our community. Subsequently our logo was changed from Triple P to the Brothers and Sisters Club, a name more suitable and relevant to the state of affairs. Presumably my perception led me to believe that no child should be left behind. As adults, it's our job to be pillars in our communities, role models to our youth, and provide positive alternative resources for them. As a woman, I stand as a role model for our children. I stand for growth and development in our communities in a positive way, and I take a great deal of pride in being able to teach our young sisters that beauty is skin-deep."

Following her speech, a smile emerged on her face as the whole congregation rose to their feet to give her a standing ovation and their blessings.

In the wake of all the hallelujahs, thank-you-Jesuses, and amens, the reverend quickly regained control over the situation and managed to get everybody back on the same page in order to get his point across.

"Thank you, Sister Charlene. Before you sit down, I have a story I would like to share with you. If you were to die today, right now in this instant, and before you were allowed into heaven, you had to convince God to let you in, would you dress like that?"

As if the air was just snatched from her lungs, Sister Charlene was baffled beyond words.

"I-I-I-I believe tha-t as a child of God, we are to come as we are, being that our true intentions lie within our heart and not on the surface."

"Sister Charlene, if you knew that God would be here today, would you have come here dressed like that?"

"Hone-stly, I-I wouldn't have," replied a cracky-voiced Charlene.

"Ya see, folk, a lot of people here today don't believe that God is in our presence every day, let alone that this is his house. No true, firm believer would enter God's throne, his house of worship, dressed like a hooker!"

The entire church could be heard whispering and chatting among each other as the reverend jumped down sister Charlene's throat.

"You are a sophisticated, intellectual, articulate businesswoman and a role model. When the Bible says come as you are, you come dressed like that. What type of message does that send to our fellow church members? I mean just look at you! I know it's hot outside, but in no way should you be showing that much skin. By the way, do you know that your blouse is see-through? Woman, you ought to be ashamed of yourself that you have the audacity to come in the house of the Lord dressed like that. The Bible says come as you are. You're a businesswoman, a role model, so dress like one. Thank you. You may be seated."

It didn't stop there; the reverend stepped away from his podium, mic in hand, and went through the mass, putting all the fakers on blast.

"Brother Stephon! Brother Stephon!" the reverend screamed at the top of his lungs as he watched a drooling, comatose-looking Stephen nod from the back of the church.

It was evident in his appearance that he was a dope addict from the countless track marks and infected-looking abscesses d i s p e r s e d throughout his entire body. His hands were the size of bear paws due to the numerous times he used the veins in his hands as the gateway to receive his daily dosage.

"Ya see, folk, brother Stephon has been coming to this church here for quite some time now. Mentally and spiritually, his mind has never been with us, and because of it, this will be his last visit until he's cleaned up. He's not coming to worship the Lord. Instead, he's coming to get a free meal, to beg for change, hoping that some of us good old church folk will bring him closer to the next high. Last week, he had the nerve to put one dollar in the collection plate and take out a twenty-dollar bill in the process. But not anymore!" the reverend snapped his finger, and two ushers came to his aid and escorted dope fiend Stephon out the front door without altercation.

"Our community is plagued with violence, drugs, and sex so bad that it's starting to overflow into our churches, and that we can't have people! I know, I know. Some of us today may say, Reverend, you are being too hard. That's not Christian-like. But guess what, folk, welcome to the real world."

Ms. Janice's heart was beating one hundred miles a minute as the reverend walked in her vicinity with his eyes locked on her.

"Sister Janice!"

She couldn't believe it; her worst fear had come true. She was being exposed.

"Will you stand for me, sister, please?"

Please, God, get me through this, and I swear I will never sin again, she silently prayed, rising to her feet.

"Sister, will you tell us what it is you do for a living and what you stand for as a woman?"

No, not you too, Rev. I thought I could trust you. Why now, when all seems right, Ms. Janice said to herself as she looked back at all the confused facial expressions worn by Smoove and her parents.

"I-I." Before she could form a word, Ms. Janice passed out, causing the whole church to go in an uproar.

"Oh my Lord! Someone call the paramedics!" her mother screamed as she knelt down to the floor to comfort her daughter.

CHAPTER NINETEEN

P ULLING UP IN her new Lexus, Wanda watched as Ms. Janice lit up with excitement as she parked next to her. This was her first time seeing Wanda since she purchased her new car.

"I'm ballin'!" Wanda said as she approached Ms. Janice. Greeting with a hug, they both were delighted to finally hang out after not seeing each other for over a month.

"Girl, you did not tell me that you bought a new car. Your dream car at that. Oh my god!"

"Yeah, girl, I feel so good to finally be on my feet," replied Wanda. After giving Ms. Janice a tour of her new car, Wanda pulled out a wad of money.

"By the way, it's my treat today."

"I hear that," Ms Janice told her, playfully snatching the money from her hand.

"No need to hold on to it then."

"Ah, bitch is balling for real. I don't care what chu do with that chump change. As long as I can work these hips of mine, I'm always good."

"Girl, I cannot believe you." Ms. Janice was cracking up, watching Wanda sway her hips side to side as they headed toward the entrance of Applebee's.

Once seated, they placed their orders then went straight to playing catch-up.

"Your stomach is getting big. Aw! I'm so happy to see you pregnant."

"Girl, I'm happy to be pregnant."

"So what is it that you have to talk about that's so important? Smoove isn't acting up, is he?"

"Where do I begin? In the midst of all the good things happening in my life, it's like I can't seem to even fully enjoy it."

With a concerned look on her face, Wanda listened attentively to Ms. Janice as she brought her up to date on things.

"I was raped."

"What? Who? Like what in the hell do you mean you were raped?"

"Just let me talk. I know it's a lot to take in, but I need you to just listen and let me vent, 'cause I literally have so much bottled up."

"Girl, like you are my best friend, so hearing some shit like this hurt like hell. Hold on." Wanda got the attention of their waiter and ordered two shots of Patron. After downing both shots, only then was she able to begin listening.

"I'm cool. I'm cool. You talk, and I'll listen."

"I'm in a sticky situation, and I don't know how I'm going to get out of it. Remember the guy Dion I told you about from Rent-A-Center?"

"Yeah."

"Well, like I told you before, I went against policy and started seeing him under the table. My thing was this. Why pay Diva's a percentage of my money to sleep with a guy I liked sleeping with. That's when my guards went down. I trusted him. He slowly became a friend and far beyond. He knew where I lived. We confided in each other, went on dates, and everything. It got to the point where it wasn't even about the money with him. I really seen him as a friend. But to make a long story short, when I told him we could no longer see each other, he blackmailed me."

"Blackmailed you?"

"Yeah. We made several sex videos"

"Oh, so he's using that as leverage to keep you at bay."

"Yeah, so on one hand, I don't feel as if he's raping me. I kinda feel like he's going through a phase because of the breakup."

"No, don't think that way. If he's taking advantage of you against your will, then that's a major problem.

"Don't get me wrong, I do know how it's easy to get it misconstrued when it's a person you deal with. Whew! I feel a little better. You had me thinking that somebody just jumped out of the bushes and started humping you."

"If you let me explain further, you'll get to fully understand my situation. As you're aware, I'm happily in love with Smoove, not to mention carrying his baby. If he were to find out, I'm sure he would kill Dion. On the other hand, if he does find out, what will happen to our future?"

"Damn, that is something to think about."

"It gets worse. The first time he blackmailed me, he came to my house while Smoove was there."

"You lying."

"Nope. He even went as far as showing me scenes from the tape we made on his phone right then and there on the front porch."

"Where was Smoove?"

"Marcus came out when he was leaving. He even started questioning me about him to the point I was scared that he heard something."

"So what was he saying?"

"He basically told me that if I kept sleeping with him, all would go well, but the minute that I stopped, the sex tape would go viral."

"Wow!"

"I know, right. So I agreed to hook up with him later, and when I did, we had sex. We came to an agreement that as long as I slept with him twice a month and talked to him on the phone, all would go well. But as time went on, I started feeling guilty, so I changed my number and no longer frequented my regular spots. Then out of nowhere, as you're aware, Smoove popped up and just moved me."

"So why if you met him and y'all had consensual sex, do you feel he raped you?"

"I'll get to that. With me moving and changing my number, he couldn't reach me, so I just abandoned our agreement by disappearing. I mean, I didn't know what else to do. How could I continue to let another man just run up in me while carrying Smoove's baby? To make matters worse, he won't wear a condom anymore."

"Y'all had unprotected sex?"

"Yes, and he came in me."

"Oh yeah, this nigga is outta pocket."

"I haven't even gotten to the worst part. Now mind you, with all kinds of things going on in my life—the baby, moving, Smoove's friend being killed, then finding out he wasn't dead, plus another guy from my old block was found dead in a house Smoove owned—now this. The last thing I was expecting was for Dion to show up at my church during a time where I'm formally introducing Smoove to my family."

"What! He showed up at your church?"

"Not only did he show up at church, he also had the nerve to pull me off to the side and rape me inside a dirty utility closet."

"Oh, this nigga is out of his fucking mind. We need to set that nigga's ass up and get him killed. The hell with the police."

"I made Charles aware of what happened. He told me not to worry, that he would see to it that he never would be able to lay a finger on me ever again."

After going over several plans to get rid of Dion, Ms. Janice shared the rest of her experience at church.

"I thought you said you slept with the preacher before?"

"I did. That's why when he called me, I passed out."

"Did he ever get the chance to say what he felt?"

"Girl, you wouldn't believe what he did! The whole time I'm thinking to myself that he was going to expose our affair. But to my surprise, he used me as an example of what a great woman was and highlighted me in a positive way."

Wanda was such a great relief to Ms. Janice. Being able to finally talk about all the turmoil in her life was therapeutic. She felt better already.

"So what's the deal with those bodies being found in a house Smoove rented out?"

"The house where him and his family grew up in burned down. Thing is, all three bodies found were killed. Two of them were the renters, and like I said, one of them was a guy named Swift that used to hang on my block."

"That's the same guy you said Smoove got into a shoot-out with a while back, right?"

"Yeah, him."

"Damn, girl, you do have your hands full. What does Smoove have to say about it?"

"He claims he has no idea how Swift knew them, but my gut tells me otherwise. He been carrying a gun on him lately, and word's been spreading round about his friend Heavy, the guy who faked his death and who was later revealed to be a snitch."

"Oh my god! I'm glad you are telling me all this because you need to relax and just allow me to hold you down while you just take care of my nephew up in there," Wanda said, touching her stomach.

"I'll be fine."

"No, I'm your friend. I'll see to it that you are fine. As much as you done for me, girl, I owe this to you. Plus I told you I'm ballin'," Wanda bragged, pulling out another wad of money.

"I love you, do you know that?" asked a teary-eyed Ms. Janice.

"Aw! I love you too."

With teary eyes, they both rose to their feet and hugged each other.

"I needed this, Wanda. Thank you so much for being here for me," Ms. Janice told her in between sobs.

"That's what friends are for. You know I'm your girl, and you know I always got your back. Don't even trip. We goin' to get through this together one day at a time," Wanda reassured her, rubbing the small of her back. "But for now, let's just enjoy the moment and spend the rest of the day having fun. We can go to the spa, get our toes done, go shopping—you know, pamper ourselves for the whole day at my expense."

"Girl, are you serious?" asked Ms. Janice as she looked at Wanda with a serious look on her face.

"As a heart attack."

"That would be so nice, 'cause I sure do need that right now."

"Good, 'cause I could use a day of pampering and chilling with my girl too. You know what I mean?"

"Come on, let's be out then. Ain't that's how you hood rats say it?"

"Hood rat. No, bitch, I'm hood rich now. And yeah, let's be out. By the way, since I'm treating, we rolling in your truck."

Jumping inside the truck, Ms. Janice pushed a few buttons on the touch-screen navigation system. She removed her flip-flops, propped her feet on the dashboard, reclined her seat back, and relaxed as Wanda took control of their destination.

CHAPTER TWENTY

F OR THE ENTIRE ride, Wanda rubbed Ms. Janice's swollen belly while Ms. Janice slept with her feet propped up on the dashboard. Wanda loved the attention they received from various guys they passed in traffic. Ms. Janice was wearing a summer dress, and while she was sleeping, Wanda took it upon herself to lift it, exposing her beautiful long legs.

Guys were honking their horns, hanging outta car windows, and on one occasion, one dude jumped out his car at the red light to get a closer look. Feeling Wanda's hand reaching inside her panties, Ms. Janice jumped out her sleep.

"Ooh! Girl, if you don't get cho hands up off of me, chile," Ms. Janice said, smacking her hand away.

"Wake up, sleepyhead, we here."

"Whoa, this is nice, Janice. Where in the world did you find this spot?"

"I seen it in the newspaper. I figured it would be a nice spot for us to check out, being that it's run by Africans"

"Mandingos!" They both said in unison, referring to the sign hanging in front of the building

Entering Mandingo's was like entering a love nest. They were in awe upon walking inside. The entire inside was custom-designed to create a euphoric feeling. From the walls to the floor, every inch was made from the material used to make therapeutic mattresses.

"I'm King Tutie. Welcome to my tribe," a half-naked African man announced from behind a counter. "Whut kud I du for tha tu lovely ladies tuday?" he asked in his deep African accent.

Ms. Janice and Wanda looked at each other and smiled. They both admired his deep accent and extremely good looks.

He was dressed like he was still living in a tent in Africa. The only part of his body that was covered was his genital area, leaving what appeared to be the buffest body they ever seen covered in chocolate exposed. Well over six feet, he had muscles over muscles.

"We would like the deluxe for two," Wanda said, handing him her credit card, along with the discount coupon she tore out the newspaper. After changing into their robes, they were led by Tutie to two massage tables where two Africans dressed in a king's attire awaited their arrival.

Right away Wanda disrobed before climbing onto the massage table. Ms. Janice quickly followed suit. She too got completely naked. With two strong men catering to every inch of their bodies, they felt like two schoolgirls doing something sneaky.

"Smoove is going to kill you," Wanda told Ms. Janice, watching her masseur massage her butt.

"What do you think big Chris is going to think about your new job?" Ms. Janice teased.

"Oh, I'm sure I would be dead too. You know he's on his way home, right?"

"Yeah."

"So right now, my main focus is to get this money, 'cause when he does get out, I'm done."

"You just make sure that you be safe. Have you been going to see my doctor?"

"Dr. Feel Good, a.k.a. head doctor. You were not lying when you said he was a certified head doctor. The only thing you didn't tell me was that he was hung like a horse too."

"I never knew, 'cause I never seen it."

For the rest of the day, they caught up on everything and continued to pamper themselves before heading back to the restaurant to pick up Wanda's car.

"Don't even trip. We are going to stick to our plan and hit that nigga where it hurts."

Wanda told Ms. Janice, reassuring her about getting even with Dion. Driving off, Wanda dialed a number on her phone.

"What's up, my princess? Talk to me," said the guy on the other end of the phone.

"Hey, daddy. You were right. It is as bad as she made it out to be."

"You didn't tell her I told you, right?"

"I told you that I wouldn't do that. That's my best friend. Stuff like that she's going to tell me anyway."

"Well, now that we know the severity of it, we need to act and act fast."

"I agree."

"Where can we meet?"

"Diva's."

CHAPTER TWENTY-ONE

"YO! I HOPE you cleaned my interior good this time,
'cause the last time, you left my upholstery unfurbished, knowing
I like my shit glistening."

"Nigga not only did I give this motherfucker the Black Manny special, I also spit-shined this bitch. Trust me, when you drive this baby up the block, you goin' to be looking like new money."

"I gotta give it to you. You brought my baby back to life." Smoove was amazed at how Black Manny was able to bring life back into a car that sat still for over a year.

The 1964 Impala he liked to call JFK was the only car he owned, and he only drove it on special occasions. Though it stayed parked in front of his cousin Jerry's house and was in his name, he never even had the privilege to take JFK for a drive. When it came to JFK, Smoove viewed the classic car as an investment that would pay off years down the line. Taking the backseat in the game, he had a lot of time to focus more on some of his other goals. Realizing the effect his departure from the game would have on those around him, Smoove devised a plan that would allow him to still live the lifestyle he was accustomed to, make money quietly, and keep those around him employed.

Instead of him leaving the game, he figured if he sold bulk quantities, he would take a lesser risk of going to prison. He no longer had to deal with the headaches associated with the game. If someone got locked up or a package came up missing, it was all A-Wax's burden. A-Wax was the only person whom he had dealings with pertaining to the streets. Through A-Wax, the streets were employed.

Business was on different terms now that A-Wax was in charge. Smoove sold weight to A-Wax at a cheap price. A-Wax would cut the dope and sell it at a higher price to different dealers throughout the city.

Nevertheless, A-Wax still had Crush Groove and all the same workers; just this time he was solely in charge of all the day-to-day operations. The only thing he went to Smoove for was to buy more drugs.

During the first stages of Smoove's transformation, he gave A-Wax two kilos on consignment. Within two weeks, A-Wax paid off his debt, made enough money to buy one, and never looked back.

"So what's been up, Smoove? I haven't seen you in a while," said Black Manny.

"That's the way I plan to keep it."

"Shit, all that money you making off that Crush Groove, you, for damn sure, can afford it. I just left from around there earlier, and, man, you should have seen that shit. It had to be at least a hundred people in line waiting to get served."

"What they got going on around there?" Smoove asked.

"I'm talking about your dope, Crush Groove."

"I don't know who's going around saying that, but I don't have nothing to do with nothing going on around there. In fact, I never sold drugs a day in my life. So it's no need for us to even talk about that."

Sensing that Smoove was feeling uneasy about his questions, Black Manny ended his debriefing and decided right then and there that he would no longer take any risky chances at trying to get information out of Smoove.

"I feel you. You're a bright kid, man. This game out here ain't got no rules."

"Who you telling? That's why I never played. You feel me?" Smoove replied before handing Black Manny a hundred-dollar bill. "I'm out, Manny. You take care of yourself out here. I'll probably see you in a week or so," Smoove lied before entering the driver side of his car.

Though Smoove didn't think Manny was working for the feds, he thought it would be in his best interest to treat everybody as such. Finding out that his old rival Swift, was the intruder whom he killed at the house he rented out only intensified how cautious he moved.

In his mind, there was no way it was a coincidence that Swift knew his tenants. He was sure their frantic calls to him the night before was to lure him there. But how? Who could've led him there? While Smoove drove away from the car wash, Black Manny got his cell phone.

"Hello."

"Yo, it's me. I got what you need." "Can you be at the spot in an hour?"

"As long as you got my money."

"Nigga, I got your money. Just be there." Removing the wire he was wearing, Manny hopped in his car to meet Heavy, putting his meeting with Agent Randolph on hold.

******

Manny arrived at his destination past the hour he predicted purposely to scope out the scene before getting into the van he knew would be waiting on him. Each and every meeting, he took every precaution imaginable to ensure that he went unnoticed. Scoping out the scene, wearing sunglasses, and wearing a pair of fake dreadlocks were the measures he took to ensure his safety.

On cue, the second he drove up, the blue van flashed its headlights at the end of the block. Catching his attention, he went in that direction. Already he earned well over $1,000 from Heavy just by giving up all the information he had on Smoove. Not to mention the money and drugs the feds gave him. With the information he had today, he knew from his previous meeting he would be walking away with $2,000, along with a portion of the drugs found upon Smoove's house being hit. Making a copy of the registration, he planned to take a copy to the feds once he left Heavy.

"So you finally have some concrete information for me, huh?"

"Do your fat ass like to eat?" Manny said, pulling his hood off, smiling.

"Fuck you, nigga. It took you long enough to get it."

"Listen, it ain't easy tryna get information outta someone as smooth as he is. Shit, they don't call him Smoove for nothing."

"If he's so smooth, then how in the hell did you end up getting some concrete information off him?"

"Because I'm a dope fiend and you promised me $2,000, that's why."

"A'ight enough with the bullshit. Here's your money. Now give me what you got."

Manny's palms started sweating as he admired the envelope full of twenties. He couldn't wait to buy a shitload of drugs with his money, so much so he had a bad case of the jitters just thinking about the drug binge he was about to go on. Manny dug in his coat pocket to retrieve the paper that was worth $2,000 then handed it to Heavy before looking on in admiration as Heavy's eyes got big. Manny felt good to finally have an address on Smoove. Out of all the cars Smoove ever brought to him to be washed, this was the first time he was able to find some documents with an address on it. All the rental cars he dropped off were addressed back to the rental car lots with the name Keisha Tillman as the renter on it.

"This here is big Manny. I gotta give it to you. You put in work this time. This here is part of the payoff."

Manny looked in amazement as he was handed a clear sandwich bag containing what looked like at least three grams of heroin.

"Oh shit, what's this, a bonus? Shit, we need to do this more often. I mean for this type of pay, I would break inside the White House and set the damn president up."

"That was just an incentive. I still need you to stay on him just in case this house doesn't lead us to nothing."

"I will, but from the looks of things, it seems like he's smelling something fishy. Not only has he been staying away from the neighborhood, he also was acting like I was the police when I was talking to him at the wash earlier."

"What chu mean?"

"I mean, I went to ask him a question like just mentioning his dope shop on Shirley, and he was like, man, I never sold drugs, I never did this or that. He knows I know he's one of the biggest drug dealers in the city."

"Mark my word, if he knew you were on to him, you wouldn't even be breathing right now. Trust me on that one."

"Well, I don't give a damn what you or anybody else feels. For this type of pay, I'll take that chance. Starting today I will be on Shirley Avenue, pressing his workers as well." Black Manny was in no mood to worry about Smoove; he had his sleeve rolled up trying to tie a knot in the rubber band he had wrapped around his arm.

"Got damn, you ain't waste no time, did you?"

"The same way you ain't waste no time meeting me here to reap the benefits from all the work I put in, is how I feel. Shit, you got what you wanted, why can't I? Now why you at it and since you being so nosy, why don't you help me tie this knot?" After tying the knot in his arm and having a few drops of water placed in his spoon, Manny placed a nice-size rock inside the spoon and used the flames from his lighter to melt down the rock substance. Once the entire spoon was filled with liquid, Manny drew back each drop into his syringe.

"That shit is going to kill you one day, you know that, right?"

"And you so ugly you will never have to dress up for Halloween, you know that, right?" replied Manny as he plucked his syringe to rid it of any air bubbles.

A rush of anxiety entered his body once he guided the needle to the awaiting vein in his arm. Once the drug entered his body, his dick got hard, his toes curled, and just as the last drop entered his vein, his entire nervous system shut down, sending him into cardiac arrest.

Seeing the fatal poison he laced the killer heroin with work through Manny's bloodstream, Heavy watched with a devilish look on his face as Manny went into convulsions. After a series of twitching, Manny was dead within minutes.

Searching his pockets to get the $2,000 back, Heavy came across the extra copy of the title, the tape recorder he was recording conversations with Smoove on, along with his cell phone. Heavy was baffled to find out that Manny was working with the police too. "Got damn, everybody snitching these days. I knew something was fishy about your stankin' ass." Suddenly a thought popped up in his head. *I can put this on Smoove. But how?* He began to devise a plan.

CHAPTER TWENTY-TWO

"ALL RIGHT! ALL right! Now listen up, gang, today is the day we put the pressure on Shirley Avenue!" Agent Randolph barked into the crowd of officers who stood before her.

"Fields, I need you to lead the SWAT team and have your guys hitting the houses from the front and the back. Shuvenski, I need you and Reid to oversee the entire operation from the sky, so gas up that helicopter." Each word she spoke, she used emphasis such as hand gestures and heightening her tone in order to get her point across.

"Jeffries, you're in charge of making sure your guys control the perimeter on the ground. Your team will be responsible for puttin' up roadblocks around the entire perimeter. Once we hit the block, nothing comes in or out until we have full control. After the houses are hit and we have everything at a standstill, Bondshock, you're in charge of the K-9 units. Get them dogs in there, and tear shit up. I want walls knocked in, mattresses ripped open, cars searched, bodies stripped. Nobody walks! Everybody gets arrested. Again, here's a picture of my number 2 informant, Dale Ahbrams. On the street, they call him Black Manny. Get familiar with this picture, 'cause he's on our side. When you see him, he is to be arrested. Treat him the same way the others are being treated. This is the only guy we have on the inside. From the last informant, we all know what the outcome can be if he gets exposed."

After ending her speech, she led her team in prayer. Afterward, all the officers went about the precinct, putting on their vests, loading up their guns, and gathering all the accessories they would be needing to successfully execute their assignment.

******

Meanwhile, A-Wax and his crew were on Shirley Avenue, pumping since 6:30 a.m. It was 7:15 a.m., and already they clocked well over a thousand dollars. Between 6:00 to 8:00 a.m., they always caught an

Early-morning rush. All the dope fiends who needed their fix in the morning so they could function were there.

A-Wax watched a series of fiends vomit, running inside the alley in their attempt to cure their morning sickness.

"Aye, man, can you go in there and get one for me?" one fiend asked A-Wax, holding a ten-dollar bill in his hand, clutching his stomach.

"Nigga, you gotta be out of your fucking mind if you think I'm risking my freedom to go in that alley for you!" A-Wax screamed at one of his regular customers.

"Come on, man! That monkey riding my back like a motherfucker. I buy from y'all all the time, man."

"Yeah, you spend twenty measly fucking dollars a day."

"Hey! What about you li'l man, can you bring me one?" he asked one of A-Wax's workers before falling to the ground.

Without giving his runner a chance to respond, A-Wax continued to bark on the customer. "Look, you bitch-ass nigga, we get money, nigga. Don't ever disrespect me or none of my niggas out here. Now you either go in there and get your own shit or get moving."

"Damn, man, this how you treat a nigga that put food on your table, you worthless piece of shit!" Before A-Wax could respond to his statement, he felt the cold steel touch his neck and looked on as the man he just verbally assassinated drew his weapon on his worker.

Fear ran through his body as he and his worker were dragged at gunpoint into the alley. He couldn't see who the perpetrator was who snuck behind him, but by the pressure he applied around his neck, he knew he meant business. It bothered him more to see that the guy he just argued with was a part of the robbery also.

They were led to the foot of the alley by gunpoint, and before they could be seen by any of the other workers, they were forced into the first backyard upon entering the alley. To make matters worse, the yard they were in had a brown picket fence surrounding it. Seeing inside the yard was impossible.

Once inside the yard, the gunman who had A-Wax shoved him to the ground, ordering him to strip.

"Look, man, ain't no need to strip me. Here's a thousand dollars right here," A-Wax pleaded.

"Strip, you bitch-ass nigga!"

After receiving two blows to the head from the butt of the gun, a dazed A-Wax did as he was told

"Now listen, this is how it's going to go. You see this pole here? The longer your runner takes to bring back all the dope y'all have out here, the further this pole goes up your ass. Now before you leave, let me warn you. If you try anything stupid or take a second longer than one minute, not only will this entire pole be up your ass, a bullet will be up there as well. Are we clear?"

"Y-eah," answered the scared and nervous li'l runner.

Before they allowed him to leave, the robbers made him call A-Wax's phone.

"Here's your phone back. You keep this phone just the way it is so while you're gone, I'll be able to hear what you're doing. The minute you hang up, I'll send that pole up his ass, and you already know what follows. You feel my drift?"

"Yeah," he replied in a frantic tone.

"Come here," the first robber said, grabbing the runner by his collar. Before they let him leave, they made him whisper the amount of drugs and money they had out there.

"I'm warning you, if your number doesn't add up to his and you try to play games, your ass is grass."

"Thirty-five hundred," A-Wax told him. He hit A-Wax with the gun again.

"Yo! Yo! Chill, he gave us a G already, so if you add that up, that's forty-five hundred!"

Satisfied, gunman number 1 synchronized his watch and sent the runner on his way.

Within fifty seconds, the runner came back outta breath with a handful of drugs and money. He was so tired that he couldn't even stand up straight. He was ordered by the gunmen to run to the foot of the alley to pose as a lookout for them while they attempted to make a clean getaway. Exiting the yard, they noticed two of A-Wax's other workers at the opposite end of the alley. Seeing their boss being led out the alley naked at gunpoint, they took off.

Making it to the foot of the alley, the gunmen had seen the coast was clear. Freeing A-Wax, they made a beeline to their getaway car. Out of nowhere police cars, the feds, and the SWAT team came from every direction, catching the robbers by surprise. Sensing they were trapped, robber number 1 instantly gave up by dropping his weapon. His gun went off, hitting the ground. All hell broke loose.

"Shots fired! Shots fired!" *Bang! Bang!! Bang! Bang!* The officers returned fire.

Within seconds, the robber whose gun went off was hit seven times in the upper body, killing him instantly. The second robber, who was the one who came from behind A-Wax, was wearing body armor, so though his upper body was hit six times, he was still running, squeezing off shots.

"Officer down! Officer down!"

The officer who was down was hit in the neck, causing an excessive amount of blood to stream onto the pavement. Agent Randolph was furious, watching her young rookie trainee fight to stay alive.

"Breathe! Breathe! Goddamn it, breathe! Help is on the way, baby. Stay with me!" Agent Randolph screamed, trying to apply pressure to his wound.

"I think he's gone," one of the other officers told her.

While she was catering to her rookie officer, her colleagues managed to put so many holes in the second robber that by the time his body hit the ground, he had fire coming from his jacket.

CHAPTER TWENTY-THREE

A GENT R ANDOLPH W A S enraged beyond belief. The very next day after losing one of her officers, she received the startling news that her number 2 informant was found dead. To make matters even worse, his body was found covered with dead rats in the same spot her rookie officer was murdered in.

"Fuck! Fuck! Fuck! When I get my hands on that son-of-a-bitch Smoove, they're going to name a prison after his ass. I promise you!" she roared through the phone before slamming it down.

She couldn't believe it. Here it was, month 6 of her investigation and with Black Manny being killed, every lead she had just went straight down the toilet. Due to the shoot-out yesterday, none of the raids were executed, leaving her entire investigation at a standstill. After being grilled over the phone by her boss, Agent Randolph headed to the hospital. She still had a few tricks up her sleeve.

During the day of the shoot-out, A-Wax was taken to the hospital. Agent Randolph put a hold on his body, along with his property, ordering that it be released to nobody but her. Because of her request, not only was he handcuffed to the bed 24-7, an armed officer stayed on guard at his bedside. Unbeknownst to A-Wax, Agent Randolph didn't even have probable cause. At this point, she knew it was either now or never.

The first thing she did upon entering the hospital was retrieve A-Wax's property. Though he was naked when they found him, a quick search of the area revealed that his clothes were a few yards away in one of the backyards. His phone was found at the foot of the alley. Sticking to her plan, she secretly planted a bug equipped with a tracking device in his phone. The fingernail-size gadget fit perfectly behind his battery.

Making her way toward his room, she walked with confidence and pride, causing heads to turn. She had no intentions on playing games. She entered his room briefcase in hand ready to handle business.

"I'm Agent Randolph. I'm spearheading a federal investigation—"

"Ma'am," A-Wax interjected, "I had nothing to do with those guys that killed that cop. As you can see, I was a victim as well. Not only was I robbed and stripped by them niggas, I got pistol-whipped also."

"Listen, Dontae Parker, a.k.a. A-Wax, Deloris and Kenneth Parker's youngest son—oh, I'm wrong, next to youngest son. Karl is the youngest. By the way, I like your new car. Damn, life must be good for you. Your big cousin Smoove left you the block, you and your girl, Jennifer, just moved into those new town houses out in Owings Mills, and you were just down Hammerjacks last weekend, making it rain in the club. You bought the bar out four weekends in a row. I know your sweet old grandmother Gale is smiling down on her baby. You're making a lot of money these days."

A-Wax was stunned by her remarks. *How in the hell does she know that?* he thought.

"Miss, I don't know what you're talking about. I'm sure my lawyer could answer all your questions. If you would kindly pass me that phone right there, I'll gladly call him for you."

Violating his Miranda rights, she kept her interrogation going even after he lawyered up. "Let's cut to the chase. I know who you are, and I know that you work for Smoove. Either you start being truthful, or you may end up just like this," she warned him before showing him a badly burned body that was beyond recognition. "Who the hell is this?"

Before he could even comprehend and digest what he just saw, Agent Randolph pulled another picture out. "This is Swift. You do remember him, right?"

"Damn, what happened to him? I thought he was locked up?"

"He was. But as you can see, Smoove thought he was a snitch and did this to him," she lied.

He was shocked to see her pulling out yet another picture. This time it was a picture of Heavy that she had taken when they first planned to fake his death.

"Oh shit! It's a rumor going around that he's still alive. But if he's dead, how come he didn't have a funeral?"

"His family is from North Carolina, so for their safety, the funeral was held up there. But yeah, it's true he's really dead." Not giving him the chance to think twice, she dug in her pocket to retrieve the picture of Black Manny.

"What the fuck! I just saw Manny the day before yesterday." "Well, he's dead all because Smoove thought he was a snitch." "What do you mean he thought he was a snitch? Look, I don't know where you're coming up with this information and what your angle is, but I'm telling you, you got the wrong guy. I don't even know anyone by the name of Smoove."

"I've had wiretaps on his phone for the last six months, and when he mentioned to someone that he suspected one of his contacts was cooperating, they ended up dead. Just recently you were mentioned. I'm trying to save your life. So wh—"

Before she could even finish her lie, A-Wax cut her off in mid-sentence. "Look, bitch, I told you I want my fucking lawyer present!"

******

Heavy's new home was located on the outskirts of the city. All complimentary of the witness protection program. Once a week, Agent Randolph paid him a visit to exchange views about the investigation. With each passing week, she became more comfortable sharing confidential information with him. With Black Manny being dead, Heavy was her only hope at this point.

Waiting on her arrival, Carlita was in the doorway when she pulled into the driveway.

"Hey, girl, look at you! That baby is ready to come out of that oven any day now huh?"

"Yes, and I am absolutely ready!" Carlita replied, rubbing her stomach.

Agent Randolph was pleased to see Carlita taking good care of herself. She stopped smoking and drugging, nor did she speak in a ghetto tone. Her home and appearance was in accordance with the new lifestyle she was living. They lived rent free, their kids were homeschooled, plus they were given $2,000 a month to cover their living expenses. In return, Heavy agreed to testify against Smoove when charges were brought up against him. He also agreed to help assist her with building a case against him. To monopolize the situation, he even coerced Carlita into agreeing to take the stand to back up his story.

Heavy was sitting in a wheelchair in front of the TV, watching a marathon of the first forty-eight hours when Agent Randolph came in.

KEVIN MILLER

"Hey, Antwon!" He was no longer restricted and confined to a hospital bed. From the looks of it, he was on a long road to recovery, Agent Randolph thought, judging by his appearance.

"What's going on?" Heavy answered before crying out in pain. "Ahh! I-I."

Hearing the screams from inside the kitchen, Carlita rushed to his aid to massage his jaw muscle.

"It's okay, baby. Just open them and close them back. Open and close. He gets those cramps in his jaws from time to time due to his jaw being broke. His doctor taught me how to massage it back together."

"Mmph." *He is all messed up*, Agent Randolph began thinking, seeing his condition. He lost massive weight, and his facial features were different, making him look twenty years older. Each visit he seemed to look worse. After nursing him back together, Carlita went back into the kitchen to finish cooking and attending to the kids. Heavy and Agent Randolph stayed in the living room, trying to devise a plan to get some concrete evidence on Smoove. Unbeknownst to Agent Randolph, Heavy formulated his own plan outside of what they planned. While locked up on his violation, he ran into Swift.

Knowing that Swift would be more than happy to have Heavy as an inside man, helping him get even with Smoove, Heavy gave him the address to the home Smoove's parents left behind. It wasn't until Agent Randolph told him that Swift was found dead along with the tenants did he find out. Heavy gave him any and every piece of information he had on Smoove. He didn't know if Smoove still lived there, owned the house, or if he sold it or not. What he did know was that was the house they lived in when he was adopted. Though Swift lost his life in the process, he didn't care. His angle was to bring Smoove down by any means.

"I'm not sure if you're aware, Antwon, but Black Manny was found dead on Shirley covered in dead rats."

"Oh shit! Black Manny. That was my man. Who killed him?"

"I never told you this, but Black Manny was working undercover, and somehow, Smoove found out, and I'm sure you know the rest," she told him, placing a photo of Black Manny dead in the middle of the street.

"Damn, we gotta get this nigga off the streets before he kills again."

"I know. That's why I'm here trying to get some type of direction from you. You were a drug dealer. Once, you were the right-hand man. What would you be thinking right now if you were Smoove?"

"How to kill me. I know how bad you want to take him down, but right now, we're at a dead end. Just give me a couple of days to think of something, and I'll get back with you."

A half hour after her arrival, Agent Randolph left, scratching her head. "Where do we go from here . . . ?"

Back inside the house, Heavy and Carlita laughed. They again bamboozled Agent Randolph.

"I told you that shit would work," Heavy told her, getting up from the wheelchair, walking toward the hall closet to get his coat.

It was no longer a laughing matter to Carlita after seeing that he was about to leave again. "Baby, where are you going now?"

"I gotta take care of something."

Fearing that she would tick him off, all she could do was cry as she watched her baby father make his way to the blue van he kept parked across the street.

CHAPTER TWENTY-FOUR

"THIS BETTER BE good," Smoove told Keisha as she led him outside and onto the patio.

Keisha, without saying a word, handed him a pregnancy test and watched as perplexity took over what was at first a calm expression. Smoove couldn't believe what he was reading. *No wonder she been acting different and going through all kinds of changes*, Smoove thought. He looked at Keisha standing before him with her arms folded across her chest, making her leg bounce. Tired and waiting for an answer, Keisha heavily sighed, causing Smoove to look her dead in her eyes. Looking into her eyes, Smoove couldn't stop the tears from coming, and in unison, they both grabbed hold of each other and embraced.

Smoove wasn't too thrilled about having two babies on the way and the situation it put him in. He was joyful for Keisha's sake.

When Keisha was adopted by his parents, they were told that she was the victim of a sexual assault by the hands of her parents. Over the years, they were told by several doctors that she would never be able to have kids. They often talked about having kids and what it would be like to have some. Never in a million years did they think she would get pregnant.

Smoove didn't know how he was going to pull it off, but in his heart, he knew that bringing both babies into the world was something he had to do. Telling Ms. Janice was an entirely different story. Keisha, on the other hand, was his least worry, knowing all he had to do to keep her happy was to allow her to keep the baby. With all they had been through, the only thing he could do was support her 100 percent. Whatever route he took, Keisha would follow. If she had to hide the baby from Ms. Janice or feed whomever a lie about the child's father that was something he was sure she would do.

"I'm not even going to lie to you, Keesh. I love you more than you even know."

"I love you too."

"Don't worry about nothing. All I need you to do is make sure that you stay focused on bringing us a healthy baby into the world. The last thing I need you doing is worrying about Janice or what others will think. We'll figure out a plan later. For now, I just need you to know that we having this baby. We been through thick and thin, so don't you dare even begin to think something can come between what we have. You already know."

Keisha looked up at her man as he spoke, and all she could do was smile. Placing her hands on his face and stepping on her tippy-toes, she placed a soft kiss on his lips.

Immediately lost in his thoughts, Smoove went into full sex mode. Picking Keisha up, she wrapped her legs around his waist before locking their lips together. In each passing second, Keisha became more antsy, causing her to moan. With her hands rubbing all over his head, Keisha was giving Smoove every indication that she needed to be penetrated, and now. Although he always kept women on the side, he always managed to fulfill her sexual desires. That was until Ms. Janice came into the picture. Their sex life drastically changed for the worst. Keisha couldn't stand her for being at the root of her sexual deprivation.

She was in a state of ecstasy due to the excessive amount of pleasure she received through the hands of Smoove. Being three months pregnant and without sex for two months, Smoove was awakening every sense within her body. Still fully clothed, Smoove carried her to one of the patio chairs, which resembled a beach chair with a cushion. Once there Smoove laid her on her back, never once breaking their kiss.

Keisha squirmed and moaned while Smoove was moving quickly to free his dick. Reaching inside her mini skirt Smoove rummaged through her underwear while using his other hand to get his pants down. The sensation that came with his fingertips touching her pussy opened up her floodgates. With each rhythmic stroke, Smoove's fingers became saturated with her juices.

"Ooh ba-by!" Keisha was so backed up she was instantly on the verge of climaxing. Sensing it, Smoove slid his dick halfway inside her then slowly rocked back and forth, massaging her clitoris along the way.

Shortly after his entrance, they both came. "Got damn! This pregnant pussy ain't nothing to be fucked with."

"Nigga, don't be acting like this the first time you done tapped out in this pussy. Now get up off me before somebody catch us out here like this. Ugh! I can't believe I let chu do it to me outside." She felt so disgusting and unladylike.

Smoove stood before her, laughing, dangling his dick, watching her scramble to get herself together and back inside the house. Out of nowhere, a tingling, sharp feeling made its way through his dick. Thinking nothing of it, he pulled his pants up and followed her.

Round 2 went well over forty-five minutes in the guest room. With Keisha laid out in exhaustion, Smoove retrieved his stash from the attic then waited on A-Wax's arrival.

From day 1, nobody outside of Keisha and Jerry knew that he kept a stash there. Once he took a backseat in the game, instead of taking the risk that came with driving around with a few kilos, Smoove led A-Wax to believe Jerry's house was just a neutral zone for them to meet and do business. Smoove also insisted that he ride the subway train instead of driving the distance, removing the risk of being followed.

He was eager to meet up with A-Wax to get the latest scoop on what happened with the police shooting, to hear what he had that was so important to tell him, and as the clock got closer to 11:00 p.m., his mind started to wander.

What if it's something about the feds? Or what if someone else got killed? thought Smoove. They had an agreement that they always stuck to: never discuss important business over the phone. All A-Wax told Smoove was that it was urgent that they spoke right away. From the urgency in his voice, it was evident that it wasn't good news.

Jerry and his family were out of town for the weekend. With Keisha being sound asleep, it was so quiet in the house the crickets from outside could be heard. With each passing minute, Smoove slipped deeper into his thoughts, sitting on the living-room couch.

Boom! Suddenly everything went haywire. The front door came crashing in, sending debris everywhere.

With flash grenades going off, Smoove couldn't see anything. The living room was covered in smoke. All he could see were the flashes that came with the gunshots that started erupting. Out of nowhere, a man wearing a gas mask appeared, standing directly over him. Before he could even brace himself for the blow, the gun went off in his face.

Boom! Smoove jumped off the sofa, sweating profusely. He laughed, realizing he was just having a bad dream.

Knock! Knock! Knock!

Hearing the knock at the door, he then remembered he didn't make it to pick up A-Wax from the train station. "That gotta be him, I know he's mad as hell," Smoove said, making his way to the front door.

"Who is it?"

"It's me, A-Wax."

Smiling from ear to ear, Smoove opened the door only to be stunned to see a battered and bruised-up A-Wax standing before him.

"Man, what the fuck happened to you?"

No sooner than the door was closed, A-Wax began telling Smoove the latest things that had occurred.

"The hell with what happened to me. You got bigger fish to fry."

As usual, Smoove advised A-Wax to turn the power off on his phone then turned the radio on to remove any unwanted listeners. With a menacing look on his face, Smoove listened attentively while A-Wax briefed him on the conversation he had with Agent Randolph.

"Man, the feds are on your ass. They tried to turn me against you and everything. This li'l police bitch was showing me pictures of dead bodies, claiming that you were responsible for them, saying I would end up like them if I didn't help bring you down." A-Wax went on to tell him all about seeing Heavy and Black Manny's dead bodies and about the incident that left three people dead, including a cop. Then he told him how he was robbed and pistol-whipped.

Smoove's mind was in disarray, trying to put the pieces of the puzzle together. "Yo, this shit is crazy. Black Manny just washed my car the other day. Then this shit about Heavy being dead, then one minute he's alive. I mean, this shit is un-fucking-believable. So did Heavy look dead?"

"Dead as a doorknob to me."

"What about Black Manny?"

"Oh, he's dead, for sure. They found him on the block in the middle of the street dead, covered in rats. Word on the streets is somebody drugged him up real good then dumped his body on the block during the early-morning hours. The motherfuckers that did it even left the needle in his arm when they left him."

A-Wax went on to tell him about the pictures she showed him of Swift, how she tried to coerce him into believing that he would be killed next, and how it would be in his best interest to help bring him down.

Smoove was in a world of his own after listening. His worst nightmare became a reality. From day 1, he tried everything imaginable to stay under the radar, only to be at the very center of an investigation. The thought alone made him sick to his stomach.

After going over more than a dozen scenarios, they still couldn't come up with a rational idea as to why the feds pointed the finger at him. He never told A-Wax that he was behind the attacks on Heavy or Swift, and he planned to keep it that way. How they came up with the idea that he was responsible was a mystery to him, one that he wouldn't be sticking around to find out.

"This is it for me, dog. I'm getting the fuck into hiding. Listen, I got two bricks left. You can take these joints now. Instead of giving me sixty each joint, just give me eighty, and you can have them both."

"Shit, what about the connect? Can you plug me in with him? Shit, I been waiting on a come-up like this forever."

"I think you should fall back once you move these last keys."

"Fall back? Nigga, is you crazy? I understand your concern, but ah nigga gotta eat. Shit, this all ah nigga know."

"Learn something else."

"My nigga. I ain't get in the game to learn how to get out of it. If anything, I'll learn how to get more money out of it. You feel me?"

"That's cool with me. Hell, I, for damn sure, didn't get in the game to be no drug counselor, so shit, suit yourself."

"So when are you going to plug me into him?" A-Wax asked with pure greed in his eyes.

"We'll get to that later. Right now I need you to get these bricks from out of here. I need to get these shits outta my possession now, 'cause I'm getting the fuck out of reach"

"Where do you plan on going?"

"I haven't made up my mind yet, but I just gotta disappear."

"What about the connect?"

"We'll take care of that before the week is out."

After making a clear understanding that A-Wax would be leaving with the last two bricks, they shook hands.

Smoove instructed Keisha to drive A-Wax to a wooded area where they were to stash the drugs. He advised A-Wax to immediately take Keisha to get the eighty thousand afterward. Before they departed, he told A-Wax to give him his phone. Keisha sat in the car in front of the house while Smoove and A-Wax said their good-byes.

"I'm getting rid of these phones tonight. You know how the feds play. They'll have your shit bugged," Smoove told A-Wax, holding their phones in his hand."

"So seriously, man, what about the connect? Don't leave without plugging me in."

"I told you I got chu. That's my word. Just do me one favor?"

"What's that?"

"Change up your whole operation. Change the name of your dope, move to a different block, and get some new workers. The last thing I need is to get blamed for your heat too."

"You got that."

Parting ways, Smoove walked away toward his car with a duffel bag full of the money he was removing from Jerry's house while A-Wax jumped in the passenger seat of Keisha's car with a book bag containing the two keys.

******

"What do you think of that?" Agent Randolph's newest field agent asked her.

"I think we're finally getting somewhere." Seeing Smoove leave out the same house that A-Wax's phone led them to put her investigation back into full swing.

"They both left the premises carrying bags, and Marcus used a key to lock that door. Damn right, we're getting somewhere."

"So now what?" asked the rookie.

Leading the case, Agent Randolph called all the shots. She kept a hungry rookie with her. Erica, her newest trainee, was as hungry as they came. "We'll find out who's the owner of this house. Tap the phone, and find out who that young lady was. Continue following that phone, put this house under twenty-four hour surveillance. I need to find out who lives there. Try to get a bug inside. Come on, rookie. You're rolling with the big dogs."

CHAPTER TWENTY-FIVE

"**D**ION, YOU CAN'T be going around taking advantage of women when they tell you it's over. That shit makes me look bad," Charles told Dion as they talked over drinks at Diva's.

"I don't know what she told you, but we were in a relationship. What me and my woman go through ain't none of your damn business."

"It is when you're being accused of stalking and harassing my former employees."

"Man, she lying! I never stalked that bitch. We're just going through the same type of shit people go through in every relationship."

"I understand that, but you gotta feel where I'm coming from. Janice called me, crying, telling me that you're trying to blackmail her, you're harassing her, and all kinds of shit, and that's shit I can't have happening in my establishment."

"Man that bi—"

"Hold up," Charles said, cutting him off mid-sentence. Sensing he would get nowhere talking, Charles snapped his fingers twice, giving Yellow the cue to put plan B into motion.

"Hey, daddy!" Yellow said, greeting Charles with two drinks in her hand.

"Dion, this is Yellow. Yellow, this is Dion." Half-naked, Yellow walked up behind Dion and placed her drinks on the bar before massaging his neck and shoulders. "I heard you like to take control of a bitch. Well, guess what? I'm going to take so much control of that dick tonight you won't even think about another bitch," she whispered in his ear.

"Look around, Dion. All these women belong to me in here. At the snap of a finger, they do as told." Snapping his fingers twice, Yellow stepped out of her see-through negligee.

Snapping them again, she placed a key with number 69 engraved on it in Dion's hand then made her way to fantasy lane.

Dion watched in excitement, looking at Yellow's petite frame walking naked toward room 69. "What's this about?" Dion asked, smiling.

"This is the deal I'm willing to make with you. Leave Janice alone, and give her back the tapes y'all made. No more harassing, no more blackmailing. In return, Yellow is yours. And trust me, she'll let you make all the tapes you like."

"Man, I appreciate your proposal, but I'm telling you Janice is lying to you. There's no tapes of us, and all the other shit she's telling you is a lie," Dion lied.

"So what are you saying, Dion?"

"Look, man, this conversation is over. You got me fucked up if you think you can come and dictate how I deal with my bitch. I'm outta here!" Dion barked, knocking the drinks Yellow left to the floor before making his way toward the elevator.

Not trying to cause a scene, Charles watched Dion leave, never once attempting to stop him. Casually, he dialed a number on his cell phone.

Stepping off the elevator on the first floor, Dion walked nonchalantly toward the front door. To his surprise, a tall man wearing a suit emerged, blocking his path. A ball of fear dropped in Dion's stomach upon hearing the man standing before him tell the person on the other end of the phone, "Yeah, he's right here."

"Oh, don't look worried now."

Dion backed up, truly frightened. Jordan took advantage of Dion's vulnerability and wrapped his hands around Dion's throat, squeezing with all his might. Dion clawed at Jordan's face but couldn't quite control his hands. Jordan kept squeezing with a look of deadly determination on his face.

"Please help," Dion said so quietly that Jordan barely heard him.

Dion dropped his hands to Jordan's and tried to pry them from his throat. He couldn't breathe! This couldn't be happening! Jordan was killing him. Knowing what he'd done to Ms. Janice, how dumb was he to even come here. Oh god, no! He watched his own hands flutter helplessly and without the strength to remove Jordan's hands.

The last thing he heard before everything faded completely was the elevator door opening.

A last thought crossed through his mind. Please God! Get me through this.

******

Waking up naked in the basement of Diva's, Dion found himself tied to a chair and was happy to be alive. He was now ready to cooperate.

"Okay! Okay! You win. Whatever you need me to do, I'm game. Please just let me live," he pleaded.

"We tried your way earlier. That didn't work, so let's try this." Dion didn't even have a chance to brace himself. From behind, Jordan dumped a pot of scolding hot water atop his head.

"Ah! Ah!"

"Scream again, and this stun gun goes off on your nuts." *Crack! Crack!* Dion was quiet as a mouse, seeing the voltage that came from the stun gun Charles held inches away from his private area. To further let Dion know he was serious, he stunned him.

Crack! Crack! Dion was so scared he didn't mutter a word outside of grunting. "Now that I finally have your undivided attention, let's get down to business," Charles said, holding Dion's keys and driver's license in his hand. "Who lives at this address with you?"

"Nobody but me."

"So where are the tapes?" asked Charles.

"There, right inside the entertainment center in my bedroom. There are three of them. They're labeled Paradise volume 1, 2, 3. Just please don't kill me! I swear I'll stay away from her." He cried.

"Now let me be clear on this. I'm going to check with Janice to make sure there are only three tapes, and if she says there are more or if I find more copies, I'm sure you can finish the sentence."

"Man, I swear to God, man, they're the only ones I have."

After calling to confirm the numbers with Ms. Janice, Charles sent Yellow and Jordan to Dion's house while he stayed to hold Dion captive.

******

During the short distance it took to get from New Jersey to Baltimore, Wanda and Jordan felt like two teenagers breaking the law. "I kinda like the name Yellow. Do you think it fit me?" Wanda asked.

"Nah. I like Wanda better."

"This shit gives me a rush. I feel like I'm part of the mob or something. Do y'all go through this kind of stuff with guys all the time?"

"Not all the time, but every once in a while, you get an asshole trying to act up. That's why it's important that you always keep your game tight so in the future you don't have to go through this. As of right now, you're our bottom bitch. Do you know what that means?"

"It means I'm at the bottom, 'cause I just started working."

"No, silly," Jordan said, laughing. "It means you're our main girl, so outside of our business dealings, we share a closeness with you that we don't share with the other women working for us."

"Why me, though?"

"When Janice retired, she told us that you would be the perfect candidate, and so far, we've seen you've been just that. That's why we involved you with this situation. We need to make sure that you're built for this life. Many can talk it, but only a few can walk it. Where are you going to fit in?"

"Wherever you need your bottom bitch to fit in, I'm there, daddy. Just always have my back, like Janice told me y'all would."

"Have your back! Baby, I got your front, side, and your back. Don't chu ever think nothing different. Come here." Reaching from the driver's side, Jordan grabbed Wanda by the face with a gentle touch.

"Baby, you're a part of our team. Taking care of you is like putting on socks every day. It comes that natural. I'm jumping as high as I can, then I'll ask, was that high enough? You need something done; you can stick a fork in it. Your kids are our kids. Your problems are my problems," he told her before placing his tongue deep inside her mouth.

Finishing up their plans, Jordan placed his gun inside his pocket. "You knock on the door acting like you're lost, then seconds later, I'll come from behind, and we'll take it from there. Put these on."

When Wanda put on the wig, sunglasses, and gloves, she felt a sense of nervousness making its way through her body once she approached apartment number 1. After knocking several times, she breathed a sigh of relief that no one was inside. Entering through the front door, they quickly found what they came for. "I got it, baby. Let's go," Wanda said, making her way to the front door. *Thank God this is all over*, she thought.

"Hold on," Jordan said, grabbing hold of her arm. "Never leave without doing a thorough job. Do you trust that these are the only copies? Not being sure will always come back to haunt you. Never forget that."

For close to a half hour, they quietly ransacked the tiny one-bedroom apartment, throwing every CD or DVD they could find inside a garbage bag.

They even took his laptop computer before leaving out quickly and quietly as they came.

******

Back at Diva's, Wanda wondered what could have happened to Dion. Again a ball of fear dropped into her stomach once she and Jordan stepped off the elevator. There she was in the same basement Dion was being held captive in. The last time she saw Dion, he was sitting at the bar with Charles. Now there he was, just a few feet away from her, strapped to a chair, naked. Things were beginning to move too fast for her. She was feeling dizzy. Every step she took toward Charles was slow and off-balance. *Come on, Wanda, keep it together. This shit is almost over*, she thought.

"Hey, Yellow, baby! Tell me you have what I need to spare his life," Charles asked Wanda.

"Yes, we got the tapes."

"No! Not in a million years could you ever have what I need to spare his life! The minute we let him out of here, everything we ever worked hard for goes down the drain. Our families, lives, our freedom—gone, just like that. He can't wait to go to the cops. Look at him."

Realizing his life was close to an end, Dion made his last plea to live. "I'm not going to the cops. I promise! Please just let me live. I'm too young to die!"

Seeing Charles approach him with a roll of duct tape in his hands, fear overtook every thought in his mind. "Help! Help! Ahh!" were his last words before tape covered his entire mouth, muffling his screams.

"Always remember, a dead man can't talk." Screwing a silencer onto his .40 caliber, Charles told Wanda with menace written all over his face. "There's one bullet in the chamber. You got one shot, one chance to secure our freedom. There are no more bullets. Our future solely depends on your shot. What are you going to do?" He told Wanda, placing the gun on the table before walking away.

Quickly following suit, Jordan headed for the elevator. Out to prove herself, Wanda walked up to Dion with the pistol in her hand. Knowing she had to protect their future, she grabbed a fistful of his hair, pressed the nozzle of the silencer against his temple, then pulled the trigger.

The single shot exited his left temple, killing him instantly. Finally, she earned her place. She was indeed a bottom bitch.

CHAPTER TWENTY-SIX

C HASE ME, OWNED by Ms. Janice, was a glamorous, upscale, clothing boutique located in the downtown metropolitan area. They sold brand-name clothes and accessories strictly for women. With the help of her financial advisor, she was able to hop on the road to success. She quickly learned the ins and outs of maintaining and expanding her business. Possessing no marketing or promotional skills, Smoove not only gave her $100,000 to open the store, he set her up with a sophisticated team of advisors.

She had a full-time life coach, a financial advisor, and a sales broker. Her father held a bachelor's degree in business; he was on her team as well. He controlled the day-to-day business operations while she took a course online to obtain her associates degree in business. She also worked hand in hand with him on a daily basis. She attended every business meeting, learned marketing strategies, got familiar with the retail and manufacturing side of the business, and was working relentlessly.

"Oh my god! Girl, these damn pumps are killing me," Ms. Janice told Wanda while attempting to free her swollen feet.

"Look at my baby! You are just swollen all over."

"I know, girl, this child is blowing me up something terrible."

"So y'all still set on not knowing the gender?"

"Yeah, 'cause it keeps the excitement level high. Plus this is our first child, so I want that excitement to go beyond just the birth."

"I feel where you coming from."

"Like, to me knowing what to expect just kills the suspense, and I'm starting to enjoy having these little mystery family talks with Smoove. Every night he's home, waiting on me just to cater to my every need. He's there rubbing my feet, my bath water is ready, and he's doing all the cooking and cleaning. It's like ever since I started getting closer to full term, my baby been spoiling me to death. I think I'm whipped."

"I-I get so weak in the knees I can hardly speak. I lose all control as something takes over me!" Ms. Janice enjoyed a laugh, watching Wanda imitate SWV.

She had her phone up to her mouth, swaying her head from side to side with a serious look on her face. Taking it to the next level, she squatted down before bouncing up and down, giving Ms. Janice the impression that she was riding an invisible man.

"Girl, if you don't get cho hind parts up off that floor like that! I told you that you can't be up in here with all that ghetto stuff."

Rebelling against her request, Wanda got on all fours and flipped the bottom of her mullet hem daringly short shirt dress over her back exposing her backside and started shaking her ass, causing tidal waves to appear.

"Girl!" Ms. Janice said, scrambling from behind her desk. Before she was in striking distance, Wanda sprinted to her feet, sending them both into a game of cat and mouse. Wanda jolted back and forth across the room, using chairs and everything within reach to clog Ms. Janice's path. Hearing a knock at the door sent them both back into work mode.

Adjusting her clothes, Wanda opened the door, greeted Ms. Janice's employee who stood before her, then sashayed off into another section of the store.

"Ms. Janice, your one p.m. appointment, Mr. Weston, is here to see you."

"Thank you, Juicy Peach. Can you tell him to give me five minutes please? I'll be right with him." Though Wanda was her girl, Juicy Peach, a nickname Wanda gave her, was Ms. Janice's prized possession.

Juicy Peach was fresh out of school. After studying to become a fashion designer, she was more than willing to intern for Janice. They met after Ms. Janice posted an ad on Craigslist, searching for an intern to help her incorporate a sense of style mixed with femininity into her establishment.

Through Juicy Peach, Ms. Janice was able to give her boutique a more unique, seductive appearance.

Being it was a boutique strictly for women; Juicy Peach designed and created a setting so feminine that the store itself had some sex appeal. The makeover she gave it had a look that was more approachable and playful, making the customers feel comfortable. Everything about Juicy Peach was fabulous. The tan nude skintight body suit with pearls lightly cluttered in different sections she wore hugged each inch of her shapely curves. Her flamingo-pink-color hair was styled into a cute crop pixie, a look that revealed her feminine yet rebellious side.

To glamorize her apparel, she added a small amount of accessories. Her neck and ears were adorned with beautiful crystal-like pearls, adding power to her goddess look. She even had the pearl bracelet and nose ring to match. Completing her outfit were the stunning Christian Louboutin laser-cut leather and open-toe wood stilettos. Juicy Peach was a certified fashion guru. Through Ms. Janice, she was able to live out her dream and make her name known within the fashion industry. Not only was she a fashion designer, she was a certified cosmetician, a stylist, and a makeup artist.

From the very beginning she convinced Ms. Janice to allow her store to partake in a 30 day promotion. One that would promote the store and showcase the many concepts and ideas she wanted to implement within her business. This was day three of their promotion and business was booming. Juicy Peach's idea was to create a place where a woman could receive a pedicure, buy beauty products, purchase fabulous clothes, get their hair and makeup done, and so much more under one roof.

During the thirty-day-trial period, she used business cards, flyers, Facebook, and Twitter, along with the local radio station. One weekend a group of her girls accompanied her to the hottest bars and clubs wearing Chase Me T-shirts. Once inside the clubs, their main objective was to hand out as many flyers as they could.

Juicy Peach had a four-girl crew, all of whom shared the same aspirations. She knew that with their hard work, creative ideas, and passion, they were on the verge of making a difference in the beauty and fashion world.

Among her were Jail Butt, Aaliyah and Cherry Pop. Although Wanda recently gave them their nicknames, they were all getting used to them. All day at work, Wanda would be teasing and joking them to death about their names.

At twenty-seven, Juicy Peach was the oldest and the mastermind behind the crew. Everything about her resembled the likeness of a juicy peach. She always came up with the juiciest ideas, her lips stayed shimmered in gloss, she was addicted to peaches, and she had a peach complexion. She was thick in all the right places, with big pink full lips, nice-size breasts, long eyelashes, and thick eyebrows. She had a butt that caused trouble. She loved showing off her voluptuous figure. Today was no exception. The body suit she wore was so thin and perfect fitting. When she walked, it was as if the suit was painted onto her body the way her ass cheeks wiggled.

Juicy Peach met Jail Butt while attending a hair show. Coincidentally, they both showed up rocking the same hairstyle and went on to win by a tie. Since then they'd been inseparable. After confiding in Wanda how she was once a correctional officer who got fired for having a sexual relationship with an inmate, Jail Butt was her new name.

Cherry Pop, Juicy Peach's younger sister, was the cool kid among the crew. She was petite and dark, with brown eyes, pink lips, natural long, wavy hair, and at seventeen years old, she was not only practicing celibacy, she was promoting it also. For that reason, she was receiving calls from several different prominent outlets wanting to give her the platform to help her voice reach the masses. She was amazed to see how kids were actively participating in sexual activities once she reached junior high.

Instead of not talking about it, she came up with a brilliant idea. She created a blog called ImNotDoingIt.com. Kids with similar stories could voice their opinions, share ideas to help spread the word, and serve as a place for virgins that would praise them for practicing celibacy. Word of her activities spread quickly. Shortly after came the phone calls from Oprah, BET's 106 & *Park*, Nickelodeon, and MTV. Opposite from making appearances on television, her story was featured in countless magazines. When Wanda gave her the meaning behind Cherry Pop, she began promoting her new name as well.

"Oh my god! You're that virgin girl who was on TV talking about you not doing it and stuff."

"Wanda!" Juicy Peach interjected. "Leave my li'l sister alone. I told you she's not with all that ghetto stuff."

"Girl, you know I'm just joking. It's actually good to see a young lady these days that hasn't gotten that cherry popped." Soon as the words *cherry pop* left Wanda's mouth, Juicy Peach shot her an angry look.

"Don't even think about it."

"Why not? I think it's a cute name."

"What? What?" Cherry Pop demanded. "What's a cute name?"

"I wanted to call you Cherry Pop because it stands for being a virgin, and I just wanted to show you that virgins can have cute nicknames too."

"Oh, I'm cool with that. Anything to support my cause."

Aaliyah, the best braider in the crew and Cherry Pop's best friend, was also a seventeen-year-old virgin. Looking exactly like the late singer Aaliyah, naming her after the pop princess was inevitable.

Hiring Juicy Peach was a plus for Ms. Janice. Along with her came her crew, all their contacts, clients, client referrals, and a constant flow of customers. She had things set up good. During the thirty-day-trial period while they were giving free pedicures, manicures, facials, and makeup sessions, they formed an elite glam squad.

Cherry Pop had her own section in the store where she set up a pamphlet station that held a collection of various informative literatures on celibacy and safe sex. She served as a directory for the youth. All the young girls who visited the store, she introduced them to her cause.

Wanda, Jail Butt, Aaliyah, Juicy Peach, and Cherry Pop worked together to keep up with the day-to-day activities. Together they gave out beauty and fashion tips, recommendations and shared secrets, and tips on products and trends. They all shared the responsibility of customer service and working the cash register.

During the thirty-day trial, each customer received custom-made product recommendations, along with an exclusive gift with their purchase. Once a day when the store was crowded, Juicy Peach randomly picked one customer with a scruffy appearance to make over. Seeing the tomboy-looking girl walking in her direction, she found the perfect target.

"Woman, are you crazy? I been dressing like a nigga all my life. I'm not fixing to be letting you make me look like no damn broad! Hell no, you can't give me no makeover!"

"In all actuality, you are a woman at the end of the day, so it's nothing wrong with showing off your feminine side."

"No, in all actuality, I'm not a woman. I'm a dom."

"So what are you doing carrying that Stella McCartney dress to the counter?" asked Juicy Peach.

"For your information, I'm doing what men do. I'm buying my girl this dress. How much is this thing anyway?"

"Oh, that's on sale for $329."

"Damn. $329!" She looked at her girl in the shoe section trying on matching shoes then thought about how much she really wanted that dress. "Don't y'all have some type of lay-away plan? 'Cause I do want this dress, but $329."

"We don't have lay-away, but for $200 and twenty minutes of your time, that dress could be yours."

"Aiight! Come on, man, just don't be long, and when you done, I'm washing that shit off."

Before getting into the chair, Juicy Peach took her picture and her measurements and sizes then sent her to Aaliyah for a shampoo.

"Attention! Attention! *Chase Me* customers and staff. I need everybody's attention!" Satisfied that she had everyone's attention, Juicy Peach went to work.

"This here is a real customer that I handpicked to give what I like to call the revolutionized experience. This is her before picture," she told them, displaying the blotchy-faced, nappy-headed dom picture on her laptop.

With four rough-looking cornrows, chapped lips, and an ashy face, she knew that once she finished rejuvenating her lifeless look, Chase Me would once again be on its way to becoming a household name.

To create a soft, romantic updo she prepped her hair with mousse while still wet then blew it dry. Following the blow-drying, she then twisted and pinned her hair. Gathering the hair at the nape of the neck, she rolled the ends under and loosely secured the knot in place, allowing a few pieces of her untamed hair to fall out naturally. The onlookers watched in admiration as they witnessed the transformation take place.

Happy with the quick hairstyle, Juicy Peach opened her makeup bag, smiling as she went deeper into her transformation. She applied a moisturizer with SPF by Garnier evenly throughout her face to help the concealer glide on smoothly. To give her perfectly even skin the speedy way, she used a foundation stick and the heat from her fingertips to blend in the foundation. With pesky zits and marks still poking through, she hid them with a layer of concealer by dabbing it onto problem areas with a pointed brush.

Instead of shading and sculpting her cheekbones with a brush and powder, Juicy Peach used her fingertips to apply the Yves Saint Laurent Creme de Blush to the apples of her cheeks and blended the berry color toward her temples with her fingers.

Going to work on her eyes, she applied a wash of sheer shimmery cream shadow from her lash lines to her brow bones using her index finger.

Next to give her eyes more depth, she used a flat shadow brush and applied a bronze and gold shade cream onto the center of her lids. Ridding her eyelids of harsh lines, she again used her fingers to smudge it down, making her work look blended and effortless. Adding more definition and intensity, with a brown pencil eyeliner, she rimmed her upper lash lines before smudging it upward with her shadow brush. She finished her eyes off with two coats of mascara on top and bottom, slowly focusing on the outer lashes with the top of the wand.

Gasps could be heard from the onlookers as they were in disbelief at how fast she was able to rejuvenate the tomboy's dehydrated-looking skin. Her skin looked velvety soft due to the flawless makeover she was undergoing. Unable to see her new look the crowd's reaction made the tomboy blush for the first time since walking inside the store.

Lastly, Juicy Peach thought of a way to conceal her dry, chapped lips plus give them a lustrous look.

"Cherry Pop!" Juicy Peach called out.

Making her way through the crowd, Cherry Pop came to her sister's aid. Juicy Peach pulled her out of earshot and sent her to retrieve a cup of ice and a damp washcloth before giving her attention back to the crowd.

"This here, ladies and gentlemen, is the final touch. Look carefully, 'cause you won't learn this in school. God forbid, you'll die before seeing this again," The crowd erupted in laughter. "That is unless you plan on coming back. Only here in the hands of me and my squad at Chase Me will you always, I mean *always*, have the opportunity to witness this kind of revolutionized experience."

Returning with the fresh cup of ice cubes and a damp washcloth, Cherry Pop smiled at the notion of what was about to transpire. Leaving no room for procrastination, Juicy Peach didn't say another word; she just got busy.

After receiving the secret ingredients she needed to give her lips a lusher, shimmery look, she gently buffed her dry, chapped lips with the damp cloth then evenly applied two layers of lip balm. Letting it sink in well, she grabbed her mini station fan and held it directly over her lips for sixty seconds before slowly blotting it with tissue to absorb the slipperiness. Using a strawberry-color lipstick by Maybelline straight from the tube, she started at the center of her mouth and slowly made her way around the perimeter of her lips.

"Do like this," Juicy Peach instructed her before poking her lips out, making a kissy face.

To help her look last, she blended the lipstick over her lips by patting the color on with her fingertips. To amp things up, she ran a cube of ice over her lips before slicking on a wet, glittery application of gloss, giving her lips a shiny, glamorous, glittering look.

"Ta-da!" Juicy Peach bowed before the patrons as they gave her an outstanding applause.

"Girl, did you see that?"

"Oh my god, she looks completely different. I thought she was a man at first."

"This place is something else."

Inside the crowd were all kinds of reactions and chatter. The funny thing to Juicy Peach was, she was just getting started. They hadn't seen anything yet.

CHAPTER TWENTY-SEVEN

RIDING IN THE backseat of his Rolls-Royce, Charles felt like royalty cruising through the streets of Baltimore. With Wanda on top of her game, his plans to expand his empire was beginning to come together.

"So what makes you feel so confident that she's what we're looking for?" Charles asked Wanda on the other end of the phone.

"I'm telling you, daddy, this girl is a magnet to success. You should have seen how this bitch commanded everybody's attention the other day. Then she don't have no kids, she's not into drugs, and her body is off the fucking chain."

"What does she look like?"

"I'll send a picture of her to your phone when we hang up."

"Okay, that's cool. Anyway, I was calling you because I was in your neck of the woods on a business trip, and before I head back to Jersey, I would like to see my pinky."

"You in Baltimore right now?" Wanda asked, full of excitement.

"Yeah."

"Oh my god! You damn right I wanna see you, daddy. What time?"

"I'm thinking maybe around nine tonight, give or take a little."

"Good! That'll give me enough time to shake my baby father's ass. This nigga only been home a week, so it's not fully registering with his brain that it's done between us."

"As good as that ass is you ain't going to get rid of him too easy. Hell, I don't even blame the brother."

"I knew I should have never given that nigga no pussy. I'm thinking if I let him live with me for free, help him get on his feet, and let him do him shit would be all good. Boy, was I wrong. He talking all this tying a bitch down shit. I love my new life. He should've tried that shit before his ass went in."

"I hear you, baby. Well, look, I gotta go, so I'll be calling you later. Pack a night bag. You staying with me tonight."

"Okay, daddy, I'll be waiting on your call. I love you."

"I love you back." Seconds after ending their call, a picture of Juicy Peach came to his phone.

"Whoa, you've really outdone yourself this time. She is official." He texted Wanda.

"This is it. I'll be waiting at the next spot for you," Jordan told Charles, holding the door open for him. Charles stepped out the backseat with his suitcase in hand then headed to the entrance of the subway station in Owings Mills. Heads turned seeing what looked like a celebrity walking in their direction. Strutting with a sense of pride and cockiness, he paid his toll then rode the escalator to the next floor.

On schedule, his train was already there. Boarding, he went for the seat located at the back of the cart, taking the window spot. Grabbing the newspaper he held under his armpit he went straight to the sports section.

In each stop, the train became more crowded, just the way he liked. Three stops in, he watched whom he came to meet board the train. After catching eye contact, he put the paper back up to his face and kept reading.

"Excuse me, sir, do you mind if I sit here?" a pretty white lady wearing a business suit asked.

"Sure. You're more than welcome."

"Thank you. I'm Sherry, by the way," she told him, extending her hand.

"I'm Charles. Pleased to meet you."

"I can tell by your accent you're not from around here."

"I'm not. Just here on business."

"Where are you from?"

"Jersey."

"This is my stop coming. You have a nice day, ma'am, and again, it's very nice to meet you." Placing his newspaper under his armpit, Charles grabbed his suitcase and proceeded to make his way through the crowded train. Sherry was unable to control it; she grabbed him by the arm.

"Maybe we can get together before you go back to Jersey or see each other the next time you're in town. We do have more to offer here in Baltimore than business."

Glancing at the fancy business card she handed him, he, indeed, would be calling Sherry the real estate broker. "I see you're a woman that goes after what she wants in life. I like that." Placing the card in his pocket, he walked away before she could respond.

Seeing a familiar face, he stopped to greet his friend. "What's up, man? How have you been?"

"I'm good, bruh," Smoove told him, putting his suitcase next to his.

"I haven't seen you since law school. We gotta keep in touch. You got a number for me?" Charles asked, releasing him from their embrace. 'The doors will be closing in five seconds," the train conductor announced over the loudspeaker. Giving Smoove the same business card the lady sitting next to him just gave him, Charles grabbed Smoove's suitcase and exited the train just before the doors closed.

Happy to have made yet another successful transaction, Charles threw on his Bulgari sunglasses then casually walked toward the exit. Minutes later, Jordan arrived in the Phantom. Once Charles placed the suitcase in the backseat, Jordan pulled off, leaving Charles on the bus stop with his legs crossed, reading the newspaper.

******

A-Wax and Smoove hopped off the train at the next stop. Both dressed in business suits, they looked more like businessmen than drug dealers.

Out in the parking lot, Cynthia, the mother of A-Wax's baby, drove away with the suitcase filled with heroin while Smoove and A-Wax drove in the opposite direction.

Twenty minutes later, they pulled into the parking lot of the train station where Charles awaited their arrival. Still reading his newspaper when they pulled up, Smoove beeped the horn. Smiling, he walked with a cool demeanor toward the car.

"Damn, that nigga look like money," A-Wax expressed to Smoove, admiring Charles's attire. Wearing a $7,000 Black Label Ralph Lauren suit, Black Label gators, a platinum Moonstruck Ulysse Nardin watch, and a pair of platinum Tiffany cufflinks set with VVS1 baguette diamonds, looking like money was an understatement. After formally introducing A-Wax to Charles, his connect; Smoove took A-Wax through his next phase.

Feeling uneasy, A-Wax was baffled as to why they were at his daughter's school. Not wanting to offend Charles or put Smoove in an uncomfortable situation, he kept his thoughts to himself.

"A-Wax," Smoove said, looking in A-Wax's direction, "as you're aware, my run in the game is over. When you need to reup, this is your go-to guy. Both you guys are family to me. This is business, nothing personal. Take us to your daughter's classroom."

Baffled, A-Wax did as he was told.

"Daddy! Daddy!" his five-year-old daughter yelled, seeing her father walk in her classroom.

"Hello, Ms. Toolie," A-Wax spoke, greeting her teacher. "I just wanted to drop by and see my baby," he told her, picking his daughter up.

"Hey, Smoove! Smoove! Smoove!" she yelled, happy to see her big cousin.

"Hey, Gigi, baby!" From his cell phone, Charles took pictures of them while they interacted in the hallway. A-Wax, still feeling uncomfortable, was beginning to figure out why they visited his daughter's school. To him it all made sense. In order to do business, Charles needed a safety net, he thought to himself. Going with the flow, he still didn't ask any questions, walking onto his mother's front porch.

As always, the house was crowded with family members. Inside was his grandmother, two aunts, one of his sisters, and his father, along with a bunch of kids. Introducing Charles as one of his long-time friends from school, Smoove ordered wings and pizza then instigated a spades tournament.

"Boy, I been playing this game before you were even born," Mrs. Bernice, A-Wax's mother, told Smoove.

"Check this out then. Me and my man Charles against whoever you want as a partner, and if y'all win, I'll give you $500. If you lose, you get no Christmas present from me this year."

"No, Smoove, that's not fair," she whined.

"Take it or leave it, Ms. I been doing this before you were born," he told her teasingly.

"Scared money don't make no money. Jerome, grab that bottle of whiskey and some shot glasses, and get them cards out the cabinet. Let's run over these young whippersnappers," she told her husband, A-Wax's father.

"Man, you suck," Smoove told Charles as they walked back toward the car.

"Shit, I never said I knew how to play. You just picked me as your partner then got us set."

"Set? I got us set? They ran a Boston on the first hand. God couldn't save us from getting set." Before leaving, Smoove discreetly asked Charles for his phone.

"Come on, y'all, let's take a family picture. It's not too often we all get together. Here, take a few pictures for us," Smoove told Charles, handing Charles back his phone. In two stops, Charles managed to have pictures and the whereabouts of A-Wax's closest associates. The next few hours were spent stopping at more locations. A-Wax's house, where he lived with his daughter and his baby mother. All his stash houses, the cars he drove, the women he slept with on the side were all shown to Charles.

Charles shook A-wax and Smoove's hand then exited the backseat of the car once they stopped in front of the Sheraton Hotel downtown. Suddenly a thought came to his mind. "I almost forgot. I need that business card I gave you back on the subway." Sherry the real estate broker or Wanda tonight? He played with the thought. *Hell, I'm that dude. I'll try both.* He decided before walking toward the lobby.

CHAPTER TWENTY-EIGHT

A-WAX FELT LIKE he was on top of the world, driving down the street in Charles's drop-top Bentley. The metallic gray over black beauty dipped in and out of traffic. Spending the weekend with Charles in New Jersey, where he met his family, took a trip down fantasy lane at Diva's, and got schooled onto bigger and better things through Charles's wisdom, changed his life.

The Bentley was his for a week, along with five more kilos of heroin on consignment. Charles's plan was to corner the drug market in the city through A-Wax, so schooling him came with it. At twenty-one, he had a lot to learn outside of Shirley Avenue. In order to corner the market, he first had to teach him how to. Today was his first task: motivate the city. Earlier he gave out two hundred testers then gave out double the dosage in his ten-dollar bags, providing a twenty-dollar bag for ten dollars.

Coming down the block in Charles's whip, everybody on Shirley Avenue became awestruck seeing a young A-Wax behind the driver's seat. The matching Bentley watch cluttered in diamonds complimented his new look. Normally dressed in rugged street wear, he looked clad in a black silk linen Valentino sweater and slacks. Wearing a Ferragamo belt, with matching shoes, he loved the attention that came with his new look. "Throwing money in the air like I don't really care. Yeah, standing on the chair like I don't really care. Got bitches by the pair. I'm baller of the year. Haters everywhere, but I don't really care," he sang along with Trey Songz and Waka Flocka, throwing a fistful of one- and five-dollar bills in the air while stopped at the intersection of Shirley and Cottage. Pulling off while the money came raining down the crowd of nearly thirty people gathered at the corner all jumped and screamed out of excitement.

"Oh shit! Yo, did you see that shit!" one kid yelled.

"My nigga shining! That's how we do it up Park Heights, nigga!" another dude chimed in. Scrambling over the money flying around, they all got the message.

Taking heed to Charles's advice, A-Wax moved his crew up the ranks. Instead of having them work the corner, he hired them to be his enforcers. Throughout the city, they were to travel with him everywhere he went. The only place they didn't go was to his new house in Jersey, which Charles rented out to him.

With the money he was about to be seeing, Charles had to see to it that he made the proper adjustments to keep the wolves off his back, not to mention the law. Before the month was out, he was sure from all the stunting he would have A-Wax doing, word would spread like wildfire. That was exactly what he wanted. He needed the city to see that if you dealt with A-Wax, you too could get money. Every week he planned to give him a different exotic car and some money to blow at the club and have a weekend sit-down with him just to school him deeper into the game. After the thirty-day ball-a-thon, his status as a street hustler would change.

"Let's get it, y'all. Thirty days from today, I'm leaving this block to one of you. Until then, I need y'all to be my enforcers. There's no room for mistakes. No more smoking weed or drinking on the block. The amount of paper we're about to be seeing is going to have niggas from everywhere trying to get on our level, and we have to set examples. That shit that happened to me when I got robbed can't happen again. Never can we slip like that. Those li'l niggas y'all been telling me about that's trying to get down, put them to work. I'll be back in a half hour. Have this shit better than this. I need everybody on their toes. Every corner needs a lookout. Guns need to be spread around. All those people being able to walk up on me is over. I'm the new president in the hood, so you niggas know how I'm tryna be moving. Shirley Avenue is over. We moving over to Spring hill."

******

Receiving word that A-Wax was spotted in the neighborhood driving a Bentley was one thing. Hearing that he and his crew were back on the block distributing narcotics at an enormous rate was another. For over a week, Agent Randolph gave an executive order to all the law enforcement agencies involved in her investigation to stay clear of the area. She needed Smoove and his crew to feel comfortable. Finding out they were on Springhill just a few blocks away from Shirley, she devised a plan.

Showing her undercover officer a picture of Smoove and A-Wax, Agent Randolph equipped her field agent with an electronic recording device, along with one-hundred-dollar department funds, before departing from their neutral location.

"These two are our main targets. Your objective for the day is to make direct contact with one of them and get them to send you in the direction where you can purchase some narcotics or get them to admit to participating in the sale of narcotics. There are numerous ways that you can do it, but once you're out in that field, only you and your experience can get the job done. There are two ways to approach the situation. Anything outside of it, you'll have to allow your natural instincts to kick in. The first way, which is the best way, is to purchase the drugs from the individual who's making the hand-to-hand transactions while avoiding contact with our targets. From my experience, I'm sure there'll be a number of people out there trying to purchase as well. It's Friday, the first of the month. Business should be pumping. All you have to do upon entering the block is pay attention to the direction where the other customers are going. Make conversation with any of the customers you come in contact with, even suggest the idea of putting your money with theirs to get a better deal. Through them, you'll blend in better. After making your buy, approach one of our targets and complain about the quantity and advise them that you're unsatisfied with the amount you received for what you paid for. What they're going to say, we're unsure of, but you'll be wearing a wire, so hopefully, they'll incriminate themselves. The other way to do it is to locate your target and simply ask one of them where they're hitting at or are they out, a street term most dealers are used to.

"If he sends you in the right direction to purchase the narcotics, then that's enough to get you that promotion you were asking for and remove you from that miserable desk duty you've been dreading."

Confident and eager to reestablish herself as an undercover officer and tired of the routine desk work she disapproved of, Officer Fenley entered Springhill Avenue from the intersection of Park Heights. Naturally, she had the physical attributes of a junkie. Weighing a little over 120 pounds, with blotchy dark skin, she was dressed in a dingy blue denim outfit. Giving her the tacky look most drug addicts had, she kept her hair in disarray and didn't shower or brush her teeth in the last three days. Not eating or drinking any fluids made her feel worse than she looked.

Just as Agent Randolph said, the block was live. She could see people running in and out of an alley that was behind the houses on Springhill. Her gut told her to stick with the first thought that came to her mind. Walking in the alley, she went unnoticed, walking straight up to the young gentlemen doing the hand-to-hand transactions.

"I got one hundred dollars. What can I get for this?" she asked him, clutching her stomach from the severe hunger pains she was experiencing.

"I'll give you ten. As big as these shits are, the deal is already in the bag," he told her, snatching her money before running toward a guy riding a bike in the middle of the alley.

"Fuck," she mumbled, witnessing the guy on the bike give the young boy a fresh package. She watched the young boy pass a stack of money in return to the guy on the bike, whom she could barely make out. The marked money she gave him was very crucial to their case. Seeing it ride off with the unknown individual almost deflated her. At the neutral location where she was to immediately meet Agent Randolph was the serial number that matched the one on the hundred-dollar bill. Therefore, upon arresting the individual who sold her the drugs, retrieving the marked money would seal the deal.

Once the young boy placed the ten bags in her hands, she went in search of her targets. Spotting A-Wax in the middle of the street throwing a football back and forth to some of the neighborhood kids, she felt relieved. Refusing to settle for less, she walked in his direction in an agitated manner. Hungry, feeling like shit, and irritated over the fact she lost track of her marked money, she was explosive.

"Excuse me! That young guy you got back there serving people told me to see you if I had any complaints," she said, pointing toward the alley she told A-Wax. "I just spent $300 with y'all, and he ain't give me no type of deal," she lied. "It's fucked up when you treat good-paying customers like that." Out of nowhere appeared a guy covered in overalls with oil stains all over him. It was evident to her that he was working on the car next to them with the hood up. Yanking her by the hair, he scared her.

"Woman, are you fucking crazy! You can't be just walking up on people while you got drugs on you. We don't have nothing to do with what goes on back there."

"But, but—"

"Look, bitch! Ain't no buts." *Crack! Crack!* Hearing the cracking sounds from the stun gun he held in his hand, Detective Fenley heeded his warnings without having to think twice.

CHAPTER TWENTY-NINE

F ROM THE MONEY Heavy made assisting the feds, he was able to purchase a few guns. With the city flooded with gangs, he quickly thought of a way to form a crew to help him take down Smoove. Standing in the middle of six bloods, he smiled at the thought of the group of six wimpy kids, which included two girls jumping him in.

"Thirty-one seconds, y'all. Let's go. My clock is running!" Overkill, the leader of the blood set Heavy was joining, screamed at the six individuals.

Rushing him, they pummeled him to the ground. In a fetal position, he covered himself the best he could. For thirty-one seconds, he was kicked and stomped only to stand up, smiling. *These weak motherfuckers*, he thought. With no scrapes, scars, or gashes, he dusted the dirt off his clothes then waited for Overkill to give him his next mission.

Cruising through the streets of East Baltimore, Heavy felt out of place riding around with a bunch of chumps. He couldn't wait to officially get brought in so he could take over the entire set.

"I told y'all, my man is a gangsta," Overkill stated, passing the lit blunt to one of the bloods. "Me and my nigga been puttin' in work since grade school. My man goin' put that work in. Ain't that right, my nigg?"

"You already know," replied Heavy, never once taking his eyes off the road.

"Take this next left coming up," Overkill said over the loud music pumping in Heavy's van. Taking the left, they parked behind a motorcycle on a small one-way street next to a row of rundown houses. Cutting the music off and killing the engine, Heavy was curious.

"So what's the deal, man? What we here for?"

"This is where this bitch-ass nigga Joey live. He been a thorn in my side for some time now. Gotta teach him a li'l lesson. That's his house right there."

Pointing at Joey's house, Overkill broke a mug just thinking about him.

"What's the plan?" Heavy asked, not caring what he did to deserve his fate.

"He normally comes out around nine thirty," Overkill said, looking at his watch. They had an hour to fully prepare.

"Do the nigga drive?"

"That's his motorcycle right in front of us. We could just snatch the nigga up soon as he jumps on his bike."

"Nah, we can't do it like that. Never snatch ah nigga in front of his house. It's one thing for a motherfucker to see you snatching somebody they don't know. Family, oh they calling the cops. I got this," Heavy said, starting the engine up. Driving down the block, he found a parking spot way at the other end of the street. Grabbing his binoculars, he smiled. "Here, take these, and let me know when he walks out," Heavy told Overkill before he went to the back window. Overkill was amazed at how prepared Heavy was.

"Got damn, nigga! You got rope, handcuffs, duct tape, and all kinds of shit back this raggedy motherfucker."

Heavy's van was perfect for any heist. Along with a ladder on the side, every window except the front had curtains. The inside was empty, just two chairs in the front and all kinds of robbery equipment in the back.

"Yo! Yo! He's coming out now!" Overkill yelled, seeing their target exit the front door just minutes after they parked. Witnessing him lock lips with the woman who walked him to his bike in her robe made his stomach turn.

"Work call. Time to put that motherfucking work in. Y'all ready?" asked Heavy.

"Let's get it. Yeah," they all chimed in.

"How many guns y'all got?"

"Guns, we didn't bring any. You got that pocket knife, Ice Pick?" Overkill asked one of the bloods.

"A fucking pocket knife? Nigga, what the fuck you plan on doing playing Pirates of the Caribbean with this nigga?"

"Naw, we were just goin' to beat his ass real bad!"

"So we just going to beat his ass and leave ourselves open for him to retaliate? Nigga, this ain't the eighties no more. Either you go all the way, or you leave it alone. The choice is yours. Shit, he don't know me," Heavy said, pulling his bandana he had tied around his neck toward his face.

"You right, yo. I never looked at it like that."

"Well, make the call, nigga. He coming down the street right now," Heavy said, spotting the motorcycle in his rearview mirror. Badly wanting him out of his life for good, he made the call.

"Aiight, let's get this shit over. You lead, man. We follow your lead," he told Heavy with pure fright in his eyes.

"Look, three of y'all, stand on each side of the street. When I knock him off the bike, y'all put these cuffs on him and throw him in the van. Hurry up! The nigga getting close!" Heavy barked, starting up his van.

Before Joey could pass the van, Heavy cut his wheel hard left, crashing into the bike. Caught off guard, Joey went flying over the hood. Landing in the middle of the street, he got up, enraged. Snatching off his helmet, he walked toward the driver's side. Before a word could leave his lips, he was rushed by all six bloods. A brief struggle ensued. Shortly after, he was handcuffed and thrown in the back of the van. Seeing Overkill, he knew his chance at survival was slim.

******

Digging a hole for over three hours, they were tired. Taking turns digging to holding flashlights, the six bloods were relieved when Heavy told them the hole was deep enough. Heavy didn't lift a finger.

From talking to them, he found out they all came from similar upbringings. Having drug-addict parents, weak family ties, no leadership skills, and no official dudes to run with, joining the bloods was the best thing that could have ever happen to them. Not one of them held a steady source of income outside of robbing and stealing. Matching their stories were the rundown, dusty-looking clothes they wore. Through their loyalty to Overkill, it saddened him to see them not be provided with better lifestyles. Hopefully, that would all change when he took over, he thought as he walked back to the van to get Joey.

"What the fuck! Nigga, what the fuck are you doing?" Heavy was shocked, seeing Overkill doing something to Joey's private area. When he left the van, Joey was handcuffed at the wrist and feet, fully clothed, with tape over his mouth. Seeing his pants down, he didn't know what was going on.

"This bitch-ass nigga won't be fucking my baby mother no more. Sucker ass was fucking my bitch while I was locked up then had the nerve to fuck her when I get out. Fuck you. Think I'm ah lame or something?"

Heavy couldn't believe his ears.

"Nigga, I know got damn well you ain't got me about to kill this nigga over no pussy? Please tell me I heard wrong?"

"Yeah, this nigga ain't goin' to be walking around after he done put dick all in my bitch."

"Nigga, are you stupid! You and your baby mother aren't even together anymore. And while you was locked up, nigga, she held you the fuck down your entire bid. Fucking came with your ass going to jail, you dumb ass nigga. Why the fuck you ain't tell me this from the start? I sure as hell wouldn't be here."

"You never asked."

"Come on, man, let's just get the fuck out of here."

As the bloods threw Joey in the hole alive, Heavy watched in anger as three of the bloods threw dirt on him. With a shit face, Overkill felt dumb as ever meditating on Heavy's thoughts toward him. Heavy made a lot of sense; he just didn't look at it that way at first. *Damn, I fucked up big time*, thought Overkill.

Finished covering him with dirt, they covered the makeshift grave with leaves and debris. Heavy dropped the six bloods off on Greenmount Avenue. Before they got out the van, he gave each of them fifty dollars then told them to meet him at the same location at five the next day.

"I got a big mission for y'all tomorrow. Guaranteed money. I respect y'all's loyalty, and unlike any of them other niggas y'all done dealt with, I'm ah make sure y'all good. Y'all down?"

"Hell yeah! Count me in." They all agreed.

Before leaving the van, they all exchanged gang handshakes with Overkill, who stayed in the van. *Look at this goofy-ass shit*, Heavy began thinking, watching the weirdest handshake ever take place.

"I'm good. I don't even know how to do that goofy-ass shit yet. Y'all can teach me later. Right now I gotta get moving. Remember, tomorrow, five."

"Woop! Woop! Su woop!" the bloods hollered, exiting the van. Still in the passenger seat, Overkill lit another blunt in hopes of cutting the tension in the air.

"Man, I can't believe you cut that man's dick off just because he fucked your baby mother. That was some real sucka shit you had me involved with. You know that, right?"

"You right, man. That was one to grow on. I let my emotions get the best of me."

"What got me fucked up is you been locked up all that time and been home for less than two weeks and you out here jeopardizing our freedom over a bitch just because she fucking."

"It's bigger than that. He was supposed to be fucking her while I was in. That shit was supposed to stop when I got out. You taking the wrong turn. My house is the other way," Overkill said, turning to look in Heavy's direction.

Boom! Boom! Boom! Still driving down the street, Heavy sent three bullets in his face, slumping him on the dashboard. To finish the job, he put the gun to the back of his head. *Boom!* Blood and brain matter splattered everywhere. Still in the middle of the street, driving, he kept a cool demeanor as he passed by other cars in traffic.

Making a right turn three lights later, he pulled onto a tiny dark street and parked. Tying Overkill's body tightly together, he stuffed his lifeless body into two large black trash bags then cleaned the inside of his van as best he could until he got home. Minutes later, he was dumping Overkill's body in a creek located at Halon Park. Taking over his set would be easier than he first thought.

CHAPTER-THIRTY

S MOOVE W A S IN a hectic situation. Having unprotected sex with two women, he didn't know whom to blame for the burning sensation that accompanied him while urinating. Not sure who was behind the cause sent his mind in overdrive. The mere thought of them sleeping around on him was mind-blowing. After leaving his doctor's office earlier, he still couldn't figure a way to approach the situation. Today was the day of his baby shower. Sitting at the car wash on Quantico, he thought of a dozen scenarios. None came close to solving his problem. With both of his women pregnant, for the sake of his children, he had to bring it to their attention. But how? It had to happen today, he decided.

"Here's your keys, man. I'm finished."

Taking his car keys from the detailer, he thought about Black Manny. For years, Manny was his go-to guy. Not seeing him felt kind of odd. On top of that, the guy who detailed his car was nowhere near as good as Manny.

"Damn homie! You got my windows all streaked up." Adding insult to injury, the new guy had the nerve to clean him out all the change he kept inside his cupholder.

"What the fuck happened to all my change? I should break your fucking neck! Come here, you bitch!" Snatching him off his feet, Smoove carried him by his neck in search of the owner. Without knocking on the door, he burst inside the office unannounced, throwing the measly detailer to the concrete floor. Weighing a little over one hundred pounds, his body rolled and tumbled into a shelf filled with car accessories. On impact, the shelf went crashing to the floor. Disregarding the meeting Tony was having with the white man wearing a business suit, sitting across from him, Smoove grabbed the owner by the collar.

"Listen! And you listen to me carefully. The next time I come to this dump of ah car wash and one of your workers dare steal out of my car again, I promise I'll wipe your motherfucking f a c e on this motherfucking concrete!" Scared shitless, Dominican Tony, without even fully understanding S m o o v e ' s fury, agreed.

"C'mon, Smoovey! We boys, man. I want no trouble with you. Whatever it is you need, man, just talk to me, and it's done. No need for the funny stuff!"

"Fire this slimeball motherfucker!"

"You got it."

Leaving out, he was pleased witnessing Dominican Tony kicking and stomping all over the detailer. Not paying attention, he bumped into two people trying to enter the office. "Excuse me, my b—" Unable to finish his sentence, he was caught off guard when the light-skin girl dressed in a security-guard uniform threw a cup of hot tea in his face. "You bitch-ass nigga!" She screamed.

Following his natural instincts, he smacked the female perpetrator so hard she was asleep before she hit the ground. The back of her skull crashed into the pavement. The impact woke her back up. Through crossed eyes, she looked up at the girl she was with, not sure what was happening. "Crystal! Crystal!" Her friend cried, shaking her face. "How many fingers am I holding up?" she asked, holding four fingers close to her face. With her eyes rolled in the back of her head, she managed to mumble "Thursday" before blacking out.

Realizing that was the same correctional officer he previously shat on, Smoove made a mental note to never go to that car wash again. Burning rubber when he drove off, he drove like a mad man, feeling stupid for even being back in the hood in the first place. "That's my word! This is the last time I'm even coming around this bitch," he said aloud, turning the volume on his radio up.

CHAPTER THIRTY-ONE

A RRIVING AT THE meeting spot five minutes late, Heavy was glad to see the six bloods waiting at the bus stop when he pulled up. Wearing the same clothes, they jumped in the van, smelling like weed and liquor.

"Anybody heard from Overkill? I been calling his phone all day," he lied.

"Nah, we been looking for him too," one of the bloods replied.

"Let me find out that he a chicken-hearted nigga. Well, that's his loss. We're about to get paid. Everybody down, right?"

"Hell yeah! That's why we're here."

"Work call!" Heavy yelled, pulling off.

******

"Wake up! Wake up!" one of the agents Agent Randolph had watching the house A-Wax's phone led her to said to his partner. "We got company. Look, there's a blue van coming in our direction." Watching the blue van drive past the house like the last car did two hours ago, his partner was mad.

"C'mon, Monteresse! How many times are you going to wake me up for these false calls? The daytime is yours. Night watch is mine. Don't bother me until you have something concrete, dude." With his shift approaching shortly, he fell back to sleep.

******

In the blue van, Heavy and the six bloods parked a few houses down from the address Black Manny gave him.

Driving by, he saw the old-school Impala sitting in the driveway, matching the description from the title he held in his possession.

"This is the plan," Heavy told them, killing the engine. "I just got the drop on a big-time drug dealer. This isn't his house. His cousin lives here, but I'm sure he keeps something stashed here or his cousin can at least lead us to him. Either way, whether we gotta kidnap his cousin for ransom, we coming away with some money. This how we goin' to do it." Seeing the blue fluorescent headlights approaching from behind Heavy turned around. When the white Cadillac Escalade stopped in front of the house, he was eager to see who was behind the driver's seat. Confused seeing a pregnant Ms. Janice climb out of the truck, he wondered what she was doing there. Parking behind her, Wanda got out of her Lexus in a joyful manner and hugged Ms. Janice. Wanda's baby father, Chris, and their kids unloaded bags and food trays from Ms. Janice's truck and Wanda's car. As they walked in the house, Keisha held the door open for them. Heavy's plan was sent in an entire different direction, one that presented better opportunities when he saw Keisha.

******

"Snap! Snap!"

"Buddy, can you be any louder! I'm trying to sleep. Enough already!" Witnessing his partner take pictures of some unknown people, he quickly began jotting down their license plate number without saying another word.

"I think we should move down the street." Watching car after car pull up, they figured it would be a good idea to park at the opposite end of the block, especially when A-Wax and Smoove parked directly behind them in Charles' Bentley. Taking pictures of them as they exited the car and walked inside the house, they both high-fived each other.

"We're on to something. Finally! Yes!"

"No, I'm on to something. You were sleeping."

"Should we call for extra surveillance?"

"For what? So somebody else can take credit for all the hard work we're putting in? No way we letting that happen. We goin' to crack this baby wide open ourselves." They agreed before driving down the street.

CHAPTER THIRTY-TWO

"**A**T NIGHT WE can't sleep. We living in hell. First, they give us the work, then they throw us in jail. Dear Lord, yeah, I'm trafficking the white. Please, Lord, don't let me go to jail tonight. Yeah! Who me? I'm ah sole survivor. Ask about me in the streets, ya boy Jeezy ah rider," Charles rapped word for word with Young Jeezy as he guided his platinum-colored Phantom down I-95 South. The smooth ride was over in less than the forty-five minutes predicted by the navigation system. Upon entering the street leading to Smoove's baby shower, he could tell by how crowded the block was with cars that it would be quite a spectacle.

Parking behind a car identical to Wanda's Lexus, he played with the thought of it really being hers. Having the same pink teddy bear hanging from the rearview mirror, he really thought of it being her car. Not wanting to be in an awkward situation, he turned his music down then dialed her number.

"Hey, daddy!" she yelled over the loud music playing in the background.

"You wouldn't be at a baby shower on Bonita Ave., would you?" he asked, reading the street name from his navigation.

"Yeah, how in the world you know that?" Wanda asked, full of surprise.

"Let me find out my man, Smoove is having a baby with my girl, Janice."

"You know Smoove? Charles, where are you right now?"

"I'm out front."

"Out front." Trying to go unnoticed by her baby father, Wanda placed her phone in her pocket then walked casually toward the front door. To her disbelief, there he was, parked out front.

"Pull off, c'mon! Go, we can't let nobody see us together! You can't be here." Smiling, he stayed parked.

"Girl, you trippin'. Ain't nobody going to know nothing. I already know where this is going. You do not have to worry about me telling Smoove about Janice. Both of them are dear friends of mine. It is funny thinking about it though," he said, laughing.

"I'm serious, Charles. Then my baby father is in there, so I think it would be too much to handle."

"All right, all right. I'm serious, baby. You know me. I'm not going to do nothing like that. I'm just messed up that I knew the entire time both of them were having babies but never once asked them by who. But yeah, that's my word. I'm staying out of y'all mix."

"Okay, Charles, I'm trusting your word. Since you not going to pull off, I'm going back inside before somebody catch us out here." Running into Ms. Janice in the backyard, she felt more at ease hearing her response.

"So you're not shocked that Smoove and Charles are friends?"

"Yeah, but I know Charles isn't going to say nothing. When I told you he was a good man. I meant it. The last thing I'm worried about is being exposed. Charles is like family, girl."

Making his way to the front porch, without knocking, Charles stepped through the front door. Dressed in a blue Tom Ford cardigan, complimented by blue linen slacks, he wore a solid white dress shirt with a blue tie to match. His brown Italian leather belt went perfect with his brown Caesar Picotti loafers. In his left ear sat a pear-shape 3½ carat solitaire diamond earring, sharing no comparison to the platinum vacheron Constantin watch with the bezel studded with baguette diamonds. Toting a colorful gift bag in his hand, he was greeted by Keisha who was in the living room, organizing the many gifts brought in.

"Charles!" she creamed, rushing to him before stepping on her front toes to hug him.

"How's my little sister?"

"I'm good." After introducing Charles to the few family members in the house, Keisha led him out back. Smoove, seeing him come through the door, was full of excitement.

"Yo! What's up, baby? You gotta meet the family," he told Charles with his arm around his shoulder before walking him throughout the yard to meet his family and friends. As if they never met, Charles greeted Ms. Janice with all smiles.

"Finally, I get to meet the very lucky lady. Hi, I'm Charles. Pleased to meet you."

"Janice. Nice to meet you. Charles, right?" Extending her hand, she smiled. Feeling more relaxed witnessing their introduction; Wanda downed a straight shot of Hennessy before placing her empty shot glass on the bar. Along with the open bar, Quick Silva, the hottest DJ in the city, worked the ones and twos from his music station. While big Chris, Wanda's baby father, held down the food on the grill. Promoting her brand, Juicy Peach and the staff from Chase Me worked the gathering to their benefit. In tight matching T-shirts with the word Chase Me colorfully spelled in the center, they took their thirty-day promotion to the baby shower.

Ms. Janice looked on in admiration while Juicy Peach wooed the crowd with her ice trick. Though Smoove never stepped foot inside the store, he heard enough from Ms. Janice to know that the store was well on its way to sending them both into retirement. Seeing Juicy Peach and her crew command the attention of the crowd was enough to seal the deal for him.

"Baby, you right, them girls are like that. We need to put a Chase Me in every state," Smoove said to Ms. Janice.

With teary eyes, she looked at Smoove as she spoke, "Right now I have something serious to discuss with you that can't wait."

Preparing to hear some type of explanation as to why he was burning, Smoove's mind went into a blur.

"You know I love you, right? And I would never do anything to hurt you. Promise me that when I ask you this question, you'll still be the young man I fell in love with."

"Can we discuss this inside or after the shower? I think there's a time for everything, and now is kind of an awkward time."

This bitch done burnt me. Shit, what if she thinks I burnt her? What the fuck is she thinking? Discuss this shit right now? he silently thought.

With her hand tightly interlocked with his, she ordered the DJ to cut the music then grabbed one of his microphones. "Excuse me, everybody! Can I have everyone's attention? From the bottom of our hearts, we truly are very appreciative for all of the gifts, the kind words, prayers, and for all the support each of you have given us. We're all one big family, so I ask that each and every one of you take the time out to get to know each other. With that said, I have something that I need to get off my chest."

Looking Smoove in the eyes without blinking she dropped the microphone in the grass then slowly got down onto her knees. Crying she reached inside her bra and pulled out a diamond-studded platinum wedding band. Trembling, she managed to mumble the words, "Will you marry me?"

"Yes! I will." All smiles, Smoove helped her to her feet after she placed the ring on his finger. Kissing her, he couldn't fully enjoy the moment with being burnt weighing heavy on his mind. Seeing the cold look on Keisha's face through the corner of his eye was yet another stinger.

The crowd broke out into a cheer. "Yes! Amen." People were crying, hugging, and constantly cheering them on. On cue, the DJ cranked things back up by playing "Let's Get Married" by Jagged Edge. Those who were unfamiliar with one another were now introducing themselves, sharing hugs, and dancing together. Making a separate line for the males and females, Ms. Janice started a soul-train line. Coming through the line first, she and Smoove captivated the crowd, dancing against each other.

Feeling the few drinks she consumed, Wanda couldn't wait to get her groove on with Charles. Three people later, they came down the line, performing out the gate. Charles, the perfect gentleman, slow-danced her down the line, wooing the crowd with his classy moves. Wanda, not having to do anything but walk and spin where he led her, felt like a princess as she was being twirled around. At the end of their classy movement, Wanda snuck a tiny peck on his lips.

Following her to the bar area, big Chris, her baby father, grabbed her by the arm. "Bitch, what the fuck is your problem? Our kids are in here! By the way, who the fuck is that lame you just put your lips on? Are you fucking him?"

"For your information, I am." Not wanting to cause a scene, he pulled her by the arm discreetly and took her to the front of the yard. Witnessing the ordeal, Ms. Janice followed them. Seeing Ms. Janice caused Smoove to follow her. Not wanting to get involved, Charles continued to entertain Juicy Peach, who was all over him.

Instead of taking the side of the house to get to the front yard,

Smoove walked through the house. Noticing Keisha sitting on the sofa

in a daze, he tried talking to her. Getting no response, he searched her purse in search of her psych medication, figuring that might have been the cause of her daze.

"Yo, what's up? Why you got that look?" Observing that all too familiar look on Smoove's face before he went into the house, A-Wax decided to follow him.

"Go check on them out front. I'm good I'll be out there in a minute." Searching her purse, he was shocked coming across the same bottle of penicillin he had in his pocket. After finding the pills he was looking for, he grabbed a bottle of water from the refrigerator then helped her take her medicine.

Hearing the commotion getting louder out front, he dropped everything then ran outside.

"Don't chu eva put cho hands on her in your life! I'm ah get my baby father to fuck you up!" Ms. Janice screamed at big Chris, trying to break free from the grip A-Wax held on her.

"You pregnant, Janice. Chill out. Let me handle it," A-Wax pleaded with her. Smoove snapped, seeing Wanda lying on the ground knocked out cold. Big Chris, as if it was nothing, walked down the street.

"A homie!" Before he could even turn around, A-Wax and Smoove jumped on him from behind. A-Wax grabbed hold of his shirt while Smoove got in front of him and unloaded a fury of punches in his face. Out of nowhere, Keisha jumped into the action. In seconds, big Chris was on the ground, bleeding as the three of them stomped him repeatedly.

From a distance, the feds watched everything unfold. Not wanting to blow their cover, they looked on. "Should we sit here and watch them pulverize the poor guy?" one agent asked.

"You see how hard he punched that lady. Besides, these will be the same pictures we'll show the jury after we bring down our indictment on him. Not to mention if they kill him. That alone would send him to prison for life."

******

Six bloods strapped with two guns, a stun gun, and one pocket knife sat inside Heavy's van. Red bandanas covered all their faces.

"Now! Go! Go!" On Heavy's call, they all jumped out the van. Toting

one gun, three bloods went directly for Smoove, two went for Keisha, while one gunman went for A-Wax.

Before Smoove could react, it was too late. *Boom! Boom!* He witnessed two shots enter the back of A-Wax skull, sending him crashing to the ground. At full speed, Smoove ran so fast the gunman on him sent six shots in his direction before deciding not to give chase.

"Get the fuck off me!" Keisha tried to fight off the three bloods. The voltage from the stun gun took every ounce of fight out of her. Defenseless, she watched A-Wax's body twitch as she was being carried to the van. The voltage took away her ability to move. She witnessed shot after shot crash into A-Wax's lifeless body.

Wanting to be sure he was dead, Heavy got out and sent every slug inside his six-shot revolver in the back of A-Wax's head. Throwing Keisha in the back of the van, the bloods, along with Heavy, pulled off.

By then the entire street was flooded with people screaming and crying. No one even noticed the feds trying to give pursuit. Even with them flashing their blue lights, they were unable to drive through the crowd. "I told you we should've intervened! Look at this shit." Knowing Agent Randolph would have them answering calls at their headquarters, the sleeping agent planned to shift all the blame on his partner. "Only if you had listened and let me call for backup. There's no way in hell we can explain this one! Fuck!" They never had a chance at saving A-Wax. By the time they were able to drive through the crowd the suspects fleeing in the van were out of sight.

******

To be continued.

Excerpt from
A Park Heights Tale II

CHAPTER ONE

W ITH ONE PERSON dead and two people clinging to life, the waiting room inside Northwest Hospital was flooded with grieving people. For over an hour, they waited impatiently to find out the status of their loved ones. Along with A-Wax being killed, Smoove and Ms. Janice were struck by the bullets the gunman sent in Smoove's direction. Having one bullet lodged centimeters away from his spine, the doctors who worked on Smoove were in the middle of making a big decision, one that would impact his life forever.

Wiping sweat from his forehead, one doctor expressed to his colleague, "I'm optimistic that we can pull it off without causing any internal damage. It's either now or never."

"I agree."

"The last thing we would want is for this guy to go about his life, then years later, the bullet travels and ends up in a vital place."

"But what are the chances of us successfully completing the operation without causing any damage? Easily he can get paralyzed or bleed to death."

Heavily sedated Smoove lay unconscious w h i l e his doctor made his way toward the waiting area to consult his future with his family.

******

Finally, a doctor wearing green scrubs came from behind the double doors that led to the operating room. In a split second, the entire room shifted their attention to him in hopes of hearing some good news. Moving h is glasses from his forehead down to his eyes he looked at his medical chart.

"Is anyone here related to a Ms. Janice Walker?" the entire room answered yes, causing her parents to come forth to speak up for their child.

"Excuse us, sir, we're her parents," Mr. Walker stated, tightly gripping his wife's hand.

"Can the two of you walk with me please? What about the child's father, is he here?"

"No, um, he was injured in the shooting also. Are they okay?" Mr. Walker inquired.

"I'm not sure of his current status, but I'll certainly check on him. That is after the two of you meet with your daughter and newborn granddaughter."

"Oh my Lord! Our baby is okay!" Ms. Walker cried out.

"Yes, she is. She's doing just fine. The single shot entered and exited her side without causing any major damage." After performing an emergency C-section, her doctor was delighted to deliver such good news to her family.

Moments later, they stopped at a window where one baby slept in Intensive care. Tubes and IVs assisted her with living.

"Surprise! There's your new grandbaby. Is she a first?" The doctor asked. Paying attention to nothing he said they looked at one another in complete shock after setting their eyes on a white baby with blonde hair.

******

Through all the years of living, Keisha never imagined her life coming to an end like this. *Not now. I'm supposed to have my baby. I can't believe they shot A-Wax all those times. He has to be dead. No, let's think positive. He had to pull through. That's A-Wax, my cousin. We were just dancing together. Damn, I feel for his mother. I cannot let them take me away from Smoove. They goin' to kill me.*

Knowing she was possibly in the final phase of her life she took in a deep breath and tried to think of an escape.

Having too much to live for, she would try.

Three of the bloods went in search of a Dodge Caravan to steal while Heavy and the other three bloods waited patiently, parked in his van in a crowded Security Square Mall parking lot. Uncovering Keisha's mouth and eyes, Heavy, knowing time wasn't on his side, wasted no time letting her know he meant business.

Thwack! With the butt of his gun, he bashed her hard across the face, piercing her cheek. Silencing her screams, one blood stuffed a dirty sock in her mouth.

"Look, bitch, I know you can lead us to some money. The faster and the sooner you get us to some money, the sooner we'll let you go." Scared to death, Keisha agreed with a nod.

For close to twenty minutes, they drilled her with every question imaginable related to money. Satisfied with her response, they all loaded into the stolen caravan upon the other bloods' arrival.

"Keep ya gloves on. Remember, in and out. Get what we came to get, and let's roll," Heavy told two of the bloods he was sending into Keisha and Smoove's apartment.

Guns in hand, they gained entry through Keisha's keys. Quickly finding the $8,000 Keisha said was there, they were pulling off in a minute less than the time they spent pulling up.

"Remember, if anybody's in there, tie them up first. You three, take the rope, and tape and tie them, while two of y'all search the upstairs for any more bodies. Pocket Knife, you go to the attic and get the money. Here's the combination to the safe and a bag."

It took them less than a minute to search Uncle Pete's house to find nobody was home. Unbeknownst to them, Smoove's uncle Pete and his family were at the baby shower. Along with the rest of the family, they were at the hospital also.

Having to put the combination in twice, Pocket Knife gasped after successfully gaining entry on the second attempt.

Throwing stack after stack of money in his bag, he saw his life change right before his eyes. "Oh shit! This nigga Heavy done came through. I love that nigga." Hearing him, the rest of the bloods ran in his direction.

"Yo, what's up there? Did you find it?" Dropping the bag of money next to them, they were full of excitement seeing the many stacks. At the bottom of the money was a fully loaded AK-47. Grabbing it, Pocket Knife felt like he was on top of the world. Putting the shoulder strap around his neck, he climbed out the attic. Toying around, he relived a scene from *Scarface.*

"You fucking cocker roaches! You wanna play with me?" Laughing, the remaining bloods got a kick out of seeing Pocket Knife wave the pretty nickel-plated assault rifle in their direction. Until they met Heavy, they never touched a gun. Not able to control it, he accidentally pulled the trigger.

The single shot slammed into Ice Pick's shoulder, knocking him to the floor. Making its way out back of his shoulder, the powerful bullet ripped through the wall, startling the neighbors next door. In a panic, they all headed for the front door.

Unable to make out any of their faces, the lady next door was able to count how many individuals she had just seen run out the house. She also gave the operator on the other end of the phone a detailed description of their van and clothes.

Jumping in the van, they rushed to the nearest hospital. "Man, what the fuck happened? Y'all got into a shoot-out?" Heavy asked, driving like a mad man, fleeing the scene.

"Ah! Pocket Knife shot me with a machine gun."

"It was by mistake. I found a machine gun. I ain't mean for it to go off. It just happened. I swear to God on my mother."

"So what the fuck happened? Did y'all get the money?"

"Yeah, we got a whole lot of money and a machine gun. Look."

Peeking behind his shoulder, Heavy almost lost control of the van seeing how much money was piled inside the trash bag.

"Bingo. I told y'all we was goin' to get that money. It's on now."

Celebrating, they were all happy to have made a come-up. Keisha, still hog-tied in the rear of the van, tried her best to detach the wires attached to the rear lights. Hopefully having no lights would draw some unwanted attention, she hoped.

"The hospital coming up around the corner. When we pull up, Pocket Knife, since you shot him, you staying with him."

"Stay with him. Man, I'm tryna go to Lincoln Park with y'all." Stopping at Northwest Hospital, Pocket Knife grabbed a bloody Ice Pick and carried him to the front entrance. Mad at how things were turning out, they never paid attention to the crowd of people in the waiting area. Unknown to them, they were at the same hospital as Smoove, Ms. Janice, and their family were.

******

Moments later they were back on the road in yet-another stolen van. After stopping at the hospital, Heavy, Keisha, and two bloods sat, parked in a crowded apartment complex two blocks away from the hospital. Knowing they exposed themselves from the gunshot too, the wild-driving Heavy quickly parked. Carlita came to pick up all the guns and money they had on them while two bloods went in search of a van to steal. Stopping at the mall parking lot where the first van was parked, they threw three shovels and two flashlights in the hatchback area. No longer in the hatchback, Keisha had the slightest idea what she was going to do to survive. From listening, she knew that the unfamiliar face was Heavy. What she didn't know was whether or not he knew it was she who shot him. Up until this point, her eyes and mouth were covered while loud music playing kept her from hearing clearly.

******

Arriving deep inside Lincoln Park, Heavy continued with his convincing. "Look, as long as you lead us to the money you said was buried, I promise you can live. It's not you that we want anyway. Hell, if you don't show us, then of course we gotta kill you, so you really don't have a choice, do you?" *Crack! Crack!*

Knowing the pain that came with being shocked with the stun gun, Keisha did as was told. In pitch-black darkness, the bloods, along with Heavy, carrying two shovels and three flashlights, led a handcuffed Keisha through the wooded area. With two bloods on each side of her, her only chance at survival was trusting that they wouldn't kill her upon getting the money she was leading them to.

Finally, the moment of truth arrived. For over an hour, they dug into the earth nonstop. Perspiration poured down the faces of the three bloods digging the hole. Determined, they kept diggin'. "Jackpot! I think we got something." Feeling his shovel hit something hard, Renegade was certain they came across something.

Flashing his light in the area, a devilish grin emerged on Heavy's face, setting his eyes upon a wooden chest. Inches into the dirt later, they were pulling the wooden chest from the hole. Wrapped around in a wool blanket inside a green trash bag was their future, separated in individual stacks of money. Closing the chest, they were eager to leave.

"Now, Keisha, I'm going to cut you loose like I said I would. I don't believe in killing women. Plus like I told you, it's not you that I want. All I ask is that you do me a favor."

Keisha was scared to speak, unable to form a word.

"Just like you gave me your word, you got mine. Tell Smoove that I'm going to kill him."

Heavy walked behind her, and her body trembled in fear as Keisha felt Heavy work to free the cuffs from her wrist. "That is when you see him in the afterlife, bitch." Heavy shoved her hard, and she fell face-first into the hole they just dug. "Work call!"

Mustering all her strength, Keisha tried her best to stand up. "Please! I got more money in the bank." The first swing of the shovel landed directly on top of her head. "I'm pregnant! Please! Don't kill me! " Blood gushed out of a gash on her head. One by one, Heavy and three bloods brutally beat Keisha with the shovels while one of them held the flashlight. Still handcuffed from behind, she couldn't block any of the skin-piercing blows. Badly beaten, she could no longer move or feel the dirt covering her body as numbness overtook her being.

******

The next day Agent Randolph sat at a round table, going over every piece of evidence she recently obtained with the help of her colleagues.

Opening his folder, the first agent, the one who had been asleep in the van, spoke. "Well, I did a thorough background check. Ran tags, did criminal searches, and gathered up all the information from the interviews at the hospital, and this is what I came up with. Charles Gibson is the owner of this Bentley, this Phantom, and this is his mug shot," he explained, showing them the pictures.

"So how does he fit into all of this, and what type of record does he have?" Agent Randolph asked, wondering, was Charles some type of major player in the drug market?

"His record is squeaky clean, outside of one DUI two months ago."

"So how do you explain these cars? Are they paid for?"

"Yup, along with four other cars he owns. Thing is, he owns an escorting service based in New Jersey, not to mention houses, clubs, and a few tanning salons."

"Mmm. He's pretty legit."

"That I'm not too certain about. Recently a guy was found bound and gagged with a single shot to the head. The homicide detectives working the case turned it over to the feds after it appeared to be a kidnapping. Once I contacted the feds in Jersey, they already had a beat on the case." Taking his iPhone from his pocket, he touched a few spots on the screen. Along with pictures of Ms. Janice exiting her truck at the baby shower, there, right in front of them, was Dion, covered in sweat, humping her from behind while her face was buried deep between the thighs of another woman.

"Ooh! That's Smoove's baby mother. That's interesting."

"What's more interesting is they found a Diva's business card inside his back pocket."

"Diva's? What's that?" Agent Randolph was curious to know.

"The name of the guy Charles's escort service. Then to top it off, the last call made to the dead guy's phone was made by Charles."

"Hmm." Scratching her chin, Agent Randolph sat attentively as she watched her case go into an entirely different direction. "So where did the tape come from?"

"Luckily, he had the app Find My iPhone. That's how it was found. Guessing the person, or persons, rather responsible called themselves, destroying the phone by throwing it in the Passaic River. After finding it, this is what else was revealed."

Every text message he ever sent Ms. Janice was made available to them. "Basically, this guy was blackmailing and forcing her to engage in sexual activities with him."

"Did you read them all?" Agent Randolph inquired, looking at what appeared to be well over two hundred text messages.

"Yeah."

"What's your conclusion?"

"That there are some more tapes somewhere." Without telling them why, he scrolled through the list in search of the same text that led him to believe there was more. Informing the group about the rest of the evidence, they were eager to hear what was next.

"As we speak, the guy"—he paused for a second as he scanned across the list again—"oh, here's his name—the feds are on their way over to the dead guy Dion's house in search of the tapes." He then went on to tell them about the multiple fingerprints on Dion's phone, along with what appeared to be DNA under his fingernails. "He was tortured before he was killed, so it's safe to say he put up a bit of a struggle and scratched somebody. Question is, who? The answer, we just have to wait for the lab results to come back."

Leading the way, Agent Randolph took over. "Whew! That was a lot. Good work." Patting him on the back, she smiled. After sending her field agents on separate missions, she walked to her car.

******

On her way to Homicide, she played with the idea of stopping at the hospital to question Smoove about the trail of blood he left behind the day his tenants were killed. At the end of the trail in a wooded area was his T-shirt covered in blood. Not wanting to reveal her hand just yet, she put away the thought.

"Hey, Ms. Randolph!" the active lieutenant at Homicide greeted her upon her arrival.

"Nice to meet you again, Lieutenant." Exchanging handshakes, they walked toward the holding cells.

"At your request, I didn't let anybody speak to them, nor do they even know why they're here."

"Well, well, well. How in the world did you two young bucks end up at the center of a federal investigation? Unlike being in state custody, the feds make you do 85 percent of your time, and there's no parole. Oh, not to mention the fees it cost to retain a federal lawyer, 'cause God forbid y'all let the federal government appoint an attorney for you.

"Humph! So this is what I suggest the two of you do. From the gunpowder residue found on your hands to your blood being at a crime scene where an AK-47 registered to the owner of the house was fired, plus here's the empty casing, and from the description the 911 caller gave us, you both clearly know that y'all are fucked. Now that's one situation. Just imagine doing 85 percent of one hundred years for killing that guy in the middle of the street then kidnapping that girl. Lead me to the girl, and you two walk. I got a bigger fish to fry."

Ice Pick and Pocket Knife were speechless. Little did they know Agent Randolph was lying. She wasn't sure if they were with the group of individuals who killed A-Wax and kidnapped Keisha. Following the procedure at the hospital, the nurses who tended to Ice Pick's wound pulled one of the many detectives working the baby-shower case off to the side, explaining to him their story. Not believing he was shot by an unknown male leaving a convenient store around the corner, the detective's antennas really went up seeing red bandannas tied around their necks. From interviewing the people at the baby shower, he was made aware that the shooting suspects wore red bandannas, concealing their faces. After testing positive for having gunpowder residue on both their hands, the detective passed the information over to Agent Randolph. Within minutes of being home, Smoove's uncle Pete filed a burglary complaint. From interviewing him, Agent Randolph was convinced that Keisha's abductors took her there in search of the money he told her Smoove kept stashed there. With the next-door neighbor's description of the intruders, her experience led her to believe that the damage done to Ice Pick's shoulder came from the high-powered rifle Smoove's uncle Pete said was missing. Not having the results from the blood found at the scene, she lied to him about it being his. Having nothing to lose, she was pulling out all the stops. Ice Pick and Pocket Knife had no idea what they were up against. Soon they would find out as her many ways of corruption were about to unfold.

TO BE CONTINUE......

Kevin Miller is currently incarcerated in federal prison working
On his next book, to stay abreast to the Rock Bottom movement you can
follow him on social media
Facebook @kevinmiller
Instagram:@rockbottoment
Email: rockbottomteam2@gmail.com

Kevin Miller 17579097
FCI Schuylkill
P.O. Box 759
Minersville PA, 17954